TOWN IN A WILD MOOSE CHASE

B.B. Haywood

CHIVERS

British Library Cataloguing in Publication Data available

This Large Print edition published by AudioGO Ltd, Bath, 2013.
Published by arrangement with the Berkley Publishing Group, a division of Penguin Group (USA) Inc.

U.K. Hardcover   ISBN   978 1 4713 2784 1
U.K. Softcover   ISBN   978 1 4713 2785 8

Printed and bound in Great Britain by
TJ International Limited

For James and Soren, as always

ACKNOWLEDGMENTS

Thanks to the many readers and fans who have embraced the residents of Cape Willington, Maine, and provided numerous creative ideas and suggestions. As you'll see, a few of those suggestions have been incorporated into this book. Special acknowledgment to Bill Hall of B&G Blueberries, who shared buckets of fresh-picked blueberries, provided valuable details about blueberry farming, and opened up his barn for a quick peek (even though he said it was too messy). Thanks to Sandre Swails and Jeanine Douphinett for their fabulous recipes and friendship, to Kae and Jon for lunch and career advice, and to Rock, Diane, and Laura Lee for continued support and good wishes. Finally, Leis Pederson's keen storytelling instincts helped make this a better book. For more information about Cape Willington, Maine, and details on current and

future books, visit www.hollidaysblueberry
acres.com.

PROLOGUE

He found the body at the bottom of a gully, lying on its side, half buried in the snow.

The white moose had led him to the spot.

It wasn't the sort of thing he'd expected to see when he set out from his fishing camp on English Pond that morning. If he'd had the good sense to let the moose be, or if he'd turned back at the edge of his property, or if he'd just stayed inside and worked on his carvings, he'd never have gotten himself mixed up in the whole blasted affair. But he walked right into it, all right. And he couldn't really blame himself, could he? The day was too nice, too welcoming, and he couldn't let the opportunity pass him by. They'd had some warmer weather lately, but it was coming to an end. Colder air and flurries were moving in, according to the almanac, which was accurate seventy percent of the time. Best get the chores done quickly while the nice weather lasted.

He'd laid up plenty of firewood for the season, but he liked to keep a good supply of kindling and lighter stock on hand too, and it needed replenishing. So he'd pulled on his light winter gear, stepped into his insulated boots, yanked the slat-sided sledge out from under the lean-to next to the woodshed, and headed out into the snowy woods, dragging the sledge behind him.

The sun was out, slanting through bare branches and wet-trunked trees, and the snow crust was freeing up, loosening from the bottom and softening at the top. As he trudged across the winter landscape, he unhooked the top two buttons of his flannel shirt, and the ones at the wrists as well. He'd worn only the shirt and an insulated undershirt with his old down vest, which had flattened considerably over the years. It was warm out for a morning in late January, so the heavier stuff wasn't required. He might have worn too much as it was. The mercury had touched forty-three degrees a couple of days ago, and had inched above forty yesterday. Temperatures were supposed to drop this afternoon, but the warmer air lingered, a few degrees above the freezing mark, continuing its gentle assault on the fringe of ice and snow that had tightly encased every single living and nonliving thing around Cape Willington for the better part of six weeks.

They'd had a couple of blizzards in early and mid-December, and a doozy of a sea storm right after the new year that left nearly twenty inches behind. The snowpack had thickened, and piles of snow driven by the hard winds had grown to chest height and beyond. But the January thaw of the past few days had cleared out some of it — enough so he could maneuver his way through the woods, going about his business.

A few birds sang high in the branches, and he looked up. A mild burst of wind brushed past his face, and he smelled the life hidden beneath the snow, aching to burst free. He looked down and swallowed. Not for the first time he missed Abby, his retriever. She'd loved days like this. She'd be in her glory if she were out here with him today. He'd had her for nearly fourteen years, but she was gone now, and he hadn't had the heart to replace her yet. He didn't know if he ever would.

So nowadays he devoted most of his attention to the animals in the woods around his camp. He knew some of them by sight and could recognize their tracks. The forest creatures had been busy over the past few days, given the warmer weather. As he headed off in his usual direction, following a narrow path that looped around the west side of the pond, he spotted their familiar marks.

Just up ahead, bird tracks circled a low berry bush. Obviously they'd found a few remnants of interest. Off to his right, he could see the bony footprints of a gray squirrel, which had ventured out from its nest in a weathered old oak. Farther on, in a grove of thick pines, he came across the tracks of a lone chipmunk, out foraging while it could. While crossing a low, reedy spot he spotted a few faint footprints with webbing between the toes — the hind feet of a beaver, which had a place nearby, on one of the streams feeding the pond. Another half mile on he spotted the five-toed footprints of a red fox, probably made sometime during the night or early morning hours. It seemed to have spent some time through here, sniffing out vole tunnels beneath the melting snow.

As he approached the stream he noticed how busy it sounded, its waters rushing under a shelf of ice that had broken open in a few places. Here he saw more tracks — a raccoon, whose prints looked like small, elongated human hands, and a thin weasel.

He found a good place to pull the sledge across the icy stream and headed up toward Cooper's Ridge, picking up kindling as he went. The weather of the past few weeks had knocked down quite a bit, and the work went quickly through the morning. Twice he returned to the camp, the sledge piled high with wood, which he stored away in the shed before heading out again, going out farther each time.

He'd inherited the camp from his uncle twenty-seven seasons ago. It had been a beat-down place when he took it over, but he'd fixed it up over the years and made it livable. The camp consisted of a one-room, open-beamed cabin right on the bank of the pond, plus a shed, chicken coop, makeshift boat shed, and a few other outbuildings. For nearly a decade he'd spent his summers here, only a few months at first, but it seemed as the years went by he was always arriving earlier in the spring and leaving later in the fall, until finally he'd just moved in full-time. He'd had two propane tanks, a hundred pounds each, installed at the back of the place, which gave him hot water, a few lights, and heat when he needed it. He made his dinners on a wood-burning cook-stove, and usually warmed the place with that and a smaller woodstove he'd had for fifteen years. It was an efficient operation, though he needed six or seven cords of wood in a season, plus all the kindling he could gather.

He'd decided to make the third trip his last, but the moose tracks caught his eye. They were easy to spot — larger than the deer tracks he often saw around his place. Deer frequently overnighted in sheltered areas on the other side of a hillock behind the cabin, but moose weren't as common around here. They tended to stay farther north, but a few wandered down on occasion to explore the woods around Cape Willington. They were shy, quiet, distant creatures, who preferred to stay pretty much on their own. They didn't seem to mind his presence, though, when he came upon them in the woods.

From the prints, this one looked like a newcomer; it had a V-shaped wedge cut out of one hoof, something he didn't recognize. The tracks were fairly fresh, headed southeast. Proceeding in a straight line that cut right between the trees.

That struck him as odd. He stood for the longest time staring at the tracks.

Rather than meandering through the trees, stopping here and there, searching out any leafy shoots that might have become unburied by the retreating snow cover, this particular moose had headed in a singular direction, unwavering, as if drawn by an invisible line to some unseen point in the woods up ahead.

He squinted through the trees, trying to see where the moose had headed. What was going on in those woods? he wondered. But the tracks disappeared into a miasma of muted browns, sullen grays, and dirty whites, giving him no clue. He knew the general direction, though.

The moose tracks were headed toward Blueberry Acres.

Candy and Doc Holliday's place.

He looked behind, knowing he should turn back. Best not to get too curious or too involved. He had the kindling he needed; he should head home. But for some reason he would never be able to explain, he turned the other direction, leaving his sledge where it sat, and trudged off through the wet, heavy snow after the moose tracks.

He soon began to sense that he and the moose weren't alone in the woods, and he felt a prickling on the back of his neck, in part because he started hearing things he couldn't quite place — an odd, distant crackle that sounded suspiciously like the crunch of snow as a boot stepped down, or the snap of a broken branch as someone passed nearby, carried on the faint wind that wove through the woods.

And then there came a single, sharp thudding sound, like an ax entering a tree. It sounded as if it had been made by a human. He'd never heard an animal make a sound like that.

There was probably a simple explanation. A few hikers or homeowners out today, gathering firewood like he'd been doing. Or kids playing hooky from school, pulling a sled or two, cutting through the woods to meet up with friends.

But something in his bones told him it wasn't that simple. Something else was going on. The vibrations were off. The air felt wrong. He stopped several times, looking back over his shoulder, willing himself to turn around and head home.

But the moose tracks drew him on. He followed them across the contours of the land.

Soon he heard a snort. He slowed his pace, moving forward cautiously. The trees parted, and quite suddenly he came upon the scene.

He froze.

Standing directly in front of him, on a rough edge of land that fell off to a gully behind it, stood a white moose.

He'd heard about them but never seen one before, though a buddy of his from up near Millinocket had seen one once, a decade or two ago, or so he said. They were more common in Canada, in places like New Brunswick, off to the east of Maine, and Ontario, to the northwest, and all the way up to Alaska. But sometimes one or two were seen around New England. He'd heard they weren't albinos but true white moose, whose coats turned darker in the summer but lighter during the winter months. It was some sort of genetic thing, someone had told him. This one had a few darker spots and smudges on its coat, which was long, thick, and a little shabby for the winter season. The animal stood about six and a half feet tall at the shoulders, he figured, and had shed its antlers, giving it a bald, almost comical look. It had ridiculously long, thin legs, which held up its thick, muscular body. The elongated head ended in a drooping snout. The hump at the top of the shoulders was particularly pronounced in this one, shown off by the wet spiked fur sticking up from the top of it.

The moose watched him with large brown eyes for a few moments, turning its head from side to side, as if agitated.

He backed away a little. He'd heard stories of people being trampled by moose. It was never a good thing to approach or upset one.

But this particular fellow remained where it was, its head turning and dipping so it could look down into the gully at its side.

Then it looked back at him.

He cleared his throat and said softly, "Hello, fella. You're a rare sight around here. You're not lost, are ya?"

If the animal understood, it gave no indication, until finally its head shook in a rapid movement, causing the dewlap — the loose patch of fur and skin hanging under its neck — to jiggle around furiously.

He took that as some indication to continue. "So . . . do you need help? You doing okay?"

In response, the white moose snorted, pushing the air out forcefully through its large nostrils, creating great puffs of mist as it turned away. It started off in long, determined strides, its two-toed hooves leaving distinctive tracks in the snow.

He was tempted to follow but hesitated.

A feeling of dread washed over him. Taking slow, cautious steps, he walked to the edge of the gully.

That's when he saw the body.
And the hatchet buried in its back.

From The Cape Crier
Cape Willington, Maine
January 21st Edition

BLUEBERRY BITS
by Candy Holliday
Community Correspondent

LET'S MINGLE AT THE MOOSE FEST!
With all the cold weather and snowstorms we've had recently, the inhabitants of Cape Willington have been in deep hibernation, surviving on stews and hot chocolate. But it's time to emerge from our cozy winter dens and embrace the season! The annual Winter Moose Fest, now in its eleventh year, promises a weekend of fun and festivities, most of it outdoors in the brisk, blustery air of coastal Maine.

The frozen fest kicks off this Friday at dusk with a Sleigh and Sled Parade, which draws participants from all around the region. Expect big crowds for this popular event, and be sure to wear your most colorful clothes! (It's a Cape Willington tradition!) The parade will include more than a dozen antique horse-drawn sleighs, decorated and lit in unique ways, plus many local kids and families pulling their own sleds.

On Friday and Saturday, stop by Town Park to watch professional ice carvers in action at an ice-sculpting exhibition, with children's activities and awards on Saturday morning. Also on Saturday morning at 11 A.M., Henry "Doc" Holliday (my dad!) will present a history of Cape Willington, focusing on some of the town's more prominent and colorful citizens over the past two hundred years. And throughout the weekend, you can stop in at the Cape Willington Historical Society for its annual baked goods and hot chocolate fundraiser. We hear the offerings will include Moose Mincemeat Pies, Moose Whoopie Pies, and Marbled Hot Cocoa. It's all for a good cause. If you'd like to contribute items for sale or volunteer to help, contact Marjorie Coffin at 555-8734, or just drop by the Coffins' farm anytime.

Of course, the highlight of the weekend will be (drum-roll, please!) the annual semiformal Moose Fest Ball on Saturday evening at the Lightkeeper's Inn. It promises to be the social event of the season. The ball is hosted by Oliver LaForce and the Cape Willington Women's Social Club, chaired by Wanda Boyle. Tickets are available at the inn, or contact Wanda at

555-6571. So break out your gowns and tuxes, and we'll see you there!

GRAB YOUR ANTLER HATS
Blueberry Bits has learned that Zeke's General Store has received a shipment of Antler Hats — baseball caps with faux antlers attached — just in time for the Moose Fest. Show your moose spirit by wearing your hat throughout the weekend!

NEWCOMERS TO CAPE WILLINGTON
Ralph Henry and Malcolm Stevens Randolph tell me they're pleased to announce the grand opening of The Bird Nest, a fine gardening and floral shop, on Friday, February 4. They plan to open weekends until April, and will then be open daily through the end of October. Please stop by, introduce yourself, and wish them well in their new venture. Think early Spring!

GREET THE MORNING WITH TAI CHI
Join Ted Coupland for his winter sunrise tai chi classes, which begin the first Wednesday in February. The classes will take place outdoors at the parking lot by the docks, and will run every Wednesday at sunrise through the end of March. It's a

great way to start the day, and to see winter in a new way.

DON'T WANT TO BE OUTDOORS? TAKE A NAP

Or, rather, a napkin-folding class. You'll learn how to fold napkins into zany and amazing shapes. Who wouldn't want their tables decorated with delightful swans and hearts? They're sure to be conversation starters. Classes begin February 10 in the meeting room at the Pruitt Library, and will be taught by Elsie Lingholt, our local hula hooper!

TIME DOES FLY WHEN YOU'RE HAVING FUN

Hickory Dickory Dock, Cape Willington's antique clock and pocket watch club, will present an exhibit of historic timepieces of local interest at the Cape Willington Historical Society during the month of February. While away the hours looking at these beautiful and notable pieces. The club meets every other Tuesday evening. All are welcome to join.

TASTY TIDBITS

Official Judicious F. P. Bosworth sightings

for the first three weeks of January:

Visible: 0 days
Invisible: 20 days

Apparently Judicious is hibernating, just like the rest of us! We hope to see you at the Moose Fest, Judicious!

Wanda Boyle and her son Bryan are selling bags of birdseed to raise money for the Cape Scouts trip to Vermont, where they will study the birds of the Green Mountains. Contact Wanda for more information or to help their worthy cause.

In other fundraising news, members of the Maine Housekeepers' Association will model household supplies in a fashion show scheduled to take place at the Elias J. Pruitt Ballroom at the Lightkeeper's Inn on Friday, January 28, at 7 P.M. These wonderful women have reportedly taken common household cleaning supplies and made stunning outfits out of them. We can't wait to see them! All money raised will go to the local food pantry.

ONE

Candy Holliday was sitting at the kitchen table, paging through seed catalogs and sipping a cup of hot tea, when she looked out the window and saw the figure emerge from the woods.

It was one of those rare days in late January when the morning sun hit the blueberry fields behind the house just right, reflecting off the layer of ice and snow that had settled across the fields like a winter patchwork quilt, sending off sparkles and shoots of light, turning everything magic. If you stepped out on the porch this morning (which you could do for a few minutes without putting on a coat), you could actually hear the ice cracking as it loosened its grip on rooftops and tree branches. You might even hear a few distinctive drip-drops here and there.

The January thaw had arrived.

Candy loved this time of year. The frantic

pace of the holidays was behind them, all traces of it carefully packed away for another year, and the days were growing noticeably longer. They'd have nearly forty-five more minutes of daylight at the end of January than they'd had at the beginning of the month. That in itself was a cause for celebration.

So Candy had set aside just an hour or two this morning to plan for spring, designing her gardens and ordering seeds. She'd slept in a little late (until eight thirty) and shuffled her father, Henry "Doc" Holliday, off to his daily ritual breakfast and jawing session at Duffy's Main Street Diner. Doc's crew was at winter staffing levels, since Finn Woodbury, a retired cop who ran several local summer theater productions as well as the annual American Legion flea market on Memorial Day, had headed south to sunny Florida with his wife, Marti.

But despite the absence of a key crew member, as well as the numerous travel difficulties caused by the vagaries of the winter season, Doc still made a beeline for the diner practically every weekday morning to drink coffee, eat doughnuts, complain about the weather (there was always something to complain about, even with the January thaw), and chew over the latest tasty tidbits of local news with his friends William "Bumpy" Brigham and Artie Groves.

Candy enjoyed having mornings like this to herself. She'd lit a fire to take the chill off the house and heated a kettle of water for tea. Then she'd settled in at the kitchen table for some serious, pleasurable work. She'd do all the ordering online later in the day, but first she wanted to take her time perusing the catalogs, drawing diagrams of her garden plots, making notes on which seeds to order, and deciding where to plant what.

It was a wonderful way to spend a quiet winter morning.

As she sipped her tea she read over descriptions of yellow crookneck squash, red burgermaster onions, Royal Mountie tomatoes, and sweet King Arthur peppers (a favorite of Doc's). She was particularly engrossed in a description of Boothby's Blonde heirloom cucumbers when, distracted by the barest movement at the far edge of her peripheral vision, she looked up and out the window — and that's when she saw the figure.

It spooked her at first, since it was such an unusual and unexpected sight, and she heard herself gasp in surprise. Unaware of what she was doing, she set the mug of tea down with a *thunk* and rose quickly from her chair, never taking her eyes from the figure and the line of trees.

She wasn't used to seeing people back there. The farm's blueberry fields extended several hundred feet behind the house, more than an eighth of a mile in some directions, and the back acres were still choked with dense stands of midsized trees and under- brush. Beyond that were undeveloped woods. The nearest houses in that direction, off toward the coast, lay perhaps three- quarters of a mile away, maybe more. It was walkable, but no one ever came that way.

In the other direction, toward the north- west, her woods linked up with conserva- tion land, and beyond that, private property stretching for miles. Mostly farms and fields occupied that upper region of the Cape. It was even more unlikely someone had come that way.

So who was this figure stumbling out of the woods and onto the downward slope at the edge of her blueberry field?

Candy instantly realized something was wrong.

She watched in growing shock and fasci- nation as the figure — a man, it looked like — staggered forward, moving awkwardly on the surface of snow and ice, weaving uncertainly around gray-black boulders left behind eons ago by retreating glaciers. As he walked, he repeatedly looked back over his shoulder. He'd taken perhaps a dozen steps when he lost his footing and dropped first to his knees, then to the ground.

He lay there, unmoving.

Before she could think about what she was doing, Candy dashed toward the door, her tea and catalogs forgotten. She paused only briefly to pull on a pair of boots and grab her jacket, and then dashed outside, along the porch, and around the side of the building toward the blueberry fields behind the house.

As she ran she kept her eyes on the fallen figure, but he didn't move. The day was clear and crisp, still chilly despite the warmer air, and almost immediately she felt her nose and the tips of her ears getting cold as she ran. Her breaths started coming quicker. She moved carefully over the snow-pack, avoiding the treacherous icy patches. She didn't want to wind up on her backside or, heaven forbid, injure herself with an awkward fall.

It took her a few minutes to reach the man, and as she approached she could hear him give out a low groan. She slowed as she moved in closer, cautious.

"Are you hurt?" she called out, taking in everything with a sweep of her gaze. "Do you need help?"

He groaned again, and a leg moved, kicking out in discomfort. He was wearing dark brown pants tucked into calf-high boots, a ratty navy blue vest, and a nondescript flannel shirt. He was bareheaded. As she approached, his head turned toward her, his eyes gazing up worriedly. She saw his salt-and-pepper beard, the thin blade of a nose, the unkempt hair. He had a red gash in his forehead. A thin, jagged trickle of blood inched down to his right eyebrow.

She gasped, recognizing the face. "Solomon Hatch!"

She took the final few steps toward him as he struggled to sit up, but his elbows slid out from underneath him and he fell back, groaning again. As she reached him, she dropped to one knee, brushing the hair back from her face as she scanned his body for any other signs of injury. "Solomon, what's wrong? It's me, Candy Holliday. Do you need help?"

She'd met him only once or twice, but she'd heard talk of him dozens of times. He was the town hermit, a shabby, bearded recluse who lived in a primitive, isolated cabin somewhere in the woods north of

Cape Willington. He was a man who kept to himself, coming into town only on rare occasions to replenish his stocks of sugar, coffee, flour, and propane.

But what was he doing here at Blueberry Acres? And what had he been doing in the woods? "Solomon, what's wrong?" Candy asked again, uncertain of what do to. "Do you need help? Should I call the police . . . or an ambulance?"

He looked at her wildly, like a cornered animal. His mouth worked, as if he was trying to speak, but no words came out. He looked terrified as he glanced again at the woods. It was almost as if he expected to see someone — or something — come crashing out from the trees, chasing him.

Candy looked toward the woods too, and when she looked back, she saw Solomon reaching out to her with a shaky arm, but she didn't back away. His fingers grasped desperately at a fold in her fleece jacket near her right shoulder. Latching on, he pulled her close, raising his head toward her as he spoke.

"Body . . . in the woods," he breathed, the words rattling in his chest. He fell back then, groaning as his eyes closed.

"What? There's a body? Where?" Candy turned again toward the dark line of trees at

33

the top of the slope.

Body. In the woods.

Candy was torn. She'd been in those woods dozens of times and knew them well. Should she investigate? Should she go look for a body?

Should she stay with Solomon?

Or should she go get help?

She looked back at the old hermit. He seemed to have fallen into unconsciousness, his thin body sprawled on the cold snow-pack.

Her first task, she realized, was to get him to a warm, safe place.

"Solomon, can you move?" She took him by the shoulder and tried to lift him, but he was too heavy for her.

She needed help.

She turned and looked back at the house. That was her best bet, she realized.

Moving as quickly as she could, her breathing loud in her ears now, she ran back down the way she'd come. She moved swiftly but cautiously, her boots crunching into the loosening snow. She nearly slipped several times as she raced over the blueberry bushes and rough ground, but she managed to keep her balance.

As she reached the house, she turned to check on Solomon before she went inside to call the police. But what she saw made her stop dead in her tracks.

Solomon was gone.

She blinked several times and refocused her gaze. But she wasn't mistaken.

The unconscious hermit she'd left lying in the snow had disappeared.

Two

Mystified, Candy raced back into the fields, up the rising slope. "Solomon!" she called as she ran, an uneasiness in her voice. "Solomon, where are you? What's going on?"

She scanned the field ahead before shifting her gaze to the woods on her right as she searched desperately for the old hermit. But she saw no sign of him. In fact, she didn't see much of anything, except for the strewn-about rocks and frozen vegetation buried beneath the cover of winter. The trees at the ridgeline stood in sharp contrast to the surrounding white landscape, like tall dark toothpicks, their bare, twisted branches tangling with one another in a dark brush of muted colors. She looked for movement among the trees but, again, saw nothing.

She hurried ahead, breathing in light huffs now.

As she approached the spot where Solomon Hatch had fallen, she slowed and stopped. She could see his tracks in the snow, the spot where he'd dropped to his knees before slumping to the ground. She also saw a new set of footprints, angling off in a different direction, away from her, before circling around to the right. She studied them with something bordering on disbelief. He must have climbed to his feet as she'd run for help and staggered up the slope, toward the trees at the edge of the barrens.

He'd gone back into the woods.

She was dumbfounded. Why would he do something like that, especially if he'd been injured? Or in danger? He'd seemed frightened, as if something in the woods was coming after him. So why go back in there? Why not follow her to the farmhouse, where he'd be safe?

She chided herself for leaving him but knew she'd had no choice. Besides, he couldn't be that far away. At most he had a few minutes on her. She might be able to catch up to him.

Moving cautiously, she started up the slope toward the tree line. At the top of the ridge she stood for several moments, staring into the woods. She heard all the typical sounds — the birds, the creak of branches, the brush of the wind. But no footsteps, no sound of someone moving or breathing. She saw no evidence of another person nearby.

Except for the footprints.

She thrust her hands deeper into the pockets of her fleece jacket and started into the woods, following Solomon's tracks. She studied them as she walked. The left foot appeared to be dragging across the snow a little, perhaps due to an injury. Or did Solomon have a limp? She couldn't remember. She didn't know him that well. She had no idea what to expect if she found him. Should she take him back to the farm? Would he be difficult to deal with? Her mind spun out a dozen different scenarios as she contemplated the wisdom of her actions. But no matter what happened, she couldn't abandon the old hermit. She had to find out what had happened to him.

After a few dozen yards the woods closed behind her, obscuring the farm and fields. The land rose to a crest before dropping to a hammocklike spot, where she spotted deer droppings among the low brush. The animals tended to linger near the fields whenever possible, hoping for a few nips of exposed vegetation. But she saw no deer today. She walked on, periodically calling out Solomon's name. The woods hushed, and her ears seemed to ring with the blanketing silence.

Abruptly she lost track of the footprints. Solomon had wandered into a shadowed area between a tight group of trees, and there the footprints had been brushed away, disappearing in midstride. She walked around the trees on either side and studied the area around her, expecting to see the continuation of the footprints farther on. But Solomon had swept his tracks clean.

Again, she was mystified. It was as if he had purposely prevented anyone from following him.

What was he up to?

She turned three-hundred-sixty degrees, searching the woods again. But the old hermit was gone.

For several tense moments she debated what to do. She was hesitant to go any farther. Solomon's footprints, and hers, provided her with a trail back home. If she moved ahead, out of view of the footprints, she might get lost and become a problem to herself and others. She knew these woods fairly well, but everything looked different when encased in snow and ice. She quickly decided to do the smart thing. She turned around, walked back to the farmhouse, and called the police.

They arrived in less than fifteen minutes.

Two squad cars rushed up the plowed driveway, followed by Candy's father in his old pickup truck. "What's going on?" Doc asked worriedly as he climbed out of the well-heated cab, slamming the door shut behind him. "Anyone hurt?"

"I don't know, Dad," Candy said, walking up to him. "That's what I'm trying to find out."

She turned toward the police cars. She didn't recognize the young, tall police officer who climbed out of the first car, but she certainly knew the middle-aged man who stepped out of the second one. It was Darryl Durr, Cape Willington's chief of police.

He nodded his head at her as he came around the front of the car. He was a rugged-looking man, with a weathered face, pale blue eyes, and salt-and-pepper hair that curled at the neck. "Good to see you again, Ms. Holliday," he said in a professional manner, with a slight nod of his head. "How's everything been going today?"

"Well, to be honest, Chief, it started out fine but then took a strange turn."

"You been having a little trouble out here?"

"You could say that."

He gave her an odd smile. "Funny, isn't it, how trouble seems to keep following you around?"

Candy folded her arms. "Yes, it is, isn't it?"

She and the chief had talked several times before, though usually under less than pleasant circumstances, and their conversations often involved some sort of lecture from the chief, warning her to stay out of trouble and to stop trying to solve murder mysteries around town.

"Well, why don't we go inside," Doc said, stepping forward briskly to shake the police chief's hand. "We can all talk where it's warm."

"Good idea," Chief Durr said with a nod, and he tilted his head toward Candy. "Hopefully we caught up with you on your baking day, Ms. Holliday. Your pies are the talk of the town."

He smiled again, more genuine this time, and Candy, realizing she'd tensed up, allowed herself to relax a little. It was true. She'd developed something of a reputation for her baked goods, especially her pies, which she sold to Melody Barnes, who ran a small cafe on River Road. She also worked part-time at the Black Forest Bakery, which Herr Georg, the German baker who ran the place, had closed for the season. But over the past year he'd taught her a lot about

41

baking, and she had been preparing for the shop's reopening in mid-April by practicing her craft as much as possible. In fact, she'd whipped up a German apple cake the day before.

She gave him a weak smile. "I'm sure I can find something to put out. Come on in and I'll warm up the coffee."

As they walked toward the house, Chief Durr indicated the tall, dark-haired officer who accompanied him. The young policeman wore a spotless, sharply creased uniform and brown utility coat. His shoes were shined to a high gloss, so they looked like black mirrors.

"This young fellow here is Officer Jody McCroy," the chief said. "He's new with the force, fresh out of the Maine State Police Academy in Augusta. Graduated near the top of his class. Thought I'd bring him out here to meet you in person."

Candy gave the chief a curious look, wondering what he meant by that, but he had already turned away to talk to Doc. When she looked around, she saw Officer Jody McCroy holding the door open for her.

"After you, ma'am," he said in an official-sounding tone.

She was surprised by how young he looked. She hesitated only for a moment, then gave him a nod and walked inside.

After she'd cut slices of cake and Doc had poured the coffee, they sat around the kitchen table. She noticed Officer McCroy had a notepad and pen set out in front of him. His hands were folded on the table. The young man looked prepared.

"So, could you tell us what happened?" he asked as Chief Durr sipped at his coffee, quietly watching her.

"Sure," and she told them, pointing out the window as she explained how she'd seen Solomon Hatch emerge from the woods behind the house, how he'd appeared injured, and how he'd told her about a body in the woods. After she'd finished her story, they all walked out to inspect the spot where the old hermit had fallen. Hands casually in his pockets, Chief Durr squinted back up at the trees at the edge of the field. "And you say you followed his footprints?"

"Yes, but he must have erased them at some point. I lost track of him."

"And he didn't say anything else about this body he thinks he found?"

Candy said that he had not.

Chief Durr turned slightly and nodded at Officer McCroy. Without a word, the young man headed back toward his car at a brisk trot.

The chief turned back to Candy. "Okay, we'll check it out. Officer McCroy's going to search the woods and see what he can find. He's just getting into his winter gear first. And I'll also send someone around to visit Solomon's camp. Most likely it's nothing," the chief said, looking Candy in the eye, "but one way or the other, we'll get to the bottom of it. If you see or hear anything else from him, you get in contact with us right away, okay?"

She nodded.

"We'll let you know if we find out anything. In the meantime —"

"I know," Candy said, interrupting him. "Whatever it is, stay out of it."

The chief smiled broadly. "You took the words right out of my mouth, Ms. Holliday. Thanks for the cake and coffee. Doc, good to see you again. Now if you'll excuse me, I have some paperwork sitting on my desk desperately awaiting my signature."

THREE

Doc looked worried. "Are you sure you're okay, pumpkin?"

Candy reached for her new tote bag, a stylish Kenneth Cole tan and brown number she'd picked up at a discount store in Bangor a few weeks ago, between Christmas and New Year's. She'd taken along her best friend, Maggie Tremont, and they'd made the rounds, looking for bargains. As soon as she came across the bag, Candy knew it was meant for her. It was casual yet classy, and gave her professional image a positive tweak.

Today, it also gave her something to do with her hands. She was grateful to see they weren't shaking as she checked the bag to make sure she had everything she needed — notepads, pens, her date book, digital tape recorder, business cards, flashlight, and her trusty cell phone, which was starting to show its age but still served her well.

"Dad, for the hundredth time, yes, I'm

fine," she said without exasperation. She knew her father was worried about her. He worried about a lot of things these days. The past couple of years had been rough, and they'd had a few close calls, financially and with the crop. They'd also had to invest in some new farm equipment, which they couldn't really afford, but they'd bought it anyway. And they'd managed to survive, thanks to small revenue streams from multiple sources — as many as they could come up with. It was the Maine way of getting by.

Doc had recently published a couple of articles in a popular history magazine, and was working on another one, which brought in a few much-needed extra dollars. And Candy held down at least four jobs herself, though some were seasonal and others required only a few hours a week.

It was her job as community reporter that had her headed out the door today.

But Doc wasn't ready to let her go quite yet. "You must have had a pretty good scare out there," he said, giving her his most concerned look.

Candy thought about that as she zipped up the bag and crossed the room to the coatrack by the kitchen door. She reached for a scarf and began to snug it around her neck. After a few moments she said softly,

"Well, yeah, I guess he caught me by surprise. And I have to admit I'm still worried about Solomon." She paused. "But the police are in charge now, right? I think it's best if I just stay out of it and go about my business."

Even as she said the words, though, she wondered if that was possible. Once again, there were mysterious goings-on around Cape Willington. And the timing was curious. *Could this have something to do with the upcoming weekend's events?* she wondered. *And if so, what is the connection?*

She pondered these questions as she began to pull on her yellow fleece jacket.

"I thought you were going to take the day off," Doc said as he watched her.

"I took the morning off."

"You get everything done you wanted to?"

"No, but I'll try again another day. For now, I have to go." She slipped the tote bag's strap over her shoulder and picked up her gloves.

"You headed to Town Park?"

Candy nodded as she took her keys from a hook by the door, and ticked off her plans for the afternoon. "The blocks of ice are arriving at around two, so I'm going to talk to some of the sculptors and watch them set things up. After that I'm headed across the

47

street to the inn, where they have a couple of the sleighs on display. Maggie gets off at four, so we're going to meet up, have a couple of drinks, maybe get something to eat."

She started toward the door but paused, turning back toward her father. "Hey, you want to come along? I could drop you at the diner while I'm doing my interviews. You're welcome to join Maggie and me for dinner later on."

Doc considered the offer briefly but finally gave her one of his patented don't-worry-about-me looks and waved his hand. "No, you go ahead. I have plenty to keep me busy around here. I have only a few chapters left of that historical mystery novel I've been reading, and I'm trying to finish up my article about Maine's role in the War of 1812. There was a lot of fighting along this coastline, you know. I just have to put some time in at the historical society."

"Well, if you go over there, steer clear of Wanda Boyle. You don't want to wind up in her blog."

"Heaven forbid!" Doc said in mock horror.

"Are you all set for your presentation on Saturday?"

"Oh, that?" He waved a hand. "Piece of

cake. I can deliver a speech like that in my sleep."

Candy laughed. "I bet you can. Well, I'll call you if I'm going to be out late. And give me a buzz if they hear anything about Solomon. I'm kind of worried about the old guy."

"Me too," Doc said, and he turned toward his office as she headed out the door.

After the biting cold they'd experienced over the past month and a half, today felt like a hint of spring, and she found she could actually breathe a little easier. She always seemed to hold herself tighter when it got really cold, as if she were freezing up herself. She didn't mind it too much, though. It was just something to get through so you could enjoy the spring.

During snowy weather she often parked her trusty old teal-colored Jeep Cherokee in the garage alongside the John Deere tractor and other farm equipment, but last night she'd left it in its summer place, in the driveway just off the back porch. She opened the cab, hopped into the seat, and headed toward town.

During the spring, summer, and fall, Cape Willington was a beautiful village, but it took on a special glow in the winter, glazed by nature's icing. It looked like a picture from a vintage Currier and Ives print. Of course, some of that icing had slipped a little with the warmer weather, covering the roads and sidewalks with an icy slosh that squelched satisfyingly under the shoe or boot.

Two town maintenance workers were out today, operating a nimble duo of industrial lawn-sized tractors equipped with snow shovels and large rotating brushes. They were clearing away some of the built-up snow from the sidewalks and parking spaces, making quick work of preparing the town for the weekend's festivities. Of the many things Mainers excelled at, clearing away snow was near the top of the list. Lord knows, they'd had plenty of practice over the years.

Candy found a parking spot at the lower end of Ocean Avenue, just past the opera house and almost directly in front of the old Stone & Milbury Insurance Agency. The place had been closed for nearly a year now, ever since Mr. Milbury, one of the firm's co-owners, absconded with hundreds of thousands of dollars in embezzled funds. They'd caught him in Arizona as he was attempting to cross the border into Mexico. Now he was serving time at a federal prison in northwestern Pennsylvania.

Stone & Milbury had occupied a fairly large space along Ocean Avenue, where it had been a fixture for more than two decades. But after the firm's implosion and the store's closure, the landlord had eventually split the storefront into two smaller spaces. A dry cleaner's now occupied the right side of the space, while a ritzy new art gallery had moved into the other side. The gallery had opened during the fall leaf-peeping season and had done a brisk business through the holidays, but Candy had heard that sales had slowed dramatically after the beginning of the year, causing the gallery to open only on weekends since mid-month. But today the store's OPEN sign was prominently displayed, and through the window Candy noticed a few folks browsing around inside. And that made her happy. With the Winter Moose Fest kicking into high gear, tourists were once again filling the town's inns, restaurants, and shops. The increase in activity was evident — and very welcome.

Grabbing her tote bag, Candy slid out of the front seat, locked up the Jeep, and carefully negotiated a narrow pathway through a chest-high streetside snowbank before dashing into the doorway on the right. Inside, her best friend, Maggie Tremont, stood behind the counter, chatting amiably with a customer. As soon as Candy entered, both pairs of eyes turned toward her.

"Well, look who's here," Maggie said, proudly extending an arm in greeting, as if the Queen of England herself had just entered the room. "Our very own town detective and star reporter, right on cue!"

Candy stopped and blinked, surprised by the sudden attention. "Who, me?"

"Of course you, silly," Maggie said with a wave of her hand as she came around the end of the counter and took her friend by the arm, leading her forward. "Someone here wants to meet you."

Candy's gaze angled to the customer who stood in front of the counter. He was an older gentleman, perhaps in his midsixties, with gray, longish hair, wire-rimmed glasses, and a tanned complexion, as if he had spent the past few months wintering under the Florida sun. He was smartly dressed in a black woolen overcoat, expensive-looking cream-colored dress shirt, gray and yellow argyle vest, and dark, sharply creased dress slacks. It was a stylish ensemble, disturbed only by the black rubber boots, encrusted with muddied, caked-on snow, poking out from under the cuffs of his slacks.

She'd never seen him before, but his boots

gave her a clue to his identity. *He's a true New Englander,* she thought.

He came toward her with his hand outstretched and one of the widest smiles she'd ever seen, framed by a thick gray moustache. "Candy Holliday, this *is* a thrill!" he said with great enthusiasm. He shook her hand warmly. "I've been looking forward to this moment for quite some time. I'm Preston Smith."

Candy gave him a guarded smile. "Hello, Mr. Smith, it's very nice to meet you." She glanced sideways at Maggie, hoping for some explanation.

"He says he's read your columns," Maggie said, as if that explained everything.

"My columns?"

"Oh yes, I'm a big fan," Preston Smith told her. "I'm quite intrigued by them. I'm from the city, you see. All that noise and traffic and people jammed together. But your columns truly capture everyday life here in this wonderful little village of yours. I've been hoping to visit for quite a while, so I couldn't be happier I've finally found the time to make the trip. And please, call me Preston."

He smiled at her so warmly she couldn't refuse. "Well, okay, Preston." She paused. "Where did you say you're from?"

"He's from I.C.I.C.L.E.!" Maggie interjected excitedly.

Candy looked confused. "Icicle? What state is that in?"

Preston Smith laughed heartily. "I see you're not familiar with this particular usage of the term," he said with a toothy grin. "It's an acronym, actually, for the International Committee of Ice Carvers and Lighting Experts."

"You're kidding me," Candy said.

Preston chuckled. "No, we're quite serious, though our name is a little mischievous, I'll admit. But we thought it would be fun and grab people's attention. We're a relatively new organization, you see, which probably explains why you haven't heard about us. In fact, not many people have. But we're growing fast. We truly believe in the beauty of carving and lighting ice. We're hoping to turn it into an international phenomenon — a type of sport, if you will, rivaling the popularity of football and baseball."

"Oh. Well, that's wonderful," said Candy, not completely convinced. Still, she thought as her reporter instincts took over, it might make a good story. "I'd love to write an article about your organization sometime."

"Perfect! To be honest, that's one reason

I'm here, Ms. Holliday. As I said, I've been reading your columns for quite some time, and I've enjoyed following all the activities and events taking place in your charming little town. One day recently, I was struck with this epiphany: what if we held one of our international ice-carving events right here in Cape Willington!"

"Oh my! What a wonderful idea!" Maggie was almost breathless.

"It could put your town on the map with the international ice-carving crowd," Preston said.

"Oh . . . is that a large group?" Candy asked skeptically.

"Larger than you might guess," Preston assured her.

"I never realized that," she replied, her voice only slightly betraying her doubt.

Preston went on. "We think Cape Willington would make an ideal setting for one of our keystone annual events. While the event you're presenting here this weekend is merely an exhibition — though an informative one, naturally — our organization could stage a worldwide competition, with awards, cash prizes, international press, that sort of thing. Think of it as a sort of Boston Marathon for Cape Willington — we believe the level of prestige would be that high. Such an event could bring widespread attention to your village, as well as a substantial amount of dollars for your local businesses."

Candy found herself becoming mildly intrigued. "When you say a *substantial amount* — just how much are we talking about?"

"Oh, well." Preston drew his head back and pursed his lips in thought. "We'd probably be talking in the tens of thousands, perhaps even hundreds of thousands of dollars spent locally." His grin grew sly as his gaze narrowed in on her. "All of it in cash, of course, running through your neighborhood businesses and giving a boost to the region's economy."

"Wouldn't that be wonderful?" Maggie said. "We could use a boost like that around here."

"We sure could," Candy agreed, eyeing Preston. "But why tell *me* this? You should be talking to the town council. They meet the second and fourth Tuesday of every month. You could talk to them next week."

"Yesss," said Preston Smith, drawing out the word in a hiss as his smile broadened again. "I certainly could. And I plan on doing just that, as soon as we can set something up. But first I wanted to talk to you — the beating heart of the village. The person who can carry my message to the masses."

"Like the town crier!" Maggie said helpfully.

Preston angled a long finger at her for emphasis. "Yes, exactly! That's what you are, Ms. Holliday. You're the town crier — and we need to talk business."

FOUR

Leaving Maggie to finish up her shift at the dry cleaner's, Candy headed out the door, slinging the strap of her tote bag over her shoulder as she angled down the street toward Town Park at the lower end of Ocean Avenue. Preston bid adieu to Maggie as well before he followed Candy out the door. He fell into step beside her, continuing the conversation, his tone turning serious and businesslike.

"We'd like to move fairly quickly on this," he told her, "but we can't go forward without the blessings of the town council and the support of local businesses and residents. Frankly, to make that happen, we need the help of the local media."

Candy swiveled her head toward him. "Ah, so that's where I come in," she said, beginning to understand her role in Preston's plan.

"Exactly. We'll need the full cooperation

of the townspeople and perhaps even some help from the state to pull this off. Some positive comments in your column should get the ball rolling in the right direction. It's completely up to you, of course. We don't wish to put any pressure on you. But if you decide to write about this . . . well, this opportunity, shall we call it? . . . the result will be worth the effort, I promise you that! The entire town will benefit in numerous ways."

"Really? You sound very persuasive," Candy admitted.

"I'm simply passionate about our organization," Preston said evenly, "and I'm hoping to pass some of that passion and excitement along. Should you decide to help us in that effort, perhaps you could mention our proposal in your newspaper. You could explain something about our organization, point out the benefits of an event of this magnitude, and help us clear a quick path to approval."

"A path to approval." The phrase had a marketing ring to it that made Candy wary. She wanted to believe his story, but something about it didn't ring quite true. It seemed just a little too perfect — and perfect plans rarely worked out as intended. "It sounds like you've given this some thought," she said after a few moments.

"Quite a bit, in fact," Preston told her bluntly. "We've been evaluating your community for the better part of a year."

That caught her by surprise. "A year? But I thought you said this was your first trip here."

"It's my first time visiting in person, yes. But as I said, I've been reading your columns — the entire newspaper, in fact. I've devoured every word of every issue for the past year or so, and I've been following news about the town on the Internet, mostly by keeping up with the postings by some of your citizens — personal blogs, tweets, Facebook pages, that sort of thing. All very informative, and perfectly legitimate in a legal sense, of course — we were just doing our homework."

"But why Cape Willington?" Candy asked, and let out a cry of surprise as she barely dodged an ottoman-sized clump of snow that rolled into her path from the top of the snowbank to her right. She stumbled sideways, her feet beginning to slip out from under her, until quick as a cat, Preston reached out and took her arm, steadying her.

"Oops, careful there," he said easily as Candy got her footing. "Are you all right?"

"I'm fine." She slipped again and reached

for his arm, absently noticing how muscular it felt underneath his coat. *He's been working out,* she thought. Out loud, she said, "I guess I'd better watch where I'm going."

"Well, if your tumbles take you my way again, I don't mind lending a helping hand," he said with a chuckle, and released his hold on her. "There you go."

"Thanks for catching me."

"Think nothing of it. I'm glad to be of service. Now, to answer your question: Why Cape Willington? Well, a number of reasons. The town is incredibly picturesque, of course, with the lighthouses, opera house, museum, and historic inns. It's a vibrant, close-knit community with a colorful, engaged citizenry. And the town is well set up to accommodate tourists in all seasons. It's the perfect place from which to launch our first competitive event."

"Your first event?"

His toothy grin returned. "Yes. Didn't I mention that?"

"I don't think so, but . . . do you have any experience doing this sort of thing?"

He laughed congenially. "Of course! I'd be happy to provide you with my credentials, if that would help." And without hesitation, he reached into a pocket, pulled out an ice-blue business card with white frostinglike lettering, and placed it in the palm of her hand. "You'll want to check my references, of course. You'll find a website and e-mail address on the card. If you send a message to my assistant, she'll make sure you get all the appropriate documentation."

Candy studied the card for a moment, reading the inscription: *Preston J. Smith, Executive Director, International Committee of Ice Carvers and Lighting Experts (I.C.I.C.L.E.)*, it read, and listed a post office box in Washington, D.C., as its address. At the bottom were the phone number, fax number, and e-mail address. She slipped the card into an outside pocket of her tote bag and pulled out one of her own, which she handed to him. "Here's mine, in case you need to contact me. So when are you thinking of launching this event?"

"As quickly as possible. A year from now, preferably, to coincide with your next winter festival."

She let out a low whistle. "That's moving pretty quickly. You're not wasting any time."

He gave her another smile, though it looked more calculated this time. She noticed a sudden glint of determination in his eyes — and something else, though she couldn't quite figure out what it was.

"We're deadly serious about this," he told

her, holding her gaze for only a few moments before looking around. "Ah, here we are!"

They had reached the bottom of Ocean Avenue and entered Town Park, where preparations were well under way for the upcoming ice-sculpting exhibition, part of the weekend's Winter Moose Fest event. Trucks had delivered huge blocks of ice, which ice wranglers were busily transporting on forklifts to two main work areas. Teams of sculptors would work nonstop to create two large ice sculptures — one a long, winding ice dragon, and the other a scene of the great Maine wilderness, complete with moose, elk, and other creatures native to the state. On Saturday morning, the sculptors would also create a number of smaller, single-block sculptures, which would remain on display throughout the weekend.

"I've heard they'll be lighting the large sculptures," Preston told her as they approached the area of activity, "though externally, not with internal lights."

"I'm looking forward to it. Everyone in town is excited about the sculptures."

"I can understand why. It should be a magnificent display."

"Do you sculpt yourself?" Candy asked him.

"I've dabbled in it," Preston said amiably, "but I realized a while ago I don't have the artistic ability required for the finer pieces. That's why I've shifted to the administrative side, where I seem to have found my niche. I've also been asked to judge a number of international competitive events, including ice art championships in Alaska, Quebec, and Colorado."

"I guess you spend a lot of time in cold places."

Preston chuckled. "Yes, that's true. I seem to follow winter around the world. A few months ago I was in Argentina for one of their winter events, and Japan before that, and Germany before that. I spend a lot of time getting on and off planes, as you can imagine. But I love the work." He pointed toward the blocks of ice. "Each block weighs three hundred pounds, you know, and measures three by four feet, with a depth of three feet. Large sculptures like the ones they're creating here this weekend will use anywhere from fifteen to twenty blocks. They'll shave and heat the surfaces first so the blocks meld easily together and let them freeze overnight into the large structures, which will serve as the foundations. They'll carve some of the extensions and detailed pieces individually and add them on with the forklifts, as you'll see. In the next couple of days, using the tools of their trade, the sculptors will reveal the art hiding inside these frozen cubes."

Candy's curiosity got the best of her, and she couldn't help assuming her reporter's role. "What types of tools do they use?"

"They'll start with chain saws, which they use to carve away larger chunks of ice and for some of the broader shaping. For detail work they'll switch to smaller, handheld power tools like sanders, grinders, and routers. Everything has to be very sharp to work with the ice, so I'm sure they'll use crowd barriers to keep observers at a safe distance. The carvers will finish with heat guns, which help smooth and round the ice, although some sculptors prefer to simply douse the finished work with a bucket of water."

Candy pointed toward the rising blocks of ice. "And how long will it take to create these sculptures?"

"Well, a skilled ice carver can create a sculpture from a single block of ice in a matter of minutes. But these works are more involved. The sculptors will be working off computer-generated designs, though more than likely they'll revert to a freehand style as the work progresses. I've met most of these sculptors at previous events. Here, let me introduce you to some of them."

But before he could start showing Candy around, a familiar yet cold voice sounded behind them, stopping them in their tracks. "Well, here you are. And I see you've found the I.C.I.C.L.E. guy. I'm sure he's discussing some important piece of news with you, but what I really want to know is, what happened to Solomon Hatch?"

Candy tried to stay calm as she turned.

There, in a wide stance with her arms crossed, stood Candy's nemesis, Wanda Boyle.

FIVE

"Late as usual." Wanda made a show of checking her silver-banded wristwatch. She'd dressed casually for the day, in a cream-colored turtleneck sweater, thick raspberry fleece vest, khaki safari-type jacket, and gray ski pants tucked into calf-high black rubber boots. Designer sunglasses perched atop her flaming red hair, and over her shoulder she carried a black canvas tote bag, not unlike the one Candy had carried before she bought her new tote. Wanda had clipped a badge that read PRESS to the collar of her vest. The spiral wire of a reporter's notebook stuck out of one of her jacket pockets.

"I've already had time to interview the ice sculptors and post my first story of the day online," Wanda continued in a self-congratulatory tone, "and here you come, traipsing in after all the hard work's been done. They've already unloaded the ice blocks, you know."

"They have?" Candy looked expectantly across the park and noticed a colony of busy worker bees hovering around large blocks of ice. She could hear the voices of the workers and sculptors as they moved and positioned the blocks into what looked like a huge, white, drawn-out Lego construction.

"They have," Wanda confirmed, "and you missed it." She gave Candy a tight, knowing smile. "So what have you been up to? Taking long walks in the woods?"

Candy turned back to Wanda, her brow falling into a questioning look. "I'm not sure I know what you're talking about."

"Oh, but I'm sure you are," Wanda said in a smooth tone. "I've heard you had some trouble out at Blueberry Acres this morning. Something involving the police. And a body, right?"

"A body?" Preston Smith interjected himself into the conversation as his expression changed to one of alarm. He looked from one face to the other. "Has someone been hurt?"

"Not that we know of," Candy told him truthfully, keeping her eyes firmly fixed on Wanda. "There's been a report of an injury, yes, but nothing's been confirmed. The police are checking it out."

"The police! Good gracious!" Preston looked around worriedly. "I hope there's no trouble — anything that might interfere with this weekend's activities."

"I'm sure everything will be fine," Candy reassured him. To Wanda, she added curiously, "How did you hear about that?"

Wanda feigned a bored look, as if the answer were obvious. "I have my sources. You're not the only one in town who has good reporter instincts, you know." She paused, tightening her birdlike gaze on Candy. "So spill the beans. What really happened out at the farm this morning with Solomon Hatch? Was he wounded, like I've heard? Or was it just something you made up to get attention?"

Where did that come from? "You think I need attention?" Candy asked as she shook her head and let out a breath. The old wounds between her and Wanda just didn't seem to want to heal, especially with Wanda always picking at them. She was still offended Candy had left her son's name out of a newspaper column more than a year ago, and despite Candy's apologies, and the fact that they had collaborated — in the loosest sense of the word — on a murder mystery last May, Wanda apparently had no intentions of letting bygones be bygones.

In fact, she'd upped the ante. Upset she hadn't been hired as the community editor for the town's local newspaper, the *Cape Crier,* Wanda had started her own online community blog and website, which she called the *Cape Crusader.* She updated the blog daily and posted news items, photos, calendar events, and other tidbits regularly, and had quickly drummed up traffic using social media sites. She was also handy with her smart phone, regularly sending out instant messages, texts, and tweets. She was a veritable digital multitasker.

Her newfound media voice had emboldened her, and she relished the fact that in some ways she'd left her rival in the dust. Candy, after all, just wrote a community column for a print newspaper that came out bimonthly in the winter. Without the frequency of writing for the paper's summer editions, which were published twice a week, Candy and the newspaper had fallen behind in the up-to-date news category. At least that's how Wanda probably viewed the situation, Candy thought, and Wanda exploited it in every way possible. Admittedly, there hadn't been much to write about over the past few weeks as winter had settled snugly into the region. But now, with the Moose Fest activities gearing up, Wanda was back in competitive mode.

Candy tried not to let herself get drawn into Wanda's world of constant one-upmanship, but there were times she couldn't help herself.

"Well, Wanda," she said, trying her best to keep her voice even, "it sounds like you're the one with all the sources, so why don't you ask them?"

And with that, she took Preston Smith by the arm and tugged him along with her as she started off toward the rising mountains of ice at a brisk pace, doing her best to tamp down her anger. She didn't look back, though she was tempted. Determined to put Wanda right out of her mind, she pointed ahead of them, twirling her finger around in the air to indicate the entire scene.

"So tell me what's going on here," she said to Preston as they followed a cleared, well-traveled path through Town Park. "I need to catch up fast, so give me all the details."

Preston gave her a somewhat bewildered look, not completely understanding everything he'd just heard. "What would you like to know?"

"Anything you can think of. How long until they get all the blocks set up? When are they going to start carving? Where do they get the designs? How long will it take them? That sort of thing."

"Oh, yes, I see." Preston nodded as he grasped the type of information Candy sought. "Well, let's see. Where should I start?" He pondered a moment as he focused in on the scene before them. "Of course, I'm not an organizer of this event — I'm merely an interested party and observer — but they've brought in a lot of very skilled people this weekend. At the moment they're setting up for two multiblock sculptures, as I understand it. The one on the right will be a dragon, which should be quite spectacular, while the other will be a tribute to —"

"Yeah, yeah, I got all that," Candy said, hurrying him along. "But where do the blocks of ice come from? And how does one get into this business? We've got a bunch of sculptors here today. Is there, like, a master carver or anything like that? A top dog? Which one would that be?" She scanned the crowd ahead of them.

"A top dog? Oh, well, now let me see." Distracted, Preston stumbled over a rough spot on the pathway. "I suppose there is, though you'd probably get some argument from the sculptors themselves. But if you look over that direction —"

"Hey, there's Ben!" said Candy, pointing

off to her left.

Ben Clayton was the editor of the *Cape Crier,* Candy's boss — and her sort-of boyfriend, though they'd kept their relationship low-key so far. He was walking toward them with long, purposeful strides, head down, hands lodged deep in his pockets. He seemed oblivious to all the activity going on around him, as if his mind were a million miles away. But when Candy called out to him, he stopped and looked up. It took him a few moments to locate her and focus in on her face, but when he finally recognized her he smiled crookedly. He waved and started toward them.

Candy felt Preston grasp her arm. "I hope you'll excuse me," he said, standing slightly behind her, "but I just remembered I'm scheduled to meet someone at the inn."

When she looked back over her shoulder, he was glancing down at his watch and already turning away. "Oh, I was going to introduce you to Ben."

He threw her a regretful smile. "I'll catch up with the two of you at another time — perhaps at the inn later this afternoon? Please give him my best for now."

Without another word, Preston Smith headed back across the park toward the Lightkeeper's Inn, head low as he turned up the collar of his coat.

Candy watched him go, shaking her head. She was about to call out, "You were going to tell me about the sculptures!" but he was too far away, and then Ben was there. He leaned toward her and kissed her on the cheek. "Hi, you."

"Hi yourself. You look like you're deep in thought. Having a good day?"

He shrugged, his smile fading. "Just a typical one so far. Hopefully it will improve now that I've run into you."

"That bad?"

"I've had better. I heard you had some trouble out at the farm."

"You could say that." It never failed to surprise her how fast word got around town when anything unusual occurred. "I had a strange visit from Solomon Hatch." Quickly she told him what had happened. "The police are supposed to be checking it out," she finished. "I think they're headed out to his camp by English Pond to see if he's all right."

"They've already been there, and found nothing," Ben told her. "A couple of officers made a cursory search of the woods, but they've already been called away by an accident up 192 toward Route 1. They said they might get back to the search later today."

"But what about Solomon?" Candy asked, concern in her voice. "They're just leaving him on his own?"

Ben nodded solemnly. "It looks that way for now. Unless you want to get a group together and organize a search ourselves."

"I've been considering that," she said. "Do you think it's something we should do?"

He thought for a few moments before he replied. "Maybe . . . if we have to. But for the time being, it's probably best to let the police do their jobs. Speaking of which" — he pointed behind her with his chin — "who's your friend?"

At first Candy thought he was referring to Preston Smith, but then she realized he was looking in a different direction. It took her a few moments to figure out who he was talking about.

Not far away stood a young, tall police officer — the same one who had been out at the farm that morning with Chief Durr. What was his name? Jody something? That was it. Officer Jody McCroy.

As she studied him, he stared right back at her, unfazed. Over his neat uniform he wore the same standard-issue brown jacket she'd seen him in that morning. He had broad shoulders, she noticed. Not muscled but firm. He looked like the type of guy who ran five miles before his Wheaties, and another five after work. With a brisk walk later in the evening, just for the fun of it. He kept meticulous records, she guessed. He had a notebook in his hands now. In fact, as she watched, he looked down and wrote something in it.

She felt a sense of apprehension as she watched him. *Is he writing something about me?* she wondered.

She turned back to Ben. "He was out at the farm today. He's supposed to be searching for Solomon. What's he doing here?"

Ben ignored the question as he took a step closer, his angular face showing concern. "Look, I'm not doubting you or anything, but are you sure Solomon was injured? Maybe he just lost his way and stumbled onto your field."

"He had a gash on his forehead and he looked dazed," she said matter-of-factly. "Something was wrong with him, that's for sure. I just hope they find him soon."

Ben looked back over at Officer McCroy, who was still watching them intently.

"Me too," Ben said thoughtfully. "Me too."

Six

As they turned away from the young police officer, leaving him to his note taking, and started off toward the rising sculptures, Candy couldn't help but shiver. Ever since she'd seen Solomon Hatch stumble out of the woods that morning and collapse in the middle of the blueberry field, she'd had a strange feeling in the pit of her stomach. Some part of her hoped the whole thing was a fluke, a mistake, nothing more than a disoriented old hermit who got spooked in the woods and overreacted. Maybe he'd let his imagination run a little too wild and mistook an animal carcass for a human body. Or something like that.

But she feared a more sinister scenario was playing out.

Twice before she'd stumbled into mysteries that had involved murder, and even though she'd eventually unmasked the villains, she'd put herself and her friends in danger. She hoped she wasn't seeing a repeat of those events.

What bothered her at a deeper level, though, was a secret she'd uncovered last May, hinting at an ominous force behind the murders eight months ago. She had linked initials written in the corner of a set of blueprints to a Boston developer named Porter Sykes. Though she couldn't prove it, she felt he had been responsible, at least in some way, for the deaths in town last year. Over the summer she'd quietly made a few inquiries and conducted what research she could, but she hadn't been able to put all the pieces together, to figure out what it all meant. Wanda Boyle still held a piece of that puzzle, in the form of the blueprints in question, but, naturally, she had refused to cooperate. So Candy had eventually let it go. And as the months passed and summer faded into fall, which slipped into winter, she'd let her concerns retreat to the back of her mind, where they'd become overshadowed by more pressing demands, like paying for the oil bill and bringing in a few more armloads of wood.

Now, those earlier concerns were again coming to the fore.

She did her best to squash her rising sense of dread and turned to face Ben.

Instantly she felt her worries ease. If anything, he was more reassuring, and more handsome, than when they'd first met. His face had aged just slightly, altering the angles and emphasizing the lines of his jaw. With the shorter, overcast days of winter, he'd lost some of his summer color, but he'd grown out his hair, giving him a shaggier, earthier appearance that fit him well. He'd kept active by cross-country skiing most weekends, and had even tested his ruggedness by camping out once or twice during the winter.

But something else had changed in him — something less tangible. She first noticed it last summer, when his demeanor had subtly shifted. Before that, he'd been guarded, cautious, at times distracted, and overall unattached. He had joked with her and been friendly enough, but their relationship had remained mostly on the surface. He'd rarely talked about his past, his beliefs, his goals, his wishes. But he'd been fun and charming and good company for her, and she'd been happy enough with that. Still, she'd often felt he was holding something back.

Then, last summer, it was as if he'd suddenly discovered a part of himself he hadn't known existed. He began to talk about his

79

concerns and reveal details he'd only brushed over before — about his childhood in Rhode Island, his engineer father, his younger sister, and his mother, who had been a social studies teacher and nourished his interest in current affairs, politics, and geography. She'd been the one who'd encouraged him to travel, to seek his destiny in the world's great spaces, and to think and write. After attending Boston University, where he studied journalism, he'd traveled to India, Sri Lanka, and Singapore before eventually landing a job with an international news organization, which took him to other countries in Africa, the Middle East, Europe, and Asia.

Much of this Candy already knew, but on one of their dates, at an Italian restaurant up on Route 1, over plates of spaghetti *mare e monti,* slices of toasted garlic bread, and glasses of a robust Chianti, he began to open up. He talked about his two marriages, and why he felt he needed to spend time on his own after his second divorce, devoting himself to the pursuit of books, knowledge, and nature in a fit of self-discovery. It was as if he was giving her an insight into his thinking over the past two years, and the reasons he'd behaved in the ways he had. And for the first time that night, he started talking about the two of them, and where they might be headed as a couple. By the end of the evening, they'd both agreed they weren't quite ready for a serious relationship (yet), but they also both admitted they were fond of each other and liked spending time together. Whether their relationship would go further than that remained to be seen.

Candy was telling the truth when she said she wasn't sure she was ready for a relationship. She was still recovering from past emotional wounds, and anyway, she continually told herself, she had too much to do out at the farm and too much to do around town, just to try to make ends meet. She also found herself increasingly drawn into the activities of her adopted coastal community, attending meetings and events, getting involved with local organizations, and helping out at the newspaper.

But over the past few months, she'd felt her relationship with Ben deepening in unexpected ways. For one thing, he'd become more demonstrative, frequently putting his arm around her waist or taking her hand when they were alone. He'd also become more involved in her life, hanging out at the farm, chatting with Doc for hours, and helping in the fields at harvest time. He'd even taken to calling her in the evenings, to say good night and make sure she was okay.

Some of that had fallen away after the beginning of the year, but even now, as they headed toward the ice sculptures, they walked so closely together their shoulders touched, and she sensed his concern for her. She wanted to reach out and take his arm, but they were always hesitant to display their affection for one another in public. After all, he was still her boss, and they wanted to maintain some professionalism between them. So, instead, she waved indistinctively toward the activity ahead. "Have I missed much?"

Ben shook his head, his longish hair shifting around his face. "They just finished unloading the blocks a little while ago. Nothing much exciting there, unless you enjoy watching beefy guys with forklifts moving around big ice cubes."

Candy gave him a mischievous smile. "Sounds like a perfect date for a Saturday night."

Ben laughed, easing the tension he seemed to be holding inside. "Funny, I always took you for more of a pizza-and-beer kind of woman."

"Pizza and beer?"

"Okay, maybe more like wine and blueberries. By the way, you're looking great today."

She gave him a demure smile and nudged him gently. "You always say that."

"Well, it's always true," he said, and grew serious again as his voice lowered. "Hey, are you sure you're okay about this thing with Solomon?"

"Yeah, I'm okay," she told him honestly, looking off toward her left, past the trees and over the rooftops, "though . . . well, what if it's true? What if he's right?"

"You mean about the body?"

Candy nodded. "What if Solomon really did discover someone in the woods — someone who's hurt or injured? Who could it be?" She paused, considering her own questions as her gaze shifted back to Ben. She gave him a quizzical look. "You haven't heard of anyone missing around town, have you?"

He thought for a moment before shaking his head. "No. Of course, if Solomon really did find a body, it doesn't have to be someone we know — or even someone local."

Candy pursed her lips as she turned toward the ice sculptures and the crowd of workers. "I was thinking the same thing. We've got lots of out-of-towners coming in this weekend. It could be anyone, from any-where."

"It sure could," Ben said, eyeing the shift-ing faces around them, "so maybe we'd bet-ter find out who's alive and then we can begin to figure out who's not."

Candy gave him another nudge and a playful smile. "Hey, that's a not a bad idea. We'll turn you into a detective yet."

He laughed again. "I think I might look pretty good in a deerstalker hat and cape."

"And a pipe," she said as she glanced over at him, studying the angles of his face and his gentle, inquisitive eyes. "You know, I think it'd actually make you look quite dashing." And she couldn't help but lean into him as they approached the ice sculp-tures.

The two forklifts were zipping around the park, whirring and beeping as they lifted and placed the big blocks of ice. Many were set down in freestanding positions, while others were stacked and fused together to form two platforms, which would serve as the foundations for the large multiblock sculptures. Once that part of the operation was complete, the carving could begin.

"I'd heard early rumors they might work through the night," Ben told her, "but I think they've decided to relax tonight instead and start at first light."

"Will they finish in time for the parade?"

He gave her one of his editor's looks. "I don't know, but I know where you can find the answer." With a movement of his hand he indicated the crowd.

She took the hint. "You're a tough taskmaster, Ben Clayton, but I guess you're right. It's time to get to work, isn't it?" She reached into her tote bag, withdrew a notebook, pen, and digital recorder, and flung the bag back over her shoulder. "I'll catch up with you later," she said, and flashing him a smile, she started off.

She began with a hollow-cheeked, pale-skinned, raven-haired woman who introduced herself as Felicia Gaspar, from upstate New York. A professional chef turned ice sculptor, Felicia was dressed in dark blue cargo pants tucked into knee-high, fleece-lined boots, and a navy blue down vest over a thick, sand-colored fisherman's sweater. She wore padded mittens and had pulled back her long, straight hair into a thick braid to keep it out of her way.

"I was born to do this," she told Candy. "When I'm working with the ice, I'm one with it. I can see the harmonics in it — the precise places to chip away the outer layers to reveal what lies beneath. And I can wield a pretty mean chain saw too," she added. "When it comes to cutting into the ice, I'll give any one of these guys around here a run for his money. I may look delicate, but I can be pretty physical."

Candy didn't doubt it. Felicia had a sinewy toughness to her, like a mother snow leopard. "I still cook as much as I can," she said, "but ice carving is my passion now. And my profession as well."

"What will you be carving this weekend?" Candy asked, holding out her digital recorder so she could catch Felicia's response.

"I'll be working on the animals in the large display — deer and moose are a specialty of mine. But my favorites are horses. I won't be doing any of those this weekend, which is a pity. They turn out so majestic in the ice. I once carved an entire team of horses pulling a wagon, for a beer company. That was one of my most challenging works. I won an award for it, you know. I won't be re-creating the entire sculpture this weekend, but I'm going to carve a life-sized sleigh, in honor of the Sleigh and Sled Parade. You'll actually be able to climb up on it. I'll also carve a few smaller pieces. I do a beautiful curling snail with a textured shell and little antennae, for instance."

"How long does all that take?" Candy asked.

"It goes pretty fast. A few hours per piece, I suppose. The larger sculptures will take longer, of course. We'll work in teams, which will help, but we'll be at it all day Friday and Friday night, and into Saturday morning."

She also talked about an international competition she'd recently attended in Alaska and an upcoming one at the Winter Carnival in Quebec. "That's my favorite event. You've been to the carnival, haven't you? No? Oh, you really should go. There's a whole circuit the ice carvers travel, you know. Some even head Down Under in the summer — a perpetual-winter sort of thing. It brings in a few extra dollars. I've been once or twice. Every little bit helps, you know? Hey, who is that guy? Is he with you?"

Caught off-guard, Candy turned to look back over her shoulder. "Who?"

"That guy there. The one with the shaggy brown hair."

Candy focused in the direction she was pointing, and felt a jolt of surprise. "You mean *him?*"

Felicia was talking about Ben.

"He's adorable," Felicia said hungrily.

"Just my type. You don't happen to know if he's available, do you?"

"He . . . what? Available?" Candy didn't know how to respond.

"Yeah, you know, is he hitched? Married? Divorced?"

"Um, yes, he's divorced . . . I think so . . . I mean . . ."

"If I lived in this town, I'd scoop him right up," Felicia said, studying Ben. But after a few moments her gaze shifted to Candy. "Are you a friend of his? I saw you two walking in together."

Candy's mind flashed through a half dozen responses, but she went with the safest, easiest, least-revealing one. "He's my boss."

"Ahh." Felicia nodded. "So you're kinda chummy with him, is that it?"

Candy allowed herself a brief smile. "That's an interesting way to describe it, but yeah, something like that."

"So you, what, kinda date and stuff but nothing too serious yet? Just a casual sort of thing, right?"

Again, Candy hesitated. She didn't know exactly what Felicia was after, and decided the best course was a cautious one. "Ben and I are good friends," she said definitively.

"Uh-huh." Felicia crossed her arms in

front of her as she turned her hawklike gaze back to Ben. "I think I understand. Wonder what he's saying to Gina."

"Who?" For the first time it registered with Candy that Ben was in the midst of a conversation with another woman — a rather plain-looking sculptor with dirty blonde hair, wearing a faded light blue jacket, unflattering jeans, and scuffed work boots. Her long knit scarf was wrapped tightly around her neck, and her hands were stuffed deep in the pockets of her jacket. She looked unhappy about something.

"Gina Templeton, of the self-absorbed Templetons," Felicia explained. She frowned and glanced at Candy. "I guess I shouldn't have said that. She's actually not that bad a person. It's just that her husband, Victor, won a few international competitions, and now she thinks she's the queen bee of the ice-carving circuit. She's a decent carver herself, though not nearly as talented as her husband. He's the true artist in that family — his stuff is fantastic."

Candy looked around, intrigued. "Is he here? I'd like to talk to him."

Together they scanned the crowd. After a moment Felicia nodded toward another group. "I don't see Victor, but have you talked to Liam yet? He's the other alpha dog out here. More than likely you can expect to see at least one blowup between him and Victor this weekend."

Candy's gaze shifted to Liam Yates, the tall, blond Vermonter, who was presently talking to Oliver LaForce, the owner of the Lightkeeper's Inn. Also with them was the inn's new executive chef, Colin Trevor Jones, a young, up-and-coming French Canadian from New Brunswick, east of Maine. With his black wavy hair, finely etched features, and quick, bright smile, Colin had set more than one heart aflutter since he'd landed in town last fall. But he'd proven to be a little clumsy around women, and somewhat tongue-tied when out in a crowd. In the kitchen, however, he was a whiz. He'd already developed a reputation around town for his "classic maritime" cuisine, highlighted by such dishes as crab crepes, lobster bisque, fish chowder, mushroom and beet salad, and French Canadian pork pie. Word was that he'd roughly doubled traffic in the inn's restaurant over the holiday season, and his daily and weekend specials were a constant draw for villagers and out-of-towners alike.

Despite Colin's shyness, Oliver LaForce was not hesitant about promoting his newly acquired and buzz-worthy chef, especially when he realized he could exploit Colin's hidden talent — ice carving. Growing up on hockey rinks in New Brunswick, Colin had taken easily to the icy art, starting in his midtwenties. Now, just a few years later, he was beginning to establish a name for himself. Oliver had taken advantage of the fact, inserting himself and his chef into the event's program.

Candy turned her attention back to Liam. He had a confident attitude, bordering on cocky, Candy decided after watching him for a few moments. She didn't even have to hear what he was saying — she could imagine his words in her head. She'd run into enough men like him — and a few women — when she'd worked in marketing down in Boston a lifetime ago. She'd been happy enough to leave that life behind, but echoes of it continually returned to her, even in this quiet seaside village.

"I haven't talked to him yet," Candy said, fixing her gaze on him, "but he's on my interview list."

"Just make sure you don't buy into his bullcrap," Felicia said, an edge of anger creeping into her voice. "He tends to lay it on pretty thick. And he's completely un-trustworthy. Don't believe a thing he says." Abruptly she caught herself, as if she'd gone too far, and clamped her mouth shut. She scanned the crowd, searching for a way to change the subject. "I don't see Victor anywhere, but he must be around. Until he shows up, you should talk to Gina."

She turned back to Candy. "In fact, I'll tell you what. If you introduce me to your hunky friend Ben, I'll introduce you to Gina and Victor."

At that proposal, Candy could only laugh. She gave Felicia a quick wave. "I think I'll take a rain check, but thanks for the information."

She started off as casually as possible, vowing to keep a sharp eye on Felicia. But for now she had another goal in mind, and someone else she needed to talk to. She had to be discreet about it, though. Her goal was to head toward a stand of trees gathered near the center of the park, but first, as nonchalantly as possible, she circled around to the other side of the work area, where blocks of ice were still being manhandled and placed. As she walked, she thought about Felicia's comments. The dark-haired woman's attraction to Ben was obvious, but Candy was uncertain of how much it bothered her.

She supposed her relationship with Ben was, well, a little strange to most people.

Generally, any single woman her age would probably work quickly to tie up an eligible bachelor like Ben. But Candy had never been much in a rush to do that, and she wasn't quite sure why. Just something inside of her, some sort of intuition, told her the timing wasn't right. Ben seemed to sense it too, which resulted in a certain comfort level between the two of them.

Or maybe they'd both become too complacent about the casual nature of their relationship. Ben had been changing lately — more involved, yet more reclusive in some ways, but nothing she considered out of the norm. Just typical for a Caper.

What a strange little group of people we are, Candy thought happily. *I hope we never change.*

When she felt an appropriate amount of time had passed, and she was sure no one was watching, she slipped off to her right, away from all the activity, and into the denser stand of trees.

Judicious F. P. Bosworth was waiting for her.

SEVEN

Half-hidden behind a tree, Judicious watched her approach with a tense expression on his face. He usually displayed a somber demeanor, though at times his mood lightened, especially on sunny afternoons in the summer. But today he looked all business. His mouth was a tight line, and his eyes were shadowed, with glints of reflected light peeking out.

He was dressed in a black woolen peacoat, long gray scarf, and a black-billed cap with earmuffs, pulled all the way down to his dark eyebrows, so it hid his unruly mop of black hair. As she drew near and came to a stop close by, he glanced warily about, as if he were about to come under attack, his bright blue eyes flicking from side to side before alighting on her again. "There're a lot of people out today," he said, settling deeper into his winter coat. "Colder weather's coming in."

"So I've heard. I haven't seen you around much lately, Judicious. Has everything been going okay?"

"There's a lot been going on," he said, "so I thought you should know."

"What?" Candy felt her sense of dread returning. "Does it have anything to do with Solomon?"

"Maybe. That's the thing — I don't know for sure. It's just a feeling I have."

Candy shivered. It always meant trouble when Judicious had a feeling. As a young man he had taken a mystical journey to Tibet, where he'd spent the better part of two decades sitting on a mountaintop, exploring the mysteries of the universe. Now he was back in Cape Willington, where he lived by himself in a small log cabin on a forested patch of land at the edge of town.

Several of her previous encounters with Judicious had come at opportune times, when she'd been deep in the middle of mysteries. His sudden appearance here, now, out in public, seemingly with a message for her, made her feel even more strongly that something was up. "Have you heard from Solomon? Is he okay?"

"I can't say for sure."

"Do you know where he is?"

Judicious looked back over his shoulder,

to the west. "He's somewhere in the woods."

"Yes, but *where?*"

He pondered the question, his eyes distant, watching. "I don't know for sure. I have a feeling he'll contact you when he's ready."

Conversations with Judicious were always a little odd, but for the most part she'd become used to them. Still, she wished he were a little less cryptic and a little more forthcoming. "Judicious, is there anything specific you can tell me about Solomon? Is he injured? Is there something I can tell the police to help them find him?"

Judicious was silent for a long time as he watched the activities in the park. He seemed fascinated by everything around them. "The police won't find Solomon unless he wants them to," he said finally. "Right now, it seems he doesn't want to be found. And that's a significant point, isn't it?"

Candy felt another chill go through her as she focused her gaze on him. "What are you saying?"

Judicious answered her question with a question. "Why does Solomon feel the need to hide?"

"I don't know. Why?"

A trace of a smile crossed Judicious's face.

"Think about it. Why did he come running out of your woods?"

She saw what Judicious was getting at. The obvious answer quickly came to her. "Because he was afraid of something."

"Yes, but what?"

"The body," she said at once. But she sensed there was something more. Solomon had acted scared, as if something had spooked him. But what could it have been? What had happened in those woods?

Candy lowered her voice as she leaned a little closer to Judicious. "What do you think is going on?"

He shook his head. "As I said, I don't know for sure. But I have a feeling the answers are all around us. You just have to find them. You're a detective, Candy. You've proved that before. You'll know where to look, if you think about it." He pointed with his head over his shoulder, in the direction of Blueberry Acres.

Candy knew exactly what he meant. "The woods."

His gaze shifted to her briefly, then back toward the crowd surrounding the ice sculptures. "There's something else you should know. It's not just me. The sisters feel the same way. They'll tell you all about it. Listen carefully when you talk to them."

"The sisters? Talk to who?" She felt her frustration rising. "Judicious, isn't there anything else you can tell me? Something that would help me figure out what's happening?"

At that, he gave her a melancholy smile. "I can't walk the path for you. You have to discover the answers for yourself. But you'll be fine. Trust your instincts. Yours are very strong, if you haven't noticed."

He did something with his left eye that might have been a wink; it went by so fast Candy couldn't be certain. She heard a shout behind her and turned back toward the crowd. The workers were gathered around one of the ice mountains — the one that would soon become a dragon — and were cheering about something. After watching them for a few moments, she realized what was happening. They'd put the last block into place. The forklifts were powering down. A mini celebration swept through the crowd.

Wanda Boyle was at the center of the scene, snapping photos with a small digital camera, like a seasoned pro.

She's right where I should be, Candy thought as a strange feeling swept through her. She realized that Wanda was moving in on her territory, and that her place in town was in danger of being usurped.

She knew she should probably be upset about that, but instead she just shook her head and sighed. *You have to give the woman some credit,* Candy thought with grudging admiration.

"I've got to get back over there," she said as she turned back toward Justice. But he was gone — as she should have expected.

She scanned the park and thought she saw his black peacoat disappearing between the trees. A moment later any remaining sign of him was blocked by a group of oncoming tourists excited about the events going on in the park.

Judicious had said his piece and made an inconspicuous exit — again.

And once again, he'd left her with more questions than answers. She put her hands on her hips and let out a breath. "Okay, so . . . can anybody tell me what that was all about?" she said to no one in particular.

Strangely enough, she received a reply. "Talking to yourself again?"

Candy twisted around. Maggie had come up behind her.

"Oh, hi, Mags. No, not really. There was someone here a few moments ago — though not right then, when I said that last sentence. I suppose I was alone then, wasn't I?

So yes, the answer to your question is yes, I *was* talking to myself. But not the whole time." She paused and made a face. "I don't suppose that makes any sense, does it?"

Maggie tilted her head. "You know, strangely enough, in a Candy Holliday sort of way, it does. If you were anyone else, I'd recommend a really good psychiatrist. I'd even call and make an appointment for you. But given what's happened around here the past few years, I've learned to avoid snap judgments. So I'm willing to give you the benefit of the doubt."

Candy drew her head back. "Wow, good answer. But I'm not sure if I should be impressed or depressed." In a lowered voice, she added, "Do I really sound that crazy?"

Maggie laughed. "Maybe just a little, but around here I don't think anyone will notice. So what's up?"

Candy shook her head. "You know, I'm not really sure. But it looks like we've got another mystery on our hands. And that's what's got me worried."

Maggie gave her a sympathetic smile and pointed with her eyes to the inn off to their right. "How about a glass of wine, and we can talk it over?"

Candy clapped a hand on her friend's

shoulder and looked around for Ben. "You've been reading my mind."

EIGHT

"So you think it's happening again?" Maggie asked.

Candy took a thoughtful sip of her second glass of white wine. She'd just told Maggie about her encounter with Judicious, and she needed a few moments to formulate an answer. Finally she let out a tense breath. "To be honest, yes. I've been trying hard all day not to overreact. I mean, that's the smart thing to do, right? To try to keep a level head about all this? But after talking to Judicious, I have to agree with him."

"What do you mean?"

"Well, we should have heard something about Solomon by now, right? The police can't seem to find him. Why not? Where is he?"

"Maybe he's just lost," Maggie said, trying to be helpful.

"Maybe. Or maybe he really is in trouble. Maybe, like Judicious said, someone's after him. Maybe he's hiding out in the woods, afraid for his life. Maybe he's injured and needs our help."

"And we're sitting here drinking wine," Maggie said, looking down at her glass.

"Exactly. The truth is, if Judicious thinks something's up, it's hard for me not to believe him. He's essentially corroborating Solomon's story. And you know what that means?"

"What?" Maggie asked.

"It means Solomon was right — there really was a body in the woods."

That seemed to surprise them both, and they sat for a few moments in silence as the other guests in the inn's lounge moved obliviously past them.

After walking over from Town Park, they'd settled into a corner booth and ordered glasses of an aromatic Chardonnay from Washington State. Ben had not yet arrived, but that had given the two of them a chance to talk about the day's events.

"So," Maggie said, trying hard not to sound too ominous, "what should we do about it?"

"I think," Candy replied, "that we need to be proactive rather than reactive."

"Meaning?"

"Meaning we need to search the woods

ourselves."

Maggie's eyes went wide. "You're not thinking of doing it right now, are you?"

"No — much as I'd like to. But it's too late in the day. By the time we got out there it'd be starting to get dark. We wouldn't have enough time to conduct a thorough search. Tomorrow, maybe, depending on what happens."

"We?"

"What?"

"You said, *By the time* we *got out there. . . ."*

"Oh yeah, I guess I did. Well, I don't think I should go alone. That would be irresponsible, right, given what we might find? So I thought about you —"

"Me?" Maggie squeaked, both excited and scared at the same time.

"— but I figured you're probably working all day tomorrow, aren't you?"

Maggie just as quickly deflated. "Oh yeah, that's right, I am. Darn, I always seem to keep missing out, don't I? Because it really would be fun, you know — tramping around the woods all day, freezing my toes off, looking for a crazy old hermit and a dead body, catching a cold, being bedridden for days or weeks, maybe dying of pneumonia. But, you know, good times."

"That's such a gracious way of putting

it," Candy said with an admiring smile.

"It is, isn't it? It's one of my skills, you know — being able to quickly summarize your little mysteries."

"Obviously you missed your calling. So, anyway, I figure I need to take someone who's the outdoorsy type, someone who's got decent survival skills and knows how to find his way out of the woods if we get lost. That's why I'm going to ask Ben to go with me."

Now it was Maggie's turn to give her friend a knowing smile. "You know, that's not a bad idea. It'll be nice for you and him to get out and do something — spend a little time together. If I didn't know better, I'd say you've been planning this."

"Actually it's a spur-of-the-moment kind of thing, but it seems like the most sensible approach. If we should happen to run into any trouble with Solomon, or whoever's chasing him, or whatever it is that's out there in the woods, at least I'll have Ben there to get us out of a jam."

"Think he'll go for it?"

"I think so. He sounds just as worried about Solomon as I am."

"Well, it's a good plan . . . as long as he shows up."

Candy checked her watch and glanced at

the door. "Hmm, you're right about that. I wonder what happened to him."

A little earlier, when they'd found Ben in the park, he'd been standing apart from the crowd, off to one side by himself, deep in thought. After Candy had told him where they were headed, he'd agreed to meet them, but so far he hadn't shown up.

"He must have gotten distracted," Candy said, reaching for her cell phone.

"Sure he did, honey. That's exactly what happened."

"I'll text him and see where he is."

"That's a good idea. I'm sure he just got sidetracked." Maggie placed her chin in the palm of her upturned hand and watched curiously as her friend flipped open her phone and began to key in a quick message. "So how are things going with you and Ben, anyway?" she asked after a few moments.

"Fine."

"You guys been doing anything . . . interesting lately?"

Absently, Candy answered, "Not really. He's been tied up with work a lot lately."

"So I've noticed. What's he working on that's so important, if I may ask?"

"He hasn't talked much about it."

"Isn't that strange? He's talked about everything else with you, hasn't he?"

Candy glanced up at her friend as she punched a few more buttons. "What are you getting at?"

"Well, since last summer he's been hanging out with you a lot, telling you all these things about his life and his family. But he hasn't said much about his work, has he?"

Candy finished keying in her message and pressed the send button. As she slipped the phone back into her pocket, she squinted over at Maggie. "So?"

"So I'm saying that this sort of thing has been happening a lot lately. For the past few weeks you've been telling me he's been distracted a lot. How many times has he canceled on you this month?"

Candy had to think about that. "Now that you mention it, there *have* been a couple of times — two or three, maybe." She shrugged. "He's a busy guy."

"Yes, but doesn't he seem busier than usual lately? When he comes in the dry cleaner's, he barely talks to me. He seems like a different person."

"He *is* a different person, after what happened last summer."

"I know that, but something else has happened lately. I can sense it in him. He seems, well, more preoccupied than usual — if that's possible. He mumbles a lot now

— have you noticed that? And he walks with his head down a lot, like he's looking for a lost fifty-dollar bill."

Candy nodded but said nothing. She'd noticed lots of changes in Ben over the past eight months or so, and most had been positive. So when he'd become immersed in some new project, she hadn't overreacted. She'd asked him about it a couple of weeks ago, and he'd told her vaguely what he was working on — something to do with the history of the town, he'd said. She hadn't pressed him on it, and hadn't thought much about it at the time, but she realized Maggie was right. Whatever he was working on, it was starting to occupy more and more of his time.

She was about to say something to Maggie when her cell phone buzzed. She fished it out of her pocket again.

Ben had texted her a message: *Got held up sorry will touch base soon.*

"Well, shoot," Candy said softly as she closed the phone and tucked it back in her pocket. "It's happened again."

"Ben?"

"He got held up."

"There you go."

"But I thought things were going so well," Candy said, a little bewildered at this most recent development. "He's been hanging around the farm so much for the past six months that I thought things were starting to get . . ."

She let her voice trail off but Maggie finished the sentence for her. "Serious?"

"Yeah, I guess that's the right word. Though I'm still not sure if that's what either of us wants."

"Girl, you and him need to have a heart-to-heart talk very soon and figure out what you want to do."

"I thought that's what we were doing."

"Maybe he had a different reason on his mind for getting cozy with you."

"Like what?"

Maggie shrugged. "He's a man. Who knows? Why don't you ask him?"

"Maybe I should," Candy said thoughtfully, trying hard again not to let herself jump to conclusions. But she couldn't help wonder, in the back of her mind, if the events of eight months ago were somehow linked to the odd behavior she'd witnessed around town today.

NINE

It was near dark when they left the inn. They chatted as they walked to their cars, hunkered down in their winter coats against the chilling air. A brisk wind had kicked up, flicking ice crystals off the tops of snowbanks and tree limbs, whipping stinging white swirls at them. Candy angled her face downward and raised her scarf around her ears and the back of her neck as she waited on the sidewalk for Maggie to climb into her ten-year-old Subaru wagon. The car whirred to life, and Maggie waved and flashed a smile as she backed out of the parking space and started down Ocean Avenue.

Candy's Jeep was only a few spaces away but she made no move toward it. With her hands stuck deep in the pockets of her coat, she turned slightly, her eyes following Maggie's car as it rolled down the street, braking at the light, where several cars waited for it to turn green.

Candy let her gaze drift over toward Town Park, which had quieted down substantially, though a few couples and families lingered, illuminated by the lights strung from trees as they examined the mountains of melded ice that had risen in their midst, and pointed out the beginnings of the ice carvings.

As Candy shifted back around, raising her left arm so she could check the time, her gaze shifted as well, raking casually along Ocean Avenue.

Officer Jody McCroy stood halfway down the street in the halo of a streetlight, watching her discreetly, notebook in hand.

Candy felt her stomach tighten, though she did her best to hide her surprise. She didn't want him to know she'd seen him. And she didn't want to look too guilty.

Though what she might be guilty of, she had absolutely no idea.

She made a show of glancing down at her watch, but she wasn't focusing on the time.

Her mind was racing. *Why is he following me around? And what is he writing down in that notebook of his?*

A wave of irritation rippled through her, and for a moment she thought of walking up to the officer and confronting him about his apparent obsession with her. But she lost her resolve when her cell phone buzzed again, breaking into her thoughts.

It was another text from Ben.

Apologies I can't make it tonite see you tomorrow luv b

Candy read the message twice before she sighed, flipped her phone closed, and slipped it back into her pocket. "My love life sucks," she said to no one in particular.

But, she knew, it just proved that Maggie was right about Ben. He was devoting more and more time to this mysterious project of his, but what could it be? He'd become so open with her over the past six months or so, talking about his life and loves and family and travels, and even occasionally his dreams. Now he was closing up again.

What had happened?

After she thought about it, she realized there might be a way to find out.

As surreptitiously as possible, she glanced back down the street in the direction of Officer McCroy. But he'd retreated to the shelter of the inn, where he hovered by the door, talking to one of the inn's security people. He was angled away from her, intent on the conversation.

Candy turned to look behind her, and saw she was standing near the door to the second-floor offices of the *Cape Crier*.

Moving quickly, she fished her keys out of her pocket and unlocked the glass door, which led to a wooden staircase. Scooting inside before Officer McCroy spotted her, she relocked the door and hurried up the stairs. A dim wall light at the top pushed back the oncoming shadows. She checked the door to the newspaper's offices and, finding it locked, used a second key to open it. Inside, she disarmed the motion-detector security system and again made sure the door was locked behind her, before she paused to catch her breath and survey her surroundings.

The place was empty.

She checked her watch again. It was still early — just after six. But the offices were all dark.

She slipped her keys back into her pocket and considered turning on the hallway lights, but decided against it, opting for a more surreptitious approach. She wasn't doing anything illegal, but with Officer Mc-Croy wandering around outside, keeping a wary eye on her, she felt it best to remain discreet.

She still had her tote bag with her, so she felt around inside for a flashlight. When she flicked it on, she kept it aimed low so no one could see it from outside.

She walked about halfway along the hall to where two doors opened on her right. One led to a small office used for storage. The space also held a couple of desks used by volunteers and interns when they worked at the newspaper.

The second door opened into Ben's office.

The room was dark except for the red, green, and amber glows of indicator lights on computer equipment, power strips, the printer, a charger, a digital clock, and the phone. Ben's beat-up brown leather chair was pushed under the desk. The flat computer screen glowed with a dim gray light. In hurrying out of the office at the end of the day, he sometimes forgot to turn off his computer, though Candy suspected he sometimes left it on overnight on purpose so in the morning all his open files, applications, and browser tabs would be right where he'd left them the night before, and he'd already be logged on to the production server. That way he could start right in, his ideas as fresh as the day. He often kept unfinished articles, notes, and layouts open on his desktop, though minimized into the dock at the bottom of the screen. Candy thought she might find a few clues there. Or she could check his e-mails or the computer files open on the desktop to see if anything interesting jumped out at her. She could also check the hard-copy files in the lower right drawer of his desk or in the old metal two-door filing cabinet pushed into one corner, with stacks of research books piled on top, many of them spewing numerous colored bookmarks and sticky tabs.

She could search in all those areas, if she wanted to. She was alone here. No one would ever know.

But *she* would know.

She hesitated by the door. Even though there might be answers here, she was reluctant to betray Ben's trust by rummaging through his office.

So she postponed the decision and instead headed to her own office. It was an interior room with no windows, so she closed the door and flicked on the overhead light.

She dropped her coat and scarf in a chair, turned on her computer, and while she waited for it to power up, fished Preston Smith's ice-blue business card out of her tote bag. He'd mentioned an assistant but had failed to give Candy the person's name. Nevertheless, she dashed off a quick message to the generic e-mail address listed on the front of the card, then turned to other matters.

She'd convinced herself that Solomon had been truthful when he'd told her he'd found a body in the woods. So who had it been? She was determined to find out.

She spent the next forty-five minutes going back through recent issues of the newspaper, as well as her own e-mails and notes, searching for clues about anyone around town who might be missing. She paid particular attention to the community pages, including her own column. But nothing unusual caught her eye, other than a senior citizen who had wandered away from an assisted living facility and a couple of missing cats.

She pulled out her cell phone and scrolled down through her list of contacts, giving each name an opportunity to spark a memory or help her make a connection. But again, nothing stood out.

She listened to the voice messages on her phone next, with similar results, and finally turned back to her computer.

She'd searched through her own and the newspaper's resources and found nothing about any missing persons, or anything that would give her a clue to the mystery Solomon Hatch had quite literally laid at her feet. But one resource remained — the one she was most reluctant to search, the one managed by the only other local news provider in town.

Wanda Boyle's website.

She had started thinking about it earlier in the day, when she spotted Wanda at the center of the group of celebrating workers and sculptors. Wanda had been plenty busy around town the past few days and had probably talked to as many people as Candy had — maybe more. She'd probably posted several items in the past few days. Her blog might hold a clue or two.

Candy realized she was holding her breath as she keyed the words *cape crusader* into the search engine window and clicked the link to Wanda's site. She'd been on it a few times before but hadn't bookmarked it. For some reason she could never quite figure out, it always made her uncomfortable.

The site loaded quickly. Candy leaned in closer for a better look.

It was a fairly simplistic yet eye-catching design, with flashy typefaces and bright lime green and fluorescent purple colors. In the upper left corner was a fairly large photo of Wanda, dressed as a pseudo-1940s reporter, wearing a rumpled trench coat and fedora, flashing a press badge, with a logo in a Superman-style typeface that read THE

CAPE CRUSADER superimposed over the image.

Other than that it was a typical blog, with daily postings down the middle, a link to other local resource sites on the left side, and a calendar of events and archive on the right, as well as a series of photo albums with digital images Wanda had taken around town.

The most recent postings — three or four, just a few paragraphs each — concerned today's ice-sculpting activities and the upcoming Winter Moose Fest. Wanda had posted snippets of several interviews with sculptors, as well as the images she'd taken just a couple of hours earlier.

She's fast, Candy thought. *And she's good.*

She'd caught Liam Yates complaining about the speed of the ice-block unloading process. Apparently, two of the hired temporary workers had failed to show; Candy made a note to check into it. Gina Templeton promised that her husband, Victor, who had been delayed, would arrive on Friday or by Saturday morning at the latest. Preston Smith told Wanda he was charmed by the event, mentioned a special sponsorship program he was promoting, and extended warm and congratulatory words for everyone who had anything even remotely to do with the event, which he was anxiously awaiting to see when it came to fruition on Saturday. Oliver LaForce was pleased to be involved in local efforts to bring the art of ice sculpting to Cape Willington, and his new executive chef, Colin Trevor Jones, expressed his enthusiasm for this great event and, flashing a charming smile (according to Wanda), added his hope for its continued growth and success.

Candy made a noise of disgust in her throat and scrolled on down.

Wanda had also interviewed a few of the folks who would be driving sleighs in the parade tomorrow, including an eighty-five-year-old farmer from New Hampshire who had been tending horses since he was three, and was driving a sleigh that had been owned by his grandparents, who had homesteaded in the state in the eighteen hundreds. Wanda included a photo of the farmer, who went by the name of Mason Parker. He stood angularly next to his horse, Jack, and both animal and master had similar disinterested expressions. Mason's family owned a maple sugar shack and pancake house between Nashua and Keene in the southern part of the state. He and Jack gave hay-wagon rides in the fall and sleigh rides in the winter through the family's property. He usually traveled with his wife, he said in the article, but she hadn't come with him this time, as she'd been feeling poorly lately.

Wanda had compiled a complete listing of all the sleighs and drivers who were scheduled to appear in the parade, and Candy skimmed through the list, searching for anything unusual, but nothing jumped out at her. It was all routine stuff. A father-and-daughter team, named the Summerfields, minus the mother, who had apparently stayed home. A teenage boy, his grandfather, and his uncle — where were the parents? But most were older couples from surrounding towns and villages — places like Ellsworth and Bucksport and Winter Harbor. Two of the entries were from Mount Desert Island, while a few had come from farther away, from the west toward Fryeburg or south toward Portland.

Wanda had done a competent, thorough job, Candy thought as she read through the blog post. She'd even kept track of those who had already arrived in town and those who had yet to arrive. The Schmidts, Carvers, Frosts, Bonvieves, and Dockenses were checked in at local hotels and inns, while the Cobbs, Franks, Hawthornes, Delamains, and Tuckers were scheduled to arrive by Friday afternoon. The stragglers would just make it for the twilight-timed parade. There were also a few other ice sculptors still due in, including Duncan Leggmeyer and Baxter Bryant, along with Baxter's wife, Bernadette.

In the next post, Wanda passed along some last-minute tips from two of the town's snowplow operators, Francis Robichaud and Tom Farmington, who described the conditions of the town's streets and sidewalks, and advised on parking for the weekend's events.

It wasn't Pulitzer Prize–winning journalism, but it was decent enough for a community blog, Candy had to admit.

In that moment she couldn't help but feel a tinge of jealousy. She, Ben, and a few volunteer correspondents had already covered much the same ground in the previous issue of the paper, but Wanda had done it all on her own, in a matter of hours. She was tenacious and driven in a way Candy couldn't completely understand. She'd seen it quite often in metropolitan Boston and New York, but it seemed out of place here in quiet, slow-paced Maine, where business suits and cold competitiveness were generally left at the border, and life was more off the beaten path, even in cities like Portland,

Augusta, and Bangor. Then again, cold competitiveness in particular could rear its head anywhere — even here in Cape Willington, Maine.

Candy scanned the rest of the posts, and about halfway down found one that drew her attention. It concerned two of the sculptors, Liam Yates from Vermont and Victor Templeton, Gina's husband.

Wanda had apparently dug up some old newspaper clippings and online postings, which detailed a fairly intense feud between the two sculptors. Tempers had flared and words had been exchanged between the two as recently as a few weeks ago. The feud seemed to stretch back several years. Candy remembered that, earlier in the day, Felicia Gaspar had alluded to animosity between the two sculptors.

Wanda also noted a year-old battle between Liam Yates and Duncan Leggmeyer, which centered on some sort of trophy for a hatchet-throwing contest, but details were sketchy. Candy scanned through it all with mild interest. Wanda promised her readers that she'd continued to dig and post more revelations as she unearthed them.

Maybe I need to do some digging around myself, Candy thought.

A long list of comments to Wanda's posts

had generally expressed interest in her revelations and curiosity about future findings, though a few posters had defended the sculptors and called the disagreements overblown. And one comment in particular, posted by someone identified only as *White-field,* thought there was something much more sinister going on.

That caught Candy's attention. Disagreements among sculptors were one thing, but *sinister?* That seemed a little extreme.

Candy read through the rest of the comments, and finding nothing else of interest, decided to give up for the night. As she logged off, she pondered the animosity between Liam Yates and some of the other sculptors. It was something she'd have to keep an eye out for the following day. She'd also try to figure out who, if anyone, was missing around town, and find out, one way or the other, what had happened to Solomon Hatch.

As her computer powered down, she glanced toward the filing cabinet against the opposite wall. She'd been in the bottom drawer only once in the past two years. It held the writings and research of a ghost. "I don't think you can help me tonight, Sapphire," she said, addressing the bottom drawer with a melancholy smile, "but thanks for the offer."

She shrugged into her coat and slipped the scarf around her neck. Turning out the light in her office, she retraced her steps to the front door, walking past Ben's office. But she didn't go in. She'd decided she wasn't about to start snooping on him, no matter what he might be up to.

Back at the farm that night, after Doc had gone to bed and the world had quieted down under its winter blanket, Candy lay awake with the lights off, turned toward her bedroom window, which looked out over the blueberry fields behind the house. The nearly full moon had risen, casting its soft blue glow on the landscape. The Native Americans called this the Wolf Moon, Doc had told her a few days ago, though sometimes it was called the Snow Moon. Either would fit, she decided, pulling the top blanket off the bed and wrapping it around her as she rose and walked to the window.

Few things in this world were more beautiful than a moonlit winter's night, she mused as she gazed out through the frost-speckled glass. In the moon's light, she could see every undulation of the landscape, every dip and swell, every shelled boulder and sugared bush.

She could also see something moving.

Startled, she took a step back into the shadows of the room, watching as . . . something . . . emerged from the woods at the top of the ridge. At first she thought it was Solomon Hatch again, until she realized it stood taller than a man, and had an elongated head.

It turned and ambled along the edge of the woods at a leisurely pace, headed in a westerly direction, away from her. After a few moments it disappeared back into the woods.

It was a white moose.

Ten

She woke in the early morning light, feeling unrested and off center. She knew she needed another hour of sleep, maybe two, but she was determined to be present in Town Park when the first chain saw bit into a block of ice. So she pulled herself out of bed and padded across the cold wood floor to the bathroom, where she struggled to force herself awake.

After her bout of midnight restlessness and the unexpected moonlit moose sighting, she had returned to her bed and burrowed under the blankets, but instead of falling asleep, she lay for what seemed like hours as everything that had happened the day before played back in her head. Her mind seemed to be searching for something — clues, connections, relationships, secrets . . . something.

When her thoughts had finally quieted down and she'd drifted into a light sleep, she'd dreamt of shadows and light and things in the woods — of Solomon Hatch and the white moose, and of something else, a presence she couldn't quite identify.

It all left her feeling unsettled, and as she dressed quietly, she cast a few wary glances out the bedroom window, at the woods and the fields behind the house. But she saw nothing unusual. It looked typically peaceful, a landscape intimately familiar to her, though she couldn't help but feel it had somehow changed in subtle ways. Her sense of safety had been breached the moment Solomon Hatch stepped out of the woods nearly twenty-four hours ago. Her gaze drifted several times toward the line of trees on the far ridge, searching into the muted shadows that faded back into ghostlike infinity.

Solomon was out there somewhere, but so was something else, deep in the woods. She knew it; she could feel it.

If there were any answers to be found, that's where she would have to look, out among the trees. But she had no time to investigate now. That would come later in the day.

As she passed Doc's half-opened bedroom door, she heard him rustling around inside, and downstairs he'd put on a pot of coffee for her. She poured a packet of sweetener into the bottom of a cup, splashed the coffee over it, took a few quick sips, and ate half a piece of buttered toast before she bundled up, grabbed her tote bag, and journeyed out into the clear, frosty morning.

Her trusty old Jeep started on the third try, and she nimbly negotiated the snow-packed roads toward town. The Jeep's four-wheel-drive system came in extra handy at this time of year, especially on the dirt road leading out to the farm, which gained a thick layer of snow and ice in mid-December that didn't melt away entirely until late March, if they were lucky.

She soon pulled into a primo parking spot on Ocean Avenue and hurried into Town Park, just as the day's events were getting under way. The temperature had dipped into the teens overnight and was barely edging into the twenties as bright morning light slanted in from out over the ocean, but that hadn't prevented a fairly large crowd of onlookers from gathering to witness the kickoff of the weekend's ice-sculpting exhibition. The crowd stood around one of the mountains of ice behind a roped barrier while a smaller group of seven or eight individuals, dressed mostly in jeans, fleece pullovers, parkas, and boots, stood inside the ropes in front of the ice. Candy recognized Mason Flint, the chairman of the town council, standing between Oliver LaForce and Colin Trevor Jones. The ice sculptors stood to one side, while on the other side was Wanda Boyle, clicking off shots with her digital camera.

As Candy approached she dug into her tote bag, pulled out her digital recorder, and flicked it on, just as Mason Flint launched into his opening remarks.

"Good morning, everyone, and thank you for coming!" he said jovially. He was a lean, elderly gentleman, with a full head of white hair hidden under a colorful knit cap. "It's very exciting to see everyone here this morning, and we thank you all for coming, especially our professional ice carvers. We're thrilled to host this very special exhibition here in our little seaside community, and we hope it leads to a larger professional event in the near future. Of course, none of this would have been possible without the generous support of local businesses, as well as the involvement of the Pruitt Foundation, which helped with the procurement and transportation of the ice. I'd also like to thank our wonderful anonymous donor, who helped underwrite the travel expenses and fees for all of our ice carvers here this weekend. Now, I'd like to briefly introduce our ice carvers, and then we'll ask Chef Colin Trevor Jones of the Lightkeeper's Inn to make the first cut."

Liam Yates gave a confident wave as his name was mentioned, and Felicia Gaspar and Gina Templeton smiled as warmly as possible, given the chilly temperatures. Next, Mason introduced two newcomers who had arrived in town overnight. Duncan Leggmeyer was an outdoorsy, construction type with a full beard and a ponytail that hung halfway down his straight, muscled back, while Baxter Bryant was a retired military man who'd spent twenty years as a cook in the navy and now specialized in barbecue during the summer months and ice sculpting in the winter. He traveled with his wife, Bernadette, in an RV, along with their little puffball of a dog, Snowball.

With the introductions complete, Mason nodded toward Colin Trevor Jones, who started up an electric chain saw. With his black wavy hair stylishly uncombed and safety goggles firmly in place, he wielded the whirring chain saw at a red line marked on a block of ice, deftly made the first cut, and the ice-carving exhibition was officially under way.

Muffled hand claps and a few bedraggled cheers and whistles rose among the sleepy onlookers, many of whom had steaming cups of coffee or hot chocolate in hand. Following Colin's cue, other chain saws buzzed to life, and the serious work began.

Candy wanted to talk to Duncan and Baxter, the new arrivals, but she knew she'd have to wait until later, as they were already busy cutting into the ice, calving off huge chunks as they began to shape the blocks. Like the other ice sculptors, they moved quickly with broad cuts; the detail work would come later.

With the ice sculptors occupied for at least a while, Candy knew she'd have to be content with another approach, so she interviewed a few of the onlookers for local flavor. After that, she cornered Oliver LaForce and pried a few decent quotes out of him about the effect of the Moose Fest on the local economy. The inn would be full over the weekend, and the local establishments along Ocean Avenue and Main Street, not to mention those all the way up along Route 192 to Route 1, would get a sizable dose of much-needed revenue. The midwinter jolt in the economic arm would be enough to hold most of them over until the spring thaw and tourist season arrived.

As far as the interviews went, it was all fairly mediocre stuff — not the hard-hitting copy she was looking for — but it was the best she could do for the moment.

She looked around and realized Wanda had disappeared. *She's probably somewhere warm, uploading photos and posting to her blog,* Candy thought grimly. *She always seems to be one step ahead of me lately.*

To make herself feel better, Candy lingered near Colin Trevor Jones for a bit, watching his graceful, precise movements as he shaved away at the ice, until he finally stepped back to take a break. When he turned her way, she gave him a quick wave. He grinned back and, ruddy-faced and encrusted in ice crystals, walked over to talk to her. Before long he was describing the exhilaration of cutting into ice and pulling out the shapes within. It was just the type of stuff she was looking for, plus it gave her an excuse to hang around Colin a while, though she realized he was probably a little too young for her.

Of course, it never hurt to enjoy the view.

When she asked him for his opinions of the other ice sculptors, he was quick and witty in his assessments, calling Liam "focused and aggressive yet nimble" and saying of Felicia, "She has the delicate touch of a painter, even when she's holding a chain saw in her mitts."

They talked a little longer, but finally he went back to work, and she stepped back to assess the progress the ice sculptors had made so far. The shapes hidden within the ice were still indistinct, though she could see a general framework beginning to emerge. Still, it was clear there was much work left to be done. This was confirmed for her by Preston Smith, who appeared suddenly at her side, two cups of coffee in hand.

"Ah, Ms. Holliday, you're looking very chilly out here this morning," he said pleasantly. "Perhaps I could interest you in a warm beverage." He held out one of the foam cups to her.

Candy took it gratefully. "That's very nice of you, Preston, and yes, thanks, I'll gladly accept."

"No cream, one pack of sugar substitute, just the way you like it," he said with a broad smile as he passed her the cup.

Candy gave him a curious look. "Well, that's . . . that's very sweet of you. But how do you know how I like my coffee, if I may ask?"

Preston was sipping from his cup and so couldn't answer immediately, but instead pointed up the street with a gloved finger. "The waitress at the diner. She told me," he said after he'd swallowed. "Such friendly people! What a wonderful town you have here! I'm confident I've chosen the right place for our new event." He paused as his expression turned to one of concern. "Unfortunately, this issue with the dead body in the woods could make us reconsider our decision — if it's true, of course. What's the status of the case? Have the police found out anything?"

Candy shook her head. "Not that I'm aware of, but I think they're still looking."

"And what about you? I've heard you're something of a detective around here. Are you conducting your own investigation?"

A brief smile crossed Candy's face. "I'm not really a detective," she said simply.

"But you've apparently had some success solving a few local mysteries. One of the waitresses over at the diner seems to think you're a local celebrity. In fact, you've developed quite a reputation with the townspeople. And from what I've heard, you're personally involved in this latest . . . episode. Surely you have some interest in it."

"Of course I do," Candy said, "but I've been asked to stay out of it."

Preston gave her a discerning look, his eyes gauging her. "Perhaps I'm prying too much. There's no reason you should betray your confidences to me, of course. Perhaps, if I tell you a little bit of news I've heard, you'll let me know a bit about your investigation."

Clever, Candy thought. "As I said, I'm not a detective, and I'm not conducting an investigation. But I'm always interested in the latest news. What have you heard?"

"Well, this isn't public knowledge yet, but I can assure you it's accurate." He leaned closer to her and said in a low, conspiratorial whisper, "Victor Templeton has pulled out of the event."

Candy's eyebrows rose. "Really?"

"Indeed." He drew back. "I received a communiqué from him just last night. He has been, well, he says he's been irretrievably delayed, but I suspect there's something else going on." He gave Candy a knowing smile.

She was intrigued. "Like what?"

"Weeeelll," Preston said, drawing out the word dramatically, "there have been rumors of, shall we say, ill feelings among some of the sculptors? Which, naturally, has led to some complications." He turned to face the sculptors, then subtly nodded with his head in their direction, a smile like the Cheshire cat's playing across his face. "See for yourself. It's quite evident if you know what you're looking for."

So Candy looked.

The ice sculptors were busy at work, chipping away at the ice, following a pattern marked on the surface in broad sweeps. Most of them seemed absorbed in their work, but Baxter Bryant was cracking jokes with one of the onlookers and, in a playful moment, tossed a handful of shaved ice into the crowd, drawing a mixture of squeals, groans, and laughter. He did it again, much to the delight of the crowd. He appeared to have quite an outgoing personality.

Duncan Leggmeyer, on the other hand, was quieter and more studious, peering intently at the ice, as if searching for the perfect form within. He was working close by Felicia, who kept glancing his way, as if trying to catch his attention. But he either didn't notice her or was trying to ignore her.

On Duncan's other side was Gina Templeton, and on the other side of her were Baxter and Colin. They were all picking away at the same sculpture, working on different parts of it, as if in a team.

That's when Candy realized what Preston

meant. Liam Yates was working all by himself on the other sculpture.

It was as if the ice carvers were allied five to one, and Candy suddenly felt a wave of fierce, unspoken competitiveness wash over the field.

They're all working together to try to beat Liam, she realized.

Liam himself appeared oblivious to what was going on around him. He had an intent expression on his face, and despite the fact that he was working alone, he was proceeding nearly as quickly as the other five sculptors combined, efficiently trimming away at the ice with a steady hand.

"What's going on?" Candy asked, turning back around. But she received no answer from Preston. He was no longer standing beside her. She twisted back and forth, searching for him, muttering under her breath about the strange behavior patterns of everyone in this odd little village, and finally caught sight of him headed away from her, turning just slightly to wave over his shoulder.

She also spotted someone else as her gaze swept the park. She focused in on his face.

It was Officer Jody McCroy, standing perhaps twenty-five feet away, almost directly in front of her, alternatively looking her way and down at his notebook. He was writing something.

Probably something about her, she thought as a flash of anger swept through her.

Before she knew what she was doing, she was marching toward him, determined to find out what was going on.

ELEVEN

She approached him at a brisk pace, bearing down on him like a bull on a matador, but he held his ground almost casually. Slipping his notebook and pen into a pocket, he shifted his body around slightly to face her full on, and pulled his coat aside as he dropped one hand to his utility belt, perhaps in an effort to draw attention to the items it held, including a flashlight, Taser, handcuffs, and pepper spray, as well as his sidearm, all within easy reach.

Candy barely noticed. She was determined to get answers.

"Officer McCroy," she called out when she was still several yards away, "will you tell me what in the heck's going on?"

He nodded curtly and professionally. "Ma'am, just calm down."

"I am calm," Candy said as she stopped a few feet in front of him, crossing her arms tightly in front of her for emphasis, "but I want to know what you're up to. You've been following me around for two days now, writing things down in that little notebook of yours and making no effort to conceal yourself. Am I under investigation?"

The police officer pressed his lips together, but otherwise his face remained stoic. "No, ma'am."

"Then why the shadow routine?"

"Ma'am?"

She let out a breath of frustration. "Why are you always standing there when I look around? Just tell me what this is all about."

"I'm not at liberty to say, ma'am."

"You can call me Candy. Who *is* at liberty to say?"

"That would be Chief Durr, ma'am, um, Ms. Holliday."

"The chief?" Candy made a face. "But why would he tell you to . . . ?

She caught herself as she suddenly realized the answer. "Does this have anything to do with that body in the woods?"

"I can neither confirm nor deny that, ma'am, pending chief's orders."

"You're trying to keep me out of trouble, aren't you? You're afraid I'm going to solve another mystery in this town and embarrass the police department, right?"

Officer McCroy remained silent. She

knew she had struck a nerve. She pressed on.

"So, what? You're following me because you think I'm investigating the mystery on my own and will stumble upon a few clues?"

"It's possible Mr. Hatch might contact you again at some point," Officer McCroy confirmed. "We want to be there if he does."

"Ah, so that's it. I'm sort of an accessory to an alleged murder?"

After a few moments, the officer said, "It's for your own safety, ma'am."

"Hmm." Candy studied him for a few moments. "Have you found Solomon yet?"

No response.

"Are you conducting any more searches today, or have you called the whole thing off?"

"I'm not at liberty to discuss police business with a civilian."

"So," Candy said, as if that proved her theory, "I'm right, aren't I? This is Chief Durr's way of keeping me in line."

Officer McCroy's gaze narrowed in on her, and as if he were echoing the chief's words, he said, "If I can give you one piece of advice, ma'am, you should leave the detecting to the detectives."

"Yeah, I've heard that before," Candy muttered under her breath as her cell phone buzzed, distracting her. She shook her head as she turned away and fished in a pocket for her phone. She didn't recognize the number that flashed on the phone's small front display screen, though it was a local area code. She flipped it open and held it to her ear. "Hello?"

"Is this Candy Holliday?"

She said that it was. "Who's this?"

"My name is Annabel Foxwell. You may have heard of me. I live at Shipwreck Cove with my sisters."

Candy had indeed heard of her. The Foxwell sisters — Annabel, Isabel, and Elizabeth — were local, middle-aged eccentrics who lived in a weathered, hundred-year-old saltbox on a seaside homestead not far from Blueberry Acres. They had quite a piece of land — somewhere in excess of ten acres, Candy remembered, some of it prime coastline — that had been handed down in their family far generations. People around town called them the Psychic Sisters and rarely disturbed them, an arrangement that seemed to be a silent agreement among all parties. Candy had caught fleeting images of them around town but had never met any of them personally.

To receive a phone call from one of them was a major coup.

"Yes, Ms. Foxwell, I've heard of you. It's wonderful to hear from you. To what do I owe this unexpected pleasure?"

When she spoke, Annabel's voice was rushed and whispery. "I don't mean to alarm you, Candy, but my sisters and I have received a message, and we have some very important information we need to share with you."

"What type of information?"

"It's not something we can discuss over the phone. We'll need to speak to you in person. As you probably know, we're not used to entertaining guests. But we've decided to make an allowance just this once. Would you be able to come out to see us at Shipwreck Cove?"

Candy blinked several times. She was surprised by the invitation. "Well, yes, of course. When were you thinking?"

"Today," Annabel said emphatically. "This morning if possible. When would be a good time?"

Candy thought quickly and glanced at her watch. It was just past nine. She still wanted to finish up some interviews here, and she'd thought about stopping in to see Doc and the boys at the diner to find out if they'd heard any news about Solomon, but that could wait until later. "About ten thirty?"

She heard discussion in the background. "That would be fine. Do you know how to get here?"

Candy said she did, and after saying goodbye, she keyed off the call.

She felt her heart beating just a bit faster. She seemed to finally be onto something, though what it might be, she had no idea. Still, she knew the clues were all around her, just as Judicious had said. She just had to follow them.

The game was on.

Out of the corner of her eye, she glanced over at Officer McCroy, who had taken a few steps away and was engaged in a conversation with one of the younger men in the crowd — a friend of some sort, Candy surmised.

If she was going to have any sort of freedom to begin her own investigation, she'd have to lose the Boy Scout.

After a few moments, she grinned to herself. "I think I have an idea."

TWELVE

She spent the next forty-five minutes darting around the ice sculptures, conducting quick, on-the-run interviews, trying to shoot a few decent pictures, and making sure she appeared as normal — and as unexciting — as possible. She spent another fifteen minutes or so mingling with the growing crowd, drinking coffee, and talking with Maggie on her cell phone as she bided her time, watching for her best opportunity.

At one point she shivered, looked up at the blue-gray sky, and took a dark wool cap from her tote bag. While she talked she absently pulled on the cap and lifted the collar of her coat, disguising most of her honey-colored hair.

When a few oohs and ahhs arose from the crowd, and a wave of warm applause and cheers swept through the park, Candy figured that was the best distraction she'd get and made her move — as casually and as discreetly as possible.

Keeping her head low so she'd blend in with the crowd, she began to drift along a broad, well-trodden pathway between the snowbanks, headed in the general direction of the inn across the street. She stayed close to groups of three or four people, using them to shield herself from any eyes that might be observing her.

In a few minutes she was out of the park. She crossed Ocean Avenue with the crowds at the red light, again mingling with chattering, excited tourists and townies headed in both directions.

On the far side of the street she continued straight ahead with eight or ten other people who were headed toward the Lightkeeper's Inn. The hotel looked like a stately, snow-wrapped princess, pale and delicate, yet steadfast against the weather, and offering the promise of a cozy respite from the chilly temperatures.

Those who entered, including Candy, were not disappointed, for a great roaring fire in the lobby helped to thaw out the inn's guests. But while the others loitered by the fire or headed for their rooms, Candy quickened her pace, threading her way through and around the guests, bags, and carts littering the lobby, and walking past the front desk, a cozy sitting area, a door that led into a small business office, and a small yet very active coffee bar tucked into a corner under the broad staircase leading to the second floor. She angled right and entered a carpeted hallway that led past some of the inn's small meeting rooms and offices.

Up to this point she'd judiciously avoided looking behind her, but it had been driving her crazy. She had to know if she was being followed, so halfway along the hall she ducked into a familiar doorway that led to a small receptionist's office and two inner offices, belonging to the innkeeper, Oliver LaForce, and the assistant innkeeper, Alby Alcott.

As she'd hoped, all three offices were empty. Everyone was busy elsewhere. She knew she probably had only a few minutes alone, but she didn't intend to linger long. She leaned back against the wall just inside the doorway, took a few moments to catch her breath, and as carefully as possible, edged her head toward the doorway so she could peek around the corner into the hallway and lobby beyond.

She scanned every face, every guest as quickly as she could, but she saw no one who looked like the police officer.

With the faint hope that she'd already ditched him, she started off again, continuing along the hallway and exiting through another door onto the side porch. Hands tucked deep into her pockets, she hurried down the stairs and angled toward the rear of the building, snuggling into her coat in an effort to appear as inconspicuous as possible. She followed a narrow pathway between thigh-deep snow to a tree-framed parking lot, which she hurried across. On the other side, she entered a narrow alleyway that ran behind the back doors of the shops along Ocean Avenue. The buildings were spaced closely together here, with only a few feet between them, and some were attached to one another.

She soon came to a walkway that led between two of the brick buildings. She slipped through as quickly as she could, since the wind funneling into the narrow space made it seem frostier than the surrounding air, and exited onto busy Ocean Avenue.

Dodging pedestrians and traffic, she crossed to a storefront on the other side and pushed through a glass door.

"There you are," Maggie said from behind the counter. She'd been reading a magazine; she had no customers at the moment. "I was beginning to think you weren't going to show."

"I was trying to throw him off my trail," Candy said as she crossed the small, carpeted reception area, staying well away from the front window. She headed behind the counter with Maggie, then sidestepped back around a corner so she wouldn't be seen by anyone looking in from the street. She peered around the corner, scrutinizing the passersby outside. "Any sign of our friendly young police officer?"

Maggie glanced out the storefront window as casually as possible, scanning the street outside. "Not a single uniform in sight — not even a Boy Scout. I think you've lost him for the time being. But I'd stay hidden if I were you. The moment he realizes you've slipped away, he'll come looking for you, and he'll probably walk right past here."

"Is everything ready?"

Maggie turned with her hands on her hips and gave Candy a look. "Well of course everything's ready. It's like a wedding. I live for stuff like this. Come on." She waved an arm as she walked past Candy into the back room, which was filled mostly with racks of cleaned, plastic-encased clothes waiting for pickup by customers. Off to one side were bins of tagged clothes, awaiting pickup for cleaning, which was done off-site.

"I did the best I could on such short notice," Maggie said, "but I think it'll all work. I even found an old wig, believe it or not, though I'm not sure you'll need it."

She paused at the center of the room and pointed. "The shirts, pants, boots, and hats are on the shelf to your right. That's the best stuff from the unclaimed bin, and most of it should fit you. I think there's a couple of flannel shirts, a really nice puffy down-filled vest, a thick cardigan sweater, and some scarves and hats with earflaps. The coats are hanging on that first rack. They should bulk you out real nice."

Rubbing her chin, Candy considered the bounty laid out before her with discerning eyes. "Yes, I think you're right," she said after a few moments. "This should work out just fine. So, where do we start?"

Ten minutes later, Candy left the dry cleaner's by the back door. The Jeep remained parked out front. She'd be taking Maggie's Subaru, which was parked up on the tail end of Main Street — perfect for Candy's purposes.

Seven or eight layers of flannel, down, cotton, and canvas gave her a huskier look, which she hoped would enable her to make good her escape undetected. She'd opted for a black and gray billed hat with thick earmuffs and a dark green scarf. She'd finished it all off with scuffed work boots, dark brown leather gloves, and wraparound sunglasses, which hid the color of her eyes.

As she walked along the lane behind the storefronts, she even tried to adjust her gait, making her steps heavier and more deliberate, to add to the illusion of being a middle-aged man. Continuing up the slope, she kept her head down but occasionally glanced around her.

She'd just navigated her way through another narrow, snow-clogged passageway between buildings and emerged onto the upper end of Main Street when she practically walked right into Officer McCroy. He had his back to her, thumbs locked into his utility belt, scanning the street in front of him — searching for her, she had no doubt. As inconspicuously as possible she turned to her right, brushing past him. She lifted her left shoulder and tucked her head down, in case he should glance in her direction, but if he did, he paid her no attention. She was just one of the townies, maybe a plumber or bus driver or oil deliverer, in worn baggy corduroys, huddled against the cold and headed home for the afternoon.

Candy slipped away unnoticed.

Rather than drive down Main Street past Officer McCroy, she headed out to the Coastal Loop, following it around past the English Point Lighthouse, Town Park and the inn, past Pruitt Manor and the Lobster Shack, and back out of town in the direction of Blueberry Acres. But instead of taking the turnoff toward the farm, she continued on, past the low brush and thin pine trees, rocky patches, and occasional glimpses of the coastline. Houses dotted both sides of the road, most sitting on several acres each, making them well spaced. Some were newer, rambling rustic or country styles, with porches and large chimneys. Others stood more upright, with long windows and steep metal roofs designed to easily shed snow and ice. She even passed small capes and saltboxes, like Ray Hutchins's place.

After a few miles she started watching for a turnoff on her left, eventually wheeling the car onto Long Heath Lane, a dirt road that ran through rocky, tree-lined bluffs before reaching the coast, where it split, leading to properties both left and right. There were some incredibly expensive places tucked in and around the coves and crags of this rugged coastline. Candy turned right, drove another few hundred yards, and parked in front of a gray ramshackle building that looked as if it'd been beaten by the sea for a hundred or more years. But it still stood, and overall looked in good repair. The sisters had done some work on it the previous summer, Candy recalled. They'd had Ray Hutchins, the town handyman, out to do the work for them.

They had a stunning piece of property, tucked on a shelf of land above the sea. There would be no basement in a place like this. The oil tank was most likely inside somewhere, in a laundry or storage room. Gray smoke wafted lazily from a stone chimney but was picked up and whisked away by the ever-present breeze coming off the sea.

As she climbed out of the car, Candy shed some of her bulkier items, including the outer canvas coat and blue down vest. She'd brought her tote bag with her, tucked under her outer coat, and now slung it over her shoulder. The pathway to the front door was well shoveled and sanded. The sea beyond looked dark blue and foamy — *sort of like blueberry froth,* she thought whimsically.

It was a sudden, happy thought, crossing her mind unbidden as she approached the small cement step and wooden door, and it

made her think of the warmest, most sensu-
ous days of summer.

Where the heck had *that* come from? she
wondered as she knocked.

THIRTEEN

Candy wasn't quite sure what she expected — a mystical aura of light surrounding the door, perhaps, or the sound of chanting voices from inside, or a black cat brushing against her legs. But she noticed none of that. Instead, hanging on the door, she saw a homemade wreath of dried, snow-dusted vines intertwined with lavender and sprigs of blueberry bushes heavy with purplish, puckered fruit. Black metal strap hinges, which extended almost the entire way across the door, had a rough, handmade appearance, as if they'd come straight from a blacksmith's shop. A black door latch replaced a standard knob, adding a charming touch.

After a few moments the latch lifted and the door creaked open.

A pleasant-looking woman with a thin face, large olive eyes, and long, brushed-out hair the color of late autumn leaves, streaked with gray here and there, greeted her. "Hello. You must be Candy Holliday," she said softly. "I'm Isabel Foxwell. Please, come in."

She opened the door wider and stepped aside so Candy could enter, then closed the door quickly behind her to keep the cold out. "You can place your boots there on the drying rug and hang your coat" — she paused as she noticed Candy's clothes — "well, your *coats* on those pegs." She smiled warmly. "Then come on into the sitting room. We have a fire going, and hot mint tea and fresh-baked cookies waiting for you."

Before she entered the house, Candy knocked the sand and muck off her boots, then stepped inside gingerly, staying to the rubber mats and rugs. She was in a short hallway converted into a mudroom, typical of most Maine homes in the winter. Against the right wall was a pine bench, where one could sit while putting on or taking off boots, and beside that stood an elegant wicker shelf for storing gloves and scarves. A row of eight or ten wooden pegs, like something you'd find in a horse tack shop circa 1900, provided a place for hanging coats. The far-left peg was available, and that's where Candy hung up her assorted items of clothing, since all the other pegs were occupied by a wide variety of colorful coats, shawls, and sweaters; apparently the sisters left only one peg free for guests.

She left on her undershirt, flannel shirt, and jeans, and in her stocking feet she padded forward, following the warming air and tempting smells of cookies and burning wood. After a half dozen paces she walked into the front sitting room, which overlooked the sea.

It was a breathtaking panorama. For a few moments Candy stood mesmerized. She'd always felt the lure of the sea, and standing in the room looking out, even on this overcast day, she was struck by the beauty and majesty of the ocean. The sisters' cottage had a rustic, organic charm about it, due in part to the bare wooden floors that gleamed in the firelight and the comfortable, overstuffed furniture arrayed around the hearth, which she noticed was a single, eight-foot-long piece of raw granite, uneven across its surface. A stack of logs for the fire sat at one end of the hearth, and a basket of kindling and a pile of newspapers occupied the other side.

"Sit here," one of sisters said, holding out her hand for Candy to shake. "I'm Annabel, the one you talked to on the phone. Welcome to our home. Sit and I'll pour you some tea." Her hair was darker and frizzier than her sister's, but she had the same slim face and olive eyes, though hers were a shade darker, flecked with brown.

The third sister sat across from Candy, on the other side of a thick multicolored rug that looked woven by hand. She gave Candy a hesitant wave and, in a soft, reserved voice, said, "Hello. I'm Elizabeth." She wore a thick, sage green knitted shawl over an ankle-length denim skirt that buttoned down the front. She had the same facial features as her sisters, though she was paler than they were, as if she rarely ventured outside, and looked like the youngest of the three. But her most striking feature was her long graying hair, parted in the middle and hanging nearly to her waist. It contrasted oddly with her supple skin, expressive lips, and deep, inquisitive brown eyes.

"You have a beautiful home," Candy said as she settled herself and accepted a warm cup of mint tea from Annabel. Isabel arrived a moment later from the kitchen with a plate of freshly baked oatmeal cookies with chocolate chips. "The chocolate mixes wonderfully with the mint tea," she said as she placed the plate on a table within easy reach of Candy. "Help yourself."

Candy hesitated. She'd gained a few pounds over the winter, and her tight-fitting jeans fit just a little too tightly these days. She'd been trying to cut back on sweets.

Still, these were freshly baked oatmeal chocolate chip cookies, and they smelled heavenly.

She limited herself to two.

Well, perhaps three.

It's a good thing Maggie isn't here, she thought with an inward smile. *She'd eat the whole plate.*

As Candy and the Foxwell sisters munched on the cookies and sipped mint tea, they chatted about the house and the view.

"It was our mother's place, and our grandmother's before that," Annabel told her. "It's always handed down to the women in the family. I guess you could say it's a tradition. Some of this furniture and many of the decorations date back to the fifties or forties, or even earlier. There are several pieces around here from the late eighteen hundreds — that table over there, for instance."

Candy surveyed the living room. It looked like a museum of antiques. "It's all very lovely," she said, "and the view is breathtaking."

159

"It's actually the third house on this site," Isabel said primly.

"A log cabin was built here sometime in the late eighteen hundreds," Annabel continued, "but it was closer to the sea, and it washed away in a storm. A second cabin was built shortly after that, more tightly anchored to the ground and farther back on the property, but it burned down in the 1920s. This one was built shortly after that. Our grandmother inherited the place from a great-aunt named Clementine, on her mother's side."

"Grandmother's name was Isabel, and she was rumored to be a witch, although in truth she was simply an herbalist and a naturalist," Isabel said frankly. She had settled herself into an ornate rocking chair to one side of the fireplace. "I was named after her, of course. She had two sisters — Annabel and Elizabeth — though Grandmother was the only one of them to marry. After her husband, Fenton, our grandfather, died during the war — though of natural causes; he was quite a bit older than she — she and her sisters lived here together."

"Grandmother was a wonderful artist and writer," the third sister, Elizabeth, said quietly, almost out of nowhere. She raised a long, narrow finger and pointed past Candy.

"We have several of her sketchbooks in the library. She worked in pencil, charcoal, and watercolors."

"Oh, I'd love to see some of her work," Candy said, twisting around to glance at the floor-to-ceiling shelves, crammed full with books of all sizes and ages, along the wall behind her.

"And we promise we will show you," Annabel said as the smile dropped from her face, "but first we must talk to you about another matter — it's why we asked you here."

"Oh, yes, of course." Candy folded her hands in her lap and looked at them expectantly.

"We have something very important we need to tell you," Isabel said, clutching the arms of the rocking chair.

"We don't want to scare you," Annabel added, "but we thought you should know."

"Know what?" Candy could feel her heart starting to beat faster.

"It's about our sister," Isabel said, indicating Elizabeth. "She's had a premonition."

"A premonition? You mean . . . a vision?"

"Perhaps you've heard what people say about us," Annabel said, giving Candy a knowing look.

It took Candy a moment to figure out

161

what she meant. "Oh, you mean about being psychic? I thought that was just a village rumor."

"Some rumors are based in truth," Isabel said cryptically.

"I saw something." It was Elizabeth's voice again, with an underlying strength despite the soft tone. "A premonition, a vision — call it what you want, though it wasn't really as defined as either of those. It was just more of . . . a feeling."

"I see. And what was this *feeling* about?" Candy asked, not sure she wanted to hear the answer.

"I don't know exactly."

"These things are often difficult to interpret," Isabel said helpfully.

"Would you like more tea?" Annabel asked, reaching for the pot.

"No I'm . . . I'm fine, thank you." Candy looked back over at Elizabeth. "Was it about me? Your premonition? Is that why you asked me here?"

"Not directly . . . but yes, I feel in some way you are connected to everything," Elizabeth answered.

Candy gulped, and suddenly her mouth was very dry. "Am I in danger?"

"We don't know," Annabel said truthfully.

"There have been no specific indications,"

Isabel clarified.

Candy focused on Elizabeth. "Can you tell me exactly what you . . . felt?"

"It was . . . a darkness," Elizabeth said in a voice barely above a whisper.

A sudden gust of wind from out over the sea pushed at the house just then, rattling the windows and whistling under the eaves and around the chimney. The fire fluttered.

Candy felt a chill go through her, though possibly it was due to a sudden draft brushing past her. She leaned forward and picked up her cup of tea. "I think I changed my mind. Could I have a refill, please?"

Annabel smiled. "Of course, dear. I think we all could use another cup. If you would like something stronger, we have some pretty good whiskey in the cupboard."

Candy couldn't help but smile. "Thank you, but I think I'll pass."

"Would you prefer beer or wine?" Isabel asked.

"We make our own blueberry wine," Annabel added. "It's quite good. We've entered it in a few contests."

"Came in second at the Fryeburg Fair," Isabel announced proudly. "Sure you don't want a glass?"

Candy politely declined. She wanted to hear more about this *darkness.*

So they told her.

"As I said," Annabel began, "some people thought Isabel — our grandmother Isabel — was a witch. But of course she wasn't." She paused. "Not really." Another pause. "As long as you don't count the premonitions."

"She had premonitions too?"

"It seems to skip a generation," Isabel told her.

Candy glanced at Elizabeth, who was watching her coolly.

"It goes back for generations, as far as we can tell from family accounts," Annabel explained. "Where it comes from, we don't know, but it's inherited. When we realized as little girls that Elizabeth had her, well, her *ability*, should we say, we decided we'd have to protect and guide her. Now we're happy here by ourselves."

"But how often do you have these . . . premonitions?" Candy asked, looking directly at Elizabeth.

She shrugged, a waifish gesture. "Not so often now. When I was a teenage girl, I had them fairly frequently, once every two or three months — mostly just little things about family members and friends, and occasionally about someone else in the community. But they're tapering off as I get older. Now I have them only a few times a year."

"Have you seen anyone about them?"

"Who would she see?" Isabel asked, sounding slightly confused.

Candy shook her head. "I don't know. A doctor? A psychiatrist?"

"She's not crazy, if that's what you're thinking," Isabel said, sounding a little defensive. "It's just a trait, like the length of an earlobe or a cleft in the chin. Except this one isn't physical or emotional — it's something else."

"I see." There was a silence in the room then, and Candy could hear the waves breaking against the rocks outside. "So how am I involved in this premonition?"

"The darkness is attracted to you," Elizabeth said.

"In what way?"

Another silence. Finally Annabel spoke. "Well, the thing is, it seems to be centered around you . . . and Ben Clayton."

FOURTEEN

Twenty minutes later she headed back out into the cold, overcast day, which had grown noticeably gloomier while she'd been inside. The air had that sharp chill to it that was an indication of imminent snow, and the day felt rawer. As she pulled out Maggie's keys and climbed inside the Subaru, she saw a few stray flakes flutter down from the sky, harbingers of what was to come. She knew it would start snowing steadily soon.

It was perfect weather for the upcoming Sleigh and Sled Parade, which would take place later that afternoon. But it wasn't ideal for what Candy had in mind next.

Still, she was determined to go through with her plans. It was time to take matters into her own hands — despite her promise to do otherwise.

She checked her watch. They were on a tight schedule. They had about an hour and a half before they had to get back to town to cover preparations for the parade.

It would have to be enough time.

Ben had called her while she'd been inside, and she'd excused herself briefly from the Foxwell sisters to take his call. The police had turned up nothing in their search for Solomon Hatch. It was as if the old hermit had disappeared into thin air. He hadn't been seen or heard from in days. His cabin had been unlocked when they'd checked it, with the wood stoves still giving off heat and dishes still wet in the sink, so he hadn't been gone for long. But there was no sign of him at the camp. They'd followed his tracks into the woods for a mile or so but lost them at a place where the snow-pack had been disturbed. It was as if someone had deliberately covered up Solomon's tracks so no one could follow him — or, at least, that's what the police surmised, Ben had told her.

"I noticed the same thing yesterday morning when I followed Solomon's footprints into the woods," Candy said softly into the phone. "He must be in danger. We have to find him."

Talking quickly in low tones, she briefly explained her unexpected summons to the home of the Foxwell sisters, and her creative solution for escaping the watchful eyes of

Officer McCroy. "I have a couple hours before I have to be back in town," she said to Ben. "Can you meet me at Blueberry Acres?"

The time had come, she'd decided, to search the woods themselves.

After she'd hung up, Candy had asked the sisters if they knew anything about Solomon's disappearance, and if it had anything to do with Elizabeth's premonition. But they had no more details for her — at least for the moment. "Elizabeth sometimes receives echoes," Isabel said, "which help us interpret the premonition in the days after."

"It's not an exact science," Annabel added helpfully, "and it sometimes takes us a while to sort through it all. But if we're all patient, Elizabeth will eventually reveal everything she has learned, and we will pass it all on to you. There will be more, I'm sure. All in good time."

All in good time . . . but what if Solomon didn't have any time left?

Ben was waiting for her when she pulled up in front of the farmhouse. In his casual yet ruggedly charming way, he was leaning back against his vintage 1980s, well-maintained cypress green Special Edition Range Rover, which he'd bought a few years ago from a retired mechanic and car collector up in Old Town. It needed a quart of oil every couple of weeks, and used too much gas, but Ben loved its angled exterior lines and functional yet comfortable interior, complete with leather seats. Plus, he often said, it could get him to the top of Mount Baxter in the middle of a snowstorm and had never failed to deliver him to his favorite fishing and camping spots, even at the height of mud season.

He'd come dressed for the weather, having switched out his standard navy blue fleece jacket for something a little weightier, and added a knit cap, gloves, and boots. The oxford shirt and conservative tie were gone as well, replaced with a flannel shirt.

He appraised her outfit as she stepped out of the Jeep, and grinned. "I guess the disguise worked."

"It worked. I almost ran into him, but he didn't recognize me."

"Maybe that's because you look a little like my Uncle Cecil."

"Is he the one who keeps pigeons in the attic of his garage?"

"That's the one."

"Well, no wonder people keep giving me strange looks. But it did its job. So far, no Officer Jody."

Ben looked back along the driveway toward the main road. "He's probably still searching for you, though. They think you're going to lead them to Solomon Hatch so they can question him about this alleged body. It's only a matter of time before Officer McCroy or Chief Durr shows up here."

"Then we should get going."

He looked her over again. "You want to change first?"

Candy shrugged. "I'm fine. These old duds are actually pretty comfortable, and they're plenty warm."

They walked side by side up through the blueberry field as the scattered snowflakes gathered into a light flurry. It wouldn't stick for a while, but it made the hard-packed surfaces more slippery.

"What did you find out from the Foxwell sisters?" Ben asked as they walked, their shoulders nudging each other on occasion.

"Well, it was sort of odd. One of them — Elizabeth — has had a premonition."

Ben gave her a wry smile. "Really? That's pretty rare, from what I've heard. The word around town is that the sisters are more eccentric than psychic, though of course that's still up for debate. There apparently were a few occurrences twenty or thirty years ago that remain unexplained."

She gave him a sideways glance. "Have

you researched them?"

He grinned. "When you're a reporter in a small town like this, you find that after a couple of years you've researched just about every possible angle to every possible story line to find something new to write about. I've talked to them on a few occasions. They seem friendly enough, and they're fairly quiet. I've checked back through the records — this was a couple of years ago — but all I found were a few old clippings on microfiche from back issues of the newspaper."

"And what did they say?"

Ben raised an eyebrow, and his tone turned more serious. "About thirty years ago, there was an outbreak of murders around town. They lasted for a period of eight or ten years, mostly through the eighties. The police couldn't solve them, so at one point they approached the sisters, to see if they could help figure out what was going on. The sisters would have been only in their early twenties then. Elizabeth was just in her teens."

"And did they help?"

"They did."

"And?"

"From what I could tell, the resolution was murky. There were a few arrests, due in part to the sisters, who helped decipher some of the clues, but the murders kept happening. There was some talk that they were all connected somehow, though I don't know all the specifics. According to the reports I read, the sisters got actively involved trying to solve the mystery and were making some headway. But that also put them in danger. They were threatened at one point, and it must have scared them a lot. They backed off and went quiet. I've tried to find out what really happened, but ran into a roadblock. The police declined to make some of the information public."

"Something scared the sisters off the case," Candy said.

"Sounds that way, doesn't it?"

"I guess that's why they've been reluctant to get involved with these new murders that have occurred in town over the past few years."

"That would explain it," Ben agreed, "but why did they decide to call you now?"

They walked in silence for a few moments as Candy thought about that, but finally the answer came to her. "Because something's changed," she said.

Ben gave her a curious look. "What makes you say that?"

Candy shook her head uncertainly. "I really don't know. Just a hunch, I guess."

More silence as Ben studied the trees at the top of the ridge ahead of them. "So did Elizabeth tell you what her premonition was about?"

"She did. She said it had something to do with us."

"Us?"

"You and me. She said it's centered around the two of us."

"Well that sounds pretty weird. Did she tell you what this *something* is?"

Candy nodded. "She called it *a darkness*."

He whistled. "That sounds ominous."

"It does, doesn't it?"

They stopped. They had reached the place where Solomon had fallen to the ground.

"He came from that way," Ben said, indicating the old hermit's now indistinct tracks, which led up toward the trees on the right.

"And he left that way," Candy said, pointing off in a different direction, also still marked by the trail of Solomon's footprints. "I followed those tracks yesterday but didn't find anything."

Ben eyed the numerous tracks that spread across the field, including those made by the police, and finally pointed to the spot where Solomon had emerged from the woods. "Let's head this way. Maybe we can

173

find out where he came from, and that will give us some clues."

She nodded, and together they started toward the top of the ridge. "We'd better stay on our toes," he told her as they walked, their breaths starting to come harder. "Glad I brought my GPS with me. I have this too."

He reached into one of his coat pockets and pulled out a small, military-style compass, which he handed to her. "I've had this since my days overseas. It came in handy a few times. Why don't you hold on to it, just in case."

He reached for her right hand, placed the compass in it, curled her fingers around it, and continued to hold her hand. "Listen, let's try to stay together, okay? If we get separated, just stay where you are and I'll double back and find you. If worse comes to worst, you have the compass, so you can find your way back out. Just head south-southeast and you should come out somewhere near the farm. And promise me," he continued, his tone turning more serious, "that if we *do* find something in there, you won't do anything crazy."

Candy gave him an amused smile. "What makes you think I'd do anything crazy?"

"Because," he said, looking into her eyes, "I know you."

FIFTEEN

The woods closed in around them.

As they followed a path of fading foot-prints back through the trees, Candy couldn't help but feel there was another world that existed here when humans weren't around. The silence of the winter forest seemed to have a sound of its own, an ever-present whisper that came from all around them, disturbed only by the crunch of their boots on the snowpack and the rattle of bare branches in the faint wind. The woodland animals were invisible in the landscape, tucked into their dens or hiding spots, shivering silently as they waited for the visitors to pass.

Or maybe they were hiding from some-thing else.

Ben must have felt it too, because he said nothing. Instead, his eyes scanned the woods ahead of them, carefully picking out the best path for them between the trees, bushes, outcroppings of rock, and fallen branches and trunks, eyes ever watchful.

"Stay close," he said to her again, in a low tone, as he detoured around a fallen pine tree with an extensive root system that had been plucked out of the ground at some point in the recent past, perhaps during one of the fierce spring storms of the past few years.

Once they were on the other side of the fallen tree, Ben had difficulty picking up Solomon's trail. There were several sets of footprints here, all moving around and across each other. It was probably a place where the police officers who had searched the woods the previous day had gathered to compare notes and decide their next move.

After studying the area for a few minutes, Ben finally pointed to a set of footprints that angled off from the others, headed back into the densest part of the forest. "It's just a hunch, but I'd say he came from that direction."

Candy followed his gaze. "Why that way?"

"Well, the pattern on the bottom of the boots looks fairly well worn. My guess is Solomon doesn't go shopping much. Plus they're more indistinct than the other tracks, so it's likely they were made earlier. And besides" — Ben pointed down at his handheld GPS device, which he'd pulled out of his coat pocket — "they lead off in the general direction of Solomon's camp."

Candy whistled. "Wow, that's impressive. You been reading a lot of mystery novels lately?"

He gave her a boyish grin. "I lean more toward James Bond and old Alistair Mac-Lean adventures. Shall we?" He tilted his head toward the miasma of grays, browns, and dark shadows at the heart of the forest, and they started off again.

The footprints changed direction several times, first heading off in a northerly direction, then angling off to the northeast before swinging northwest. "It's like he couldn't decide which direction to head," Ben said. "He was stumbling around."

"Maybe he was injured."

"Or scared."

"Because he was being chased?"

Ben raised an eyebrow but didn't answer.

They followed the tracks into a low area, where they managed to cross over the thin ice of a frozen stream without falling in, and climbed up the bank on the other side. Here the trees were less dense, and the woods opened up, so they could see all the way to a rocky outcropping a few hundred yards away, at the top of a gradual slope.

But Solomon's tracks had disappeared.

They searched the high bank in both directions, but all signs of him were gone.

However, they soon came across another set of the large prints in the snow.

"Too big for deer, and not quite the right shape," Ben said, crouching down to get a better look. "They're moose tracks."

Candy felt a chill go through her. "A moose? Out here?"

Ben straightened. "That what it looks like, and from the size of the tracks he must be a big fellow."

Candy blinked several times and turned in both directions, searching the woods around them, suddenly alert.

"Something wrong?" Ben asked, watching her.

"I don't know. It's just . . . I saw a moose last night."

Ben grinned. "You did? Where?"

"Behind the farm. I had trouble falling asleep, so I got out of bed to look out the window. And I saw it. It walked right out of the woods and turned up along the edge of the field, sauntering along as if it didn't have a care in the world. So you think it's the same one?"

"It could be. What did it look like? How big?" Ben asked, gesturing with his hands.

"Big," Candy said. "No antlers. And it was white."

"White?"

"Well, at least that's how it looked in the moonlight."

Ben sounded impressed. "I haven't heard of a white moose sighting in this area for years. I wonder what it's doing around here."

"Maybe it senses something strange going on in the woods," Candy said, speaking before she had a chance to think about what she was saying. "Maybe . . . maybe it's here for a reason. Maybe it was drawn here because of —"

She broke off when she saw the strange look on Ben's face. "But that's crazy, isn't it?" she said after a few moments.

"What's crazy?"

She hesitated but decided she might as well finish what she'd started saying. "That the white moose has something to do with Solomon's disappearance. That it's here for a reason. Something drew it here, something that's not right. It came here to . . ." But she stopped herself again, as if she'd just listened to what she was saying. "Okay, yeah, that does sound a little crazy."

Ben let out a breath. "I think we're both letting our imaginations get away from us.

But I have to be honest with you. After what's happened around this town the past few years, I've learned to discount nothing. At least, not until we know what's going on." He took her hand and squeezed it. "Come on, let's keep looking."

They followed the moose tracks in silence so they could tune in to the sounds of the forest. The woods grew dense again, with thick undergrowth and dark gray branches overhead. Flakes of snow filtered down through the canopy. The day had turned colder. Candy was starting to feel it in her bones.

Ben stopped her suddenly and put a finger to his lips. "Shhh."

He pulled her aside, behind the thick trunk of a tall pine.

"What's wrong?" she whispered.

"I think we're being followed."

"By who?" Cautiously, she stuck her head out from behind the tree. She studied the woods they'd just come through. "I don't see anyone."

"I know. Listen."

They were both silent as they huddled together against the tree, his arms around her.

When the sound came, from their left, their heads turned toward it in unison.

"I heard that," Candy whispered, alert for any movement.

"Me too."

"What do you think it is?"

"I don't know," Ben said.

They heard it again, a rattling in the woods.

"I think we should check it out," Candy said. "It might be Solomon."

Ben thought about that. The concern was clear on his face. "*I'll* check it out," he said after a few moments. "You stay here. I'll be right back."

She grasped his arm. "Where are you going?"

"To investigate."

"But you said we should stay together."

"I'll feel better if you stay here." He patted her hand. "Don't worry. It's probably just a deer or something. I'll be right back."

He headed off through the trees and was gone.

Candy found herself strangely calm as she waited, alone. She'd been in these woods many times before. She knew them well. But she also knew there were all sorts of creatures around, including black bears and even a few wolves.

She felt strangely unprotected, and wished she had a weapon. Maybe a knife. Or maybe just a heavy iron frying pan, which she could use to deliver a good blow if she needed to.

She heard another sound, coming from the other direction, opposite from the way Ben had gone.

"Ben!" she whispered loudly. "Is that you?"

There was no answer.

"Ben!" More sharply this time.

She heard the sound again.

It was coming from somewhere off to her right, behind a dense stand of brown bushes.

She saw movement then and jumped back, hugging the tree.

When she looked again, she saw a section of the bushes swaying.

Something's back there! she thought.

She looked around the tree in the opposite direction.

Ben was nowhere to be seen.

She thought of calling out to him again but hesitated. She didn't know what was in the woods with her. Best to keep a low profile.

Taking a deep breath, she edged around the curve of the tree so she could get a better look at the surrounding landscape. If she moved off to her right, she could circle around behind the bushes so she could see who — or what — was back there.

She stepped out as stealthily as possibly, placing her boots down slowly to minimize their crunch. The bushes were rattling again. Something was pushing against them and yanking at them.

It took her several minutes to move into position, crossing patiently from tree to tree, taking her time. She heard a snort and the rustle of something pawing at the ground. The bushes snapped.

As Candy stepped behind the final tree trunk, she heard heavy footsteps shuffling nearby, then coming toward her. In a moment of panic she knew she'd been spotted. She thought of running but kept still, until the footsteps stopped.

She slid slightly to her left, cautiously rounding the tree trunk, trying to look beyond the curve of the tree, but at first she could see nothing. Mustering up all her courage, she scooted farther around the trunk.

And found herself face-to-face with the white moose.

Sixteen

It was so close she could practically reach out and touch it. But she didn't. Keeping her hands at her sides, feeling the tree bark reassuringly at her back, she returned the way she'd come, scooting along the curve of the trunk until she was just out of the animal's line of sight.

That, she thought, might do the trick. Out of sight, out of mind, right? It would probably just head off in the opposite direction, sauntering away in search of the next low bush or outcropping of grass, and paying her no further attention.

She'd heard stories of moose charging humans and trampling them, especially when the big animals felt threatened or cornered. It had happened last fall, when a bow hunter up near Lincoln had shot at one. Startled and injured, the moose had planted its legs, lowered its antlers, and charged the man with surprising speed and agility, knocking him down onto his back, though he'd managed to escape unharmed. She'd watched the video online a half dozen times, both fascinated and amused by the scene.

Moose were generally shy, quiet creatures, of course, who kept to themselves and usually preferred that humans do the same. When encountered in the wilderness, they were best left to their own.

And that's exactly what Candy planned to do. No sense tempting fate and risking a run-in with a startled or aggressive moose.

So she waited, counting to thirty in a slow, controlled manner, before she permitted herself another peek around the side of the tree.

The moose was still there, head turned slightly, thick ears standing straight up.

It was watching her.

This animal didn't act startled or spooked or even mildly upset. Instead, it looked . . . curious.

"Hi," Candy said.

In response, the moose let out a quick blast of air through its large nostrils, creating billowing clouds of condensation as it exhaled into the cold afternoon.

"Oh!" Startled, Candy backed away, around the curve of the tree.

This time the moose followed her, circling the tree with slow, deliberate steps. When it had her in its line of sight again, it drew itself to a stop as nonchalantly as possible.

Candy stood rooted to the spot, thrilled and terrified to be so close to a wild animal of this size. It was a magnificent creature, standing more than six feet at the shoulder, with a wide front torso and a thick neck. The fur along its face was snowy white, which darkened to a cream color along its hump and back, and turned to light gray along its back legs.

"I won't hurt you," Candy squeaked, "if you don't hurt me."

The moose snorted and swung its head in the other direction.

"Okay, so . . . we have a deal, right?"

The white moose stood stoically, its large dark eye flicking back and forth, as if considering the matter. But it gave no indication that it intended to cause her any trouble. Instead, it seemed to be enjoying the temporary companionship with another living being.

Maybe it's lost, Candy thought. *Or lonely.*

"Are you doing okay, fella?" she asked in a soft voice.

She sensed the animal was male, a bull, but once she thought about that, it seemed obvious, due to the animal's size. Still, without the antlers, it was sometimes hard to tell.

Looking restless, the moose shook its head, making the fur-curved flap of skin under its chin, which Candy had heard was called a bell or dewlap, jump and shiver. The moose began to look about and then, as if it had suddenly forgotten she was there, sauntered over to a low branch with a few leaves left on it, tentatively sniffed at them, and began to nibble.

They both heard it at the same time, a crack that echoed through the trees.

Abruptly the moose lifted its head, sniffed at the wind, and swung its body about, starting off toward the shelter of the trees.

"Hey, where are you going?" Candy asked.

But it paid her no more attention and trotted off to her right, into a thick stand of trees.

A few moments later Ben called out for her, from the forest to her left. Relieved, she called back, and they soon found each other.

He gave her a hug. "Are you okay? I got worried when I couldn't find you."

"Sorry. I didn't mean to make you worry. But yeah, yeah, I'm fine, I . . . I just thought I heard something, so I went to check it."

"Find anything?" He looked out into the

forest around her, and surreptitiously she glanced at the spot between the trees nearby where the moose had disappeared. There was no sign of it.

"It was . . . just a forest creature. A raccoon or something."

For a moment she felt guilty at the little white lie. She didn't really know why she wasn't ready to tell him about the moose, but for the moment she wanted to keep her encounter with the animal to herself.

Ben nodded, apparently satisfied. He looked back at her and gave her a smile. "So how are you doing? Staying warm?"

At his gaze, she indeed felt a sudden warmth inside. She smiled back. "I'm doing fine."

"So, do you want to press on? There's a chance we can still pick up Solomon's trail."

She quickly shook her head. "It's getting late, and we both need to get back to town. Besides, I'm not sure this was such a good idea. These woods . . . well, it's a lot of ground to cover."

Ben agreed. "Okay, but if you feel up to it tomorrow, we can try it again then."

Candy nodded as she took his arm. "Thanks, but I think I'm good. Maybe the chief's right — maybe we should leave the searching to the police."

Ben tilted his head as he looked at her. "Good advice, but that doesn't sound like the Candy Holliday I know. You're not giving up yet, are you? You're just getting started."

"Okay, you're probably right about that," she said with a wry grin as she tugged him along, "but enough of the woods today. We've got a parade to catch, right?"

"Agreed, but I want you to know I'm with you on this," he said earnestly. "Whatever happens and whatever you decide to do, I'll back you up."

She squeezed his arm tighter. "Thanks, partner, I appreciate that."

"And don't worry too much about Solomon," Ben continued. "He's gotten pretty good at taking care of himself. I have a feeling he's just holed up somewhere in these woods, and if he's out here, we'll find him sooner or later."

Back at Blueberry Acres, Candy made a quick dash inside to change her clothes. She put all her borrowed items into a plastic shopping bag for return to the dry cleaner's and jotted down a brief note to Doc. Outside again, she walked over to Ben's Range Rover. He sat in the driver's seat with the engine running and the heater on full blast, but he had the window rolled down. "You headed to Town Park?" he asked.

Candy nodded. "I'm going to make a quick stop at the dry cleaner's first, and after that I'll check out the ice sculptures and see how much progress they've made. Want to come along?"

He sighed. "Unfortunately, I have to take a rain check. I need to finish up a few things in the office — write a few headlines, copy-fit a few stories. But why don't we meet up later and watch the parade together? Who knows, maybe I'll even spring for a glass of wine afterward."

"Hmm, that would be heavenly."

"Shall we rendezvous at the inn then?"

She leaned in the window and gave him a quick peck on the cheek. "It's a date," she said, "and thanks for helping me out today." Then, as Ben wheeled around the Range Rover and headed back out the lane, she walked over to Maggie's car, climbed inside, and cranked up the engine.

The streets leading into town were busier than usual, thanks to the influx of tourists for the weekend's festivities. Most of the license plates that weren't local were from the New England region, primarily Massachusetts and New Hampshire, although she spotted a few plates from New Jersey and New York. The crowd for this weekend's festivities wouldn't be nearly as large as those at summer events, but Candy knew they would be no less enthusiastic, and were no less important to the town's proprietors and shopkeepers.

On the trip back to town, the snow started to fall heavily, and by the time she found a parking spot on Main Street, not too far from where she'd found the car, the town was already blanketed under a thin yet rapidly growing layer of fresh snow. She grabbed her tote and bag from the passenger seat, locked up, and hurried to the corner and then down along the busy sidewalk, aswarm with chattering tourists in colorful winter garb. Many of the shops she passed were crowded as well, with patrons slipping in and out of their front doors, and she smiled with a sense of relief and happiness. It would be a good weekend in Cape Willington, Maine.

Halfway down the block, she entered the dry cleaner's, only to find the front room empty. She heard Maggie puttering around in the back, humming happily to herself.

"Hello in there," Candy called out. "It's me."

"Oh, hey, there you are!" Maggie called excitedly as she emerged from the back room wearing a very stylish, and very expensive looking, embroidered Scandinavian sweater. "So how did it go? Did the costume work?"

"It did."

"And did you talk to the Psychic Sisters?"

"I did. And I got to hang out a little with Ben in the woods."

"That's good, honey. I'm real happy for you. Hey, what do you think about my new sweater? Isn't it a beaut?" She put her hands on her hips and turned back and forth, modeling it for Candy. "I've been getting all kinds of compliments on it. Everyone who comes in here loves it. So, how do I look in it?"

Candy studied the sweater with a calculating eye. "It fits you great. Is it yours?"

Maggie waved a dismissive hand. "I'm just borrowing it."

"You're not shopping the racks in the back, are you?"

"No . . ."

"Mags, we talked about this, remember?" Candy leaned in closer as she lowered her voice. "It's not a good idea to wear clothes that other people bring into the store for cleaning, see? It's not considered good manners, even though —"

Maggie was about to say something in her defense, but Candy beat her to it: "— *even* though, yes, I know they're cleaned before you wear them, and yes, you send them back for cleaning again after you wear them. But it's still not something normal people do."

Maggie pursed her lips. "But no one really minds," she said in an assuring tone, "and besides, it's no different than wearing clothes that came from a thrift shop, when you think about it — although, yes, *technically* these have to go back to their owners."

"So, in other words, you *are* completely sane, and you *do* understand what you're doing."

"You're making it out to be a bigger deal than it really is."

"That's because it *is* a big deal," Candy insisted.

"Well," Maggie said with a touch of indignation in her tone, "I guess we'll just have to agree to disagree."

"Maggie," Candy said, coming around the counter and giving her friend a big hug, "I love you, but you can't wear it anymore. You have to take it off."

"But it's been hanging around the racks for weeks, even months," Maggie protested, "and the owner hasn't come in to pick it up. I've called —"

"It doesn't matter," Candy said, cutting in

for emphasis. "People get upset about things like this."

"But it's sooo pretty," Maggie said, dragging out the word for dramatic emphasis, "and it's been calling to me. Oh yes, I've heard it back there, whispering to me, telling me not to let it be forgotten. Clothes are made to be worn, Candy. That's one thing I've learned since I started working here. Clothes must be worn regularly, and if they're not, it makes them unhappy." She tapped her friend lightly on the forearm. "Come on, admit it, you have some unhappy clothes in your closet, right? They're begging to be worn, and you really, really would like to wear them, but something about them just doesn't work — the color's not quite right, or the fit's off just a bit in the shoulder — but they're such *nice* clothes, they're like your family, and you can't get rid of them. Right?"

She was beaming, as if she'd just made the game-winning point.

Candy's gaze narrowed to a thin slit. "So . . . I was mistaken, then, right? You really, really *are* insane."

Maggie looked at her expectantly. "Does that mean I can keep wearing it?"

"No!" Candy threw up her hands. "Haven't you heard a single thing I've said?"

"Sure, I've been listening. So . . . ?"

"You're incorrigible, you know that."

"So I've been told."

"Look, just do me one favor, okay?"

"You got it."

"Don't ever wear anything from this shop again, ever. But if you do, please, please, please don't tell me about it. Promise?"

Maggie beamed and held up three fingers in a Boy Scout salute. "I promise!"

SEVENTEEN

An hour later, the snowfall lightened as dusk fell, and Cape Willington turned into a magical winter wonderland.

Strings of lights, some left over from Christmas and some hung especially for the Moose Fest, made the town seem to glow under its fresh glazing of snow. Streetlights and store windows, benches and tree trunks were all alight, reflecting off the surrounding snow and ice, making everything sparkle. Even many of the townies and tourists who had gathered for the parade, decked out in their most colorful hats and scarves — a Moose Fest tradition — wore lighted necklaces and bracelets, or carried flashlights wrapped in green or blue or orange cellophane, turning the oncoming night even more colorful and festive.

Candy barely noticed the gathering crowds and building buzz, for she was deep in a conversation with Duncan Leggmeyer, who was confirming information she'd heard from several other people during the past hour as she'd made her rounds in Town Park.

"I just hope they keep it all on the up and up," Duncan was telling her, the intensity strong in his dark chocolate eyes. "We really don't know what's going on. It's been a fairly secretive process, which concerns me a lot."

He'd taken a break from finishing up work on a one-block sculpture of a bear cub, part of the larger ice display depicting Maine wildlife, when Candy had asked for a few moments of his time. It had turned into a nearly twenty-minute conversation, with Duncan doing most of the talking and Candy doing most of the listening. He'd started off discussing the general stuff — the art and craft of carving ice — but when Candy had asked him about Preston Smith's organization, the conversation had taken a serious turn.

"Have you talked to Preston personally about this sponsorship issue?" Candy asked.

"I've mentioned it to him a couple of times, but I got the feeling pretty quickly that I wasn't going to get any straight answers." Duncan seemed resigned to his fate. "He's been pretty fuzzy about the whole thing from the beginning, but he says he's talking to a chain-saw company that's interested in sponsoring one of us — sort of an official spokesperson type of thing. You know, we'd use their products and wear ballcaps with their logos on them, that sort of thing. Apparently they're getting ready to make a lucrative offer, and they've asked Preston for his recommendation. He still hasn't said who's involved or how much we're talking about, but he let us know that he will be finalizing his decision any day now."

"How come I haven't heard anything about this before?" Candy asked. "Was there an official announcement?"

Duncan shrugged. "I don't know. You'd have to ask Preston about that."

Candy pursed her lips and made a note. "Maybe I will."

"A bunch of us have been talking," Duncan continued as he watched her scribble down a few quick lines, "and we're all pretty much in agreement that whatever's going on, Liam probably has the inside track on it. Either him or Victor. Those two are the most competitive of the group, though some of the women do a pretty good job keeping up with them." Casually he nodded toward Felicia Gaspar and Gina Templeton.

Candy didn't disagree with him. She'd talked to both of them, as well as to Liam. Gina in particular had seemed driven, yet at the same time distracted and even evasive, when Candy had spoken to her and asked about her husband, Victor.

"I've heard he's pulled out of the event," Candy had said casually to Gina, who was covered in ice crystals at the time and chipping away at the face of a young female figure, who was beginning to emerge from a block of ice.

"I'd prefer not to talk about that," Gina had replied, barely looking at Candy, her gaze affixed on the frozen visage before her. "It's a private matter."

"Are you going to continue to participate in the exhibition yourself? According to the schedule, you and Victor are supposed to be giving an ice-carving demonstration tomorrow morning. Are you still participating?"

A look of genuine surprise crossed Gina's face, as if she'd completely forgotten about the event, though she quickly moved to force her emotions below the surface. "Well, um, yes, of course. I'll be there!"

These last few words sounded forced to Candy, but she let it go, suspecting there was more Gina wasn't telling her, but guessing it had something to do with Gina's marital relations with her husband. And perhaps she was right — it probably *was* a private matter.

As Gina went back to carving, practically attacking the ice, Candy backed off and finally turned away. But as she did so, she noticed Gina glance first at Liam and then at Felicia, before returning to her task with renewed effort.

Her conversations with Felicia and Liam hadn't gone much better. To Candy, they all seemed strangely driven yet disconnected, like they were trying to reach an unknown destination without a map. Pedal to the metal with no idea where they were going. Only Baxter Bryant and his wife, Bernadette, seemed truly to be having a good time today. Baxter in particular always had a crowd around him as he worked, as he frequently took the time to talk about what he was doing and show off some of his techniques. He was definitely popular.

And so was Colin Trevor Jones. Candy had talked to the young chef as well, and his enthusiasm and love for his craft, as well as his skill in shaping the ice, gave her a new appreciation of him, and made him a favorite with the crowd.

Candy thanked Duncan for taking the time to talk to her and started flipping back through the pages of her notebook as she walked away. Several of the folks she'd just interviewed, including Liam and Baxter, also had mentioned this spokesperson thing to her, though they all seemed reluctant to talk about it. Perhaps they were afraid of some sort of repercussion or backlash, though from whom she couldn't imagine. Preston Smith? Could he possibly have that much power? she wondered as she made her way back to the dry cleaner's.

Preston was a bit of an odd fellow, yes, but he seemed relatively harmless. Still, on the two occasions she'd met up with him, he'd exhibited some strange behavior too. He seemed to have a way of ducking in and out of conversations, and now that she thought about it, he had a knack for avoiding certain people, like Ben. What was that all about?

She reminded herself to check for a response to the e-mail she'd sent off to Preston's assistant the night before, as soon as she had the chance. Maybe that would provide some answers, or at least verify his credentials. But for now, she had a parade to catch.

As she made her way up the street, she looked around as casually as possible.

She spotted him almost at once.

Officer McCroy was back on her trail.

He trudged up the street in the midst of the crowd, perhaps twenty feet behind her, wearing the same police-issue coat and hat with a solemn expression on his face, as if he was running down Al Capone.

"Well, that's just great," Candy said to herself. And resigned to the fact that she'd probably have a shadow for the rest of the weekend, she turned halfway around and gave him a casual salute.

He nodded back, the look on his face growing more stern, as if to say, "I have you in my sights. You won't get away from me again that easily, Ms. Holliday."

Candy hesitated a moment. Perhaps, she thought, she could use this situation to her advantage.

With a shrug, she turned fully around and started toward him, threading her way through the tourists crowding the sidewalk.

When he saw her coming, he stepped aside, waiting, obviously wondering what she was up to.

He must have thought she was going to confront him again, but she had a different idea in mind this time.

She approached more slowly, in a non-threatening manner, and even pulled a hand out of her pocket and waved tentatively.

"Hi . . . ah, Officer Jody. If I may call you that?"

"It's Officer McCroy, ma'am," he corrected in a stoic manner.

"Yes, well, Officer McCroy, I wonder if I can ask you a question."

He gave her a scrutinizing look. "I've already told you, ma'am. You have to talk to Chief Durr about that."

Candy shook her head and waved a hand. "No, it's . . . it's not about that. It's about" — she couldn't help glancing around and lowering her voice just slightly — "Preston Smith."

He gave her a confused look. "Who?"

"Preston Smith. You know, the" — she pointed uncertainly toward Town Park — "the I.C.I.C.L.E. guy."

He looked at her as if she were speaking a different language. "Ms. Holliday, I have no idea who you're talking about. My assignment is to keep an eye on you in case —"

"I know, I know," Candy said, interrupting him. Flipping her head around, she started back up the street. "You're waiting for me to lead you to Solomon Hatch."

"It's for your own protection, ma'am," Officer McCroy called after her.

She didn't respond. Part of her chafed at the surveillance by the young police officer, but another part of her was grateful for it. She'd found herself in serious trouble on at least two occasions before when solving mysteries around town. Maybe operating under the watchful eye of the authorities wasn't such a bad thing after all.

And, as she walked back up the street, she felt some satisfaction, as she had uncovered another small piece of the puzzle. Officer McCroy had confirmed what she had already guessed about Preston — that he was trying to avoid certain people, the police included.

She couldn't decide if that was significant or not.

Maggie was just locking up the store when Candy arrived yet again at the dry cleaner's. Pulling her quickly into the back room, Maggie said, "Here, we need to get dressed up for the parade," and she dug into a shopping bag full of colorful clothing she said she'd brought from home. "I promise all this stuff is mine," Maggie said in response to Candy's inquisitive expression.

If Maggie had supplemented the clothes with a few unclaimed items she'd found lying around the store, she wasn't saying.

Within ten minutes she'd outfitted both Candy and herself. Maggie wore a red jacket trimmed in white faux fur, a bright green scarf, a multicolored, multispiked jesterlike hat with bells at the tips of the cloth spikes, and bright yellow boots (definitely borrowed from her daughter, Amanda), while for Candy she'd selected a bright pink down jacket, a red and white striped scarf, a purple knit cap, and mauve fur-lined boots.

"Now you sort of look like a stick of bubblegum, which is exactly how someone named Candy should look," Maggie announced proudly as she studied the fruits of her labor. On an impulse, she gave her friend a quick hug. "This is going to be so much fun. Are you sure you don't mind if I tag along tonight?"

"Maggie, I insist."

"But won't I intrude on your little thing with Ben?"

"Of course not. We haven't planned much anyway. Well, he did offer to buy me a glass of wine afterward . . ."

Maggie's expression turned suddenly serious. "If you two need some time alone tonight, just give me the signal and I'll quietly slip away," she promised. "The last thing I want to do is get in the way of true love."

Candy laughed. "I don't know if it's progressed quite that far, but this strange little mystery out in the woods does seem to have brought us closer together."

"Then we should have more strange little mysteries around here!" Maggie announced brightly.

Candy gave her a dubious look. "Maybe, but let's solve this one first."

"Have you found any clues yet?"

"A few," Candy confirmed, "although I still don't know how they all fit together. But my instincts tell me I'm on the right trail."

"Well, that's good to know," Maggie said, her voice suddenly turning serious. "The only question is, where does the trail lead?"

On that ominous observation, they locked the door behind them and started down the street toward the Lightkeeper's Inn. Ahead of them, out over the ocean, the sky was near dark, while remains of the sunset still lightened the western sky behind them. All the voices and other sounds around town had taken on hushed, expectant tones as the onlookers who had gathered on the sidewalks awaited the arrival of the winter parade. Vendors were walking along the edge of the street, selling lighted necklaces and glow sticks. A group of individuals off to one side was singing "Sleigh Ride" in three-part harmony. True to Ben's prediction, a few snowballs flew back and forth across the street, causing the targeted teens, dressed in dark colors and doing their best to appear cool, to dodge adeptly side to side and bark with laughter or feigned annoyance.

As Candy and Maggie neared the inn, the crowd thickened, but with a little bit of patience they managed to negotiate their way through the pressing bodies and reach the inn's porch just as the jingling of bells and the first clip-clops of horse hooves echoed down from Main Street.

"Here they come!" Maggie said excitedly, clapping her hands together.

Ben had staked out a primo spot on the porch with excellent views up Ocean Avenue and across to Town Park, so they wouldn't miss a thing. And he had a treat for them. "Freshly made hot chocolate with homemade whipped cream, courtesy of Chef Colin," he said as he pointed to a small silver serving tray on a table nearby, with a large steaming pot and several heavy mugs set out. "Ladies, can I interest you in cup of cocoa?"

Warming their hands around the mugs and basking in the mellow aromas coming off the hot chocolate, they sipped away in deep pleasure as the first sleighs turned down Ocean Avenue.

Almost immediately Candy made a face. When she spoke, her tone was edged with uncharacteristic coolness. "I should have figured."

"What?" Maggie followed her friend's gaze, craning her neck to see. When she finally realized what Candy meant, she made a face as well. "Oh, it's *her!* What's she doing *there?*"

At the front of the procession of sleighs and sleds was a magnificent restoration of an antique Hudson Valley sleigh, with a family of five passengers in two rows, tucked under warm blankets and waving to the crowds. The sleigh was lit only by a discreet string of white lights edging the upper rim of the body of the sleigh. It was pulled by a single black draft horse and sat high on its framework of metal runners with thick tubing from front to rear. A wreath of entwined blueberry sprigs was hung from the front of the sleigh's body, and garlands of pine branches swooped along its recently repainted sides.

And planted firmly in the front row, wedged comfortably between the driver and right-side passenger, was Wanda Boyle.

She was dressed like a big snowflake, Candy thought, in a fluffy white, high-collared coat, white knit cap, white ear-muffs, and white scarf. As the sleigh came down the street, greeted by the cheering crowds, Wanda alternatively waved pleasantly to the crowds and snapped photos with her digital camera.

Behind them came another dozen sleighs, including two-row bobsleds, half-roofed doctors' sleighs, Albany-style open sleighs with their oval-shaped bodies, and two-passenger Portland cutters with black runners and tufted upholstery. One crowd-pleaser was a small, black single-passenger child's sleigh, driven by Lyra Graveton and pulled along by a small, brown-furred pony with a long blonde mane.

The sleighs were lighted in unique ways. Some had electric lights powered by batteries, while others opted for glow sticks, and several had charming dual lanterns hung from hooks on poles along the sides of the sleighs. Many of the passengers tossed out candies and beads to those lining the street, sending children and their excited parents scampering.

As the front sleigh passed the inn, Wanda scanned the assembled crowd, looking for someone to impress. Her gaze alighted briefly on Candy but just as quickly flitted away without a hint of recognition. Instead, she waved to Oliver LaForce, the inn's proprietor, and blew a kiss to Colin, the chef, before snapping his photo for her blog.

Behind the sleighs came neighborhood kids and families, pulling sleds and toboggans filled with siblings, friends, family members, and pets.

Up the street, however, Candy heard a sudden hush fall over the crowd, and then what sounded like a collective "Awwww!" moved through the assembled throng like a wave. A smattering of applause rippled down the street as well.

"What is it?" Maggie asked, leaning out over the porch railing to catch a glimpse of whatever might be coming down Main Street toward the Ocean Avenue intersection.

At first all Candy saw was a swarm of kids, teens, and their sleds, skimming over the ice, usually pulled by an older sibling, or a parent in some cases. But they scattered when they saw what was coming behind them, heading for the curb and any shelter they could find along the sides of the street.

Thus giving the white moose a clear path as it ambled down Ocean Avenue toward the inn and the sea.

EIGHTEEN

The moose sauntered down the street as if it hadn't a care in the world and came to a stop directly in front of Candy.

Once again a hush fell upon the crowd, as voices dropped to whispers, and even those pulling sleds and driving carriages paused and looked around to see what was happening. For the space of a few heartbeats, the entire town came to a standstill. Moose weren't necessarily rare around these parts of Maine, but still, when one walked through the center of your village, it was worth at least a few raised eyebrows.

But the moment soon passed, as children giggled and teenagers called out to the creature, and couples started talking excitedly to one another about the majesty of the animal standing in their midst, so close they could reach out and touch it.

For the moose's part, if it had any opinions about the momentous nature of its presence here in Cape Willington, it wasn't giving anything away. It stood nonchalantly, barely acknowledging the surrounding crowd. It was angled sideways, almost parallel to the porch upon which Candy stood, perhaps twelve feet away, with its right side toward her and its head pointed down the street toward the ocean. It flicked its thick ears, sniffed the air, let out a frosty breath through its big nostrils, and almost imperceptibly turned its head in Candy's direction, its right eye not quite making contact with her.

Candy was flabbergasted. "Are you *following* me?" she asked the moose.

Maggie nudged her in the side. "Friend of yours?"

"We've met," Candy said curtly. "He's been hanging around the farm."

"And you didn't tell us about it?" Maggie asked, feigning shock. "You're holding out on us!"

Ben eyed Candy warily. "You know, Maggie, I think you're right." To Candy, he added, "Is this the same moose you said you saw the other night?"

She nodded.

"Well, you were right," Ben said, studying the creature with admiration. "He certainly is a big guy. It's a bull, all right. Fully grown. Probably five or six years old. At the peak of his life and all that. He seems to have an affection for you."

It took a few moments for Ben's words to sink in. "He what?"

"He's saying the moose is in love with you," Maggie interpreted for her.

"He's courting you, or at least that's my guess," Ben clarified.

"You're both crazy," Candy retorted, crossing her arms. She suddenly realized everyone on the porch was looking at her. Someone in the crowd catcalled, another whistled, and others were chuckling.

"He's giving you his best dreamy-eyed look," Maggie observed. "It's sweet, really. I wish I had a boyfriend with eyes like that."

Candy frowned, unamused. "Isn't it a little early for mating season?"

"Love knows no bounds," Maggie opined.

"He's probably just a little confused," Ben said. "It happens sometimes. Moose tend to fall in love with all sorts of things. Cows. Lawn ornaments. Pickup trucks."

Candy's brow furrowed. "Did you just compare me to a pickup truck?"

"I think he compared you to a cow," Maggie said helpfully.

Ben chuckled. "Well, not exactly. But it's the same principle. He must have seen you around the farm and got curious. Maybe he was attracted by your hair or your scent or something like that."

"Hey, you're not wearing that Eau de Moose perfume I gave you for a joke gift last Christmas, are you?" Maggie asked with all seriousness.

"No," Candy said curtly. At moments like this, brevity was probably the best response, she decided. She didn't want to encourage Maggie and Ben any further. "So how do I get rid of him?"

"He'll eventually wander away on his own."

And sure enough, as if he had suddenly forgotten her, the white moose gave a snort, turned his head about, and started off down the street, following the horses and sleighs, eyeing the lighted trees curiously, and doing his best to stay clear of the curious onlookers. The crowd respectively made room for him, and as he reached the bottom of Ocean Avenue, he turned left up the Loop, following the parade on its way to Fowler's Corner.

"Well, that was just about the strangest thing that's ever happened to me," Candy said as the moose ambled away, half hidden behind the trees of Town Park.

"Not really," Maggie began. "You're

forgetting that time —"

But Candy cut her off quickly. "Thank you very much, Miss Tattler, but I don't need anyone reminding me of my past transgressions, whatever they may be."

"Just trying to help," Maggie said glumly. Candy gave her friend a playful jostle.

"Well, now that the excitement's over," Ben said, rubbing his gloved hands together, "shall we retreat to a warmer spot inside?"

Maggie heaved a deep sigh and put on her best forlorn look. "You two go ahead. I have some sewing to catch up on."

She started away, but Candy took her friend's arm, pulling her back. "Oh, don't be silly. Stay a while."

"I won't interfere?" Maggie asked hopefully.

"The more, the merrier. Come on, join us for a glass of wine, and I'll tell you about this real jackass who once fell for me." She glanced at Ben, then back at Maggie. "And no, it's no one you know."

The inn's lounge was packed, but they managed to squeeze into a tight spot at the far end of the bar, and for the next hour, as a cold, crisp night settled over Cape Willington, they chatted about the day's events over glasses of a tart Pinot Grigio (although Ben eventually switched to vodka martinis) and a cheese, fruit, and marinated olive plate they'd ordered to snack on. Still feeling like a third wheel, Maggie tried to sneak away once or twice, in an effort to "leave the two lovebirds alone," only to be repeatedly pulled back. But eventually it was Ben who bowed out early.

"I apologize, ladies, but I really have some work I need to finish up tonight."

"Really? On a Friday night?" Now it was Candy's turn to act glum.

He gave her a warm kiss on the cheek. "I took some time off this afternoon to help a friend, remember? I just have to catch up a little. I'll call you tomorrow and we'll meet up," he told her before heading out into the cold night.

"There he goes again," Maggie said, raising a wineglass in salute to Ben's disappearing back. Turning to Candy, she added, "You should have let me go, honey, so you and Ben could've had some time together. Maybe get a bite to eat at a candlelit table."

"Oh, it's all right. Besides, he probably wouldn't have stayed much longer anyway," Candy mused with a sigh. "Too much work."

"And not enough time," Maggie finished for her, grabbing the nearly empty bottle of wine and freshening their glasses.

"It's the story of my life."

"Mine too."

They were both silent for a few moments. Then Maggie brightened. "Well, look, if things don't work out with Ben, there's always the moose."

Candy raised her wineglass. "To the moose!"

"To the moose!"

As their glasses clinked together, Candy saw Chief Darryl Durr enter the lounge. He took off his hat as he looked around the room, spotted her, and started threading his way through the chatting patrons to their end of the bar.

"Oh, oh, here comes trouble," Maggie said, following Candy's gaze. "Looks like you've been busted."

Candy tried to discreetly hide her face behind her hands. "Me? What did I do?"

"Blocking traffic with a live moose?"

"But I had nothing to do with that!"

"Don't tell me! Tell him!"

"Ms. Holliday," Chief Durr said as he slid onto a bar stool that suddenly opened up next to her.

Maggie jumped to her feet and grabbed her purse, which was sitting on the bar. "If you'll excuse me, I have to go to the little girl's room," she announced.

But Chief Durr pointed with his pinky at the bar stool she had just vacated. "If you wouldn't mind waiting a few minutes, Mrs. Tremont. I'd like to speak to you as well."

Maggie gulped noticeably as she returned to her seat, her purse clutched protectively in front of her.

"It's come to my attention," Chief Durr said without further preamble, "that you two have been playing games with my police officer."

"Excuse me?" Maggie said, blinking quickly.

"Officer McCroy," the chief clarified as he focused in on Candy. He leaned closer, lowering his voice. "He's there for your protection, Candy. I know he's been a little conspicuous —"

"He's been a little spooky, to tell you the truth," Candy told him flatly.

Chief Durr held up both hands, as if to calm her. "That was my call, just so you know the truth, and I had a reason for it. I wanted it to be obvious to others that you were being watched."

"Others?" Candy's voice suddenly turned concerned. "What others?"

"We wanted a visible police presence," Chief Durr said, evading her question. "Now, there's nothing to be concerned about. We're just being thorough."

"Thorough? What are you talking about?"

"Is Candy in danger?" Maggie asked worriedly.

"Not that we know of. At least, we've had no specific threats."

Candy didn't like the sound of that. "Have you had unspecific ones?"

"No." A look of amusement flashed through Chief Durr's eyes and he allowed himself a smile. "None of those either. Nonetheless, we'd appreciate your cooperation until we get to the bottom of this little . . . mystery. I'll instruct Officer McCroy to give you a wider berth, but for now I want him out in the open — and close by, in case Solomon tries to contact you."

"Or in case something more serious happens to me," Candy added, thinking about the times in the past when she'd run afoul of a murderer or two.

Chief Durr nodded his head. "We have an agreement then. I'll keep him off Blueberry Acres for now, to give you a little privacy, but you have to promise me that you'll contact us immediately if you see anything else out in those woods."

Candy thought about that and finally nodded. "You have my promise."

"Mine too!" Maggie piped in.

"Good!" Chief Durr slapped the bar with a hand, rose, and put on his hat. But before he left, his expression turned serious again. "I'll hold you to that — both of you. Now you ladies have a good evening." And with that, he gave them a well-practiced smile and walked away.

"Friendly guy," Maggie observed.

"Secretive too. I wonder what he's sitting on."

"A bar stool?" Maggie offered.

"Information," Candy replied. "He knows something we don't."

"About Solomon?"

"About something."

"What do you think it is?"

"I don't know."

"Then we'll figure it out, won't we?"

"We will," said Candy, checking her watch, "but not tonight. Ready to head home?"

Twenty-five minutes later, Candy was sitting beside the dying embers of a fire Doc had made, sipping a relaxing cup of the blueberry green tea she'd bought earlier in the week at a new organic and herbal shop in town, and finishing a warmed-up cup of lobster stew, made with a famous recipe. They had the TV on with the sound down low, turned to a cable cooking show, but they really weren't watching it. Doc had his nose deep in a history book about lost Maine coastal schooners, and Candy was absently flipping through a regional magazine, glancing at stories about skiing, sea glass, covered bridges, and the preservation of historical state photos.

By eleven the TV was off and Candy was in bed, though Doc stayed up a while reading. Eventually, though, she heard him make his way up the stairs and quietly close his bedroom door.

She fell into a deep sleep and awoke only when her alarm clock went off. It took her a few moments for her to realize it was Saturday morning.

But I didn't set my alarm clock to go off, she thought groggily.

She heard the ringing again and realized it was the phone downstairs. It rang a couple more times before the answering machine, an antiquated device Doc insisted on keeping, went off. After the recorded message, Candy could hear a voice talking frantically into the machine. It sounded like Finn Woodbury's voice. She thought she heard him say the words *police, road,* and *dead.*

She tried to roll out of bed, but Doc beat her to it. She heard him open his door and pad down the stairs. A few moments later she could hear him listening to the message, rewinding it, and listening again.

Almost immediately he headed back up the stairs.

A moment later he knocked on her door.

"Pumpkin?" he called, opening the door a crack. "You awake?"

She poked her head out from underneath the warm, cozy covers. "Yeah, Dad, what is it?"

"They found a body."

NINETEEN

For an hour Candy fretted, wandering around the house in her fluffy pink slippers and thick bathrobe, wondering if the body they'd found at dawn along the Coastal Loop just outside of town was Solomon Hatch.

She could think of no other scenario that might fit, and blamed herself for it. She should have done a better job searching for him. She should have spent more time in the woods, looking behind every tree and beneath every rock. She should have done whatever she needed to do to find him, wherever he'd been hiding. But she'd been too distracted, and she hadn't devoted the time to the search she now felt she should have. If she'd been more focused on the woods behind her house than on Town Park, she might have found him — and maybe saved his life.

But Doc warned her not to jump to

conclusions. "Let's wait until we hear back from Finn before we go about burying Solomon," he told her in his thick morning voice. He'd been on the phone several times since he'd woken, and still hadn't had his first cup of coffee. Candy offered to make him a pot, but he waved her off. "Just give me five minutes," he told her, "and we'll get in the truck and head to the diner."

But five minutes came and went several times as Doc stayed on the phone and Candy paced nervously. Finn Woodbury had an inside connection in the local police department and usually was able to get information before anyone else. Even though he was wintering in Florida, at an RV park about an hour south of Orlando, Finn stayed connected to Cape Willington and was working the phones, trying to find out more about this latest mystery. But so far he'd heard nothing definitive about the identity of the body, or how the person had died.

Tired of waiting, Candy jumped in the shower. By the time she'd toweled off, dried her hair, and dressed in her regular jeans, turtleneck sweater, and fleece jacket, Doc was ready to go. "We're reconvening at the diner," he informed her as she grabbed her tote bag.

Duffy's Maine Street Diner was hopping with activity on this Saturday morning, due to the influx of tourists in town. All the booths as well as most of the seats at the counter were occupied, but Artie Groves and William "Bumpy" Brigham, the two members of Doc's inner circle who had remained in town for the winter, had managed to hold the horseshoe-shaped corner booth for them.

"Anything new?" Doc asked as he slid into the red-upholstered seat next to Artie, who was digging into a tall plate of pancakes dripping with maple syrup. He had grown a goatee for the winter and sported a new pair of silver-rimmed glasses, which replaced his previous horn-rimmed ones, giving him a nattier appearance. Naturally, the rest of the crew had endlessly commented on Artie's new look. Even Finn had weighed in from Florida after Artie posted a new photo on his Facebook page. Rumor was that he had cleaned up his look because he had a new girlfriend, though so far he had neither confirmed nor denied that point.

Candy slipped into the booth on the other side, next to Bumpy, who had packed on some extra weight for the winter, which he called his "insulation." Apparently he felt as if he'd packed on a little too much insulation, however, since he'd decided to forego the pancakes this morning and had settled instead for oatmeal and fruit. From the furtive glances he cast across the table at Artie's plate, it was clear he wasn't completely satisfied with his breakfast choice.

Candy had barely sat down when a steaming cup of hot coffee magically appeared before her.

She looked up. Juanita Perez, one of the diner's longtime waitresses, beamed down at her. "I've already ordered a toasted English muffin for you, just the way you like it, with blueberry jam on the side," she told Candy before she hurried away to check on her other customers.

Candy graciously accepted the premium customer service, even though Doc and the boys still sometimes kidded her about it. Ever since Juanita had won a cook-off contest the previous summer, for which Candy had been a judge, the waitress had made her gratitude well known, telling Candy she had "an endless cup of coffee and anything she wanted" whenever she stopped by the diner. Candy had protested at first, to no avail. And, truth be told, she kind of liked the way it made the boys in the corner booth jealous, especially when Juanita sent her home with a special treat, such as a thick slice of chocolate cake or a bowl of the diner's newly famous lobster stew.

It was a benefit she'd secretly come to enjoy, and even at times to relish.

Today, though, she was less concerned with the food and drink, and more focused on hearing the latest information.

"I just got a text from Finn. We now know who discovered the body," Artie said, dousing his pancakes with more syrup. "It was Francis Robichaud."

"The snowplow driver?" Candy asked.

Bumpy nodded. "He was plowing that stretch of the Loop up past Fowler's Corner right after daybreak and saw the body lying by the side of the road, halfway stuck in a snowbank, right there in front of him. They had to dig the body out, from what we've heard. How it got in there, no one knows.

"We still don't know if it was an accident or something more serious, like homicide," Artie continued evenly while Bumpy scooped up another spoonful of oatmeal. "They've got the area blocked off and the police are checking it out now."

"Do they have any idea who it is . . . or was?" Candy asked.

"No word yet," Bumpy said, "but Finn's on it."

"He said he'll let us know as soon as he hears something," Artie added.

"I can't believe it," Doc said, shaking his head. "Another mysterious death in town. This makes how many?"

"Not that we're keeping score, but that's five in less than two years," Artie said, adjusting his glasses.

"That's just great," Doc said. "If this keeps up, they'll start calling us the murder capital of Maine."

Juanita brought Candy's English muffin, along with a small plate of homemade blueberry jam, and she delivered Doc's coffee and took his order, joking with him and the boys the entire time. That got them going, and they fell into their typical morning chatter session, which today focused on a variety of pertinent topics, including the mysterious body, the Moose Fest, Doc's historical presentation later in the morning, parking in town, taxes, the weather, the latest eBay trends, and the upcoming spring baseball training season. "Twenty-two days until pitchers and catchers report," Artie cheerfully informed them, and he proceeded to give his impression of the upcoming baseball season.

Candy listened for a while but soon lost interest, as she often did when they fell into their guy talk. She put her chin in the palm of her hand and gazed out at the winter scene beyond the diner's windows. The streets were starting to fill up, and she noticed a police car slowly moving along Main Street. She looked around for Officer McCroy but saw no sign of him. *Probably directing traffic around the dead body,* she thought, darkly amused. That's why she hadn't seen him on her tail this morning.

It made her feel suddenly very free . . . and strangely vulnerable. Her safety net apparently had been called away to other duties.

She sighed. She was back on her own, trying to solve a mystery.

Deciding she needed to do something, she took a last few gulps of coffee and slid out of the booth. "I'll be right back," she told Doc and the boys, though she wasn't completely sure if they'd heard her as she left the diner.

Maggie was just opening the dry cleaner's, so she slipped in to say a quick "hi" before heading back down to Town Park. The ice-sculpting exhibition was scheduled to officially kick off at ten, but several sculptors, including Duncan Leggmeyer and Baxter Bryant, were already on the scene, laying out their tools and preparing for the day's events. But so far there was no sign of Liam Yates, Felicia Gaspar, or Gina Templeton. Had she withdrawn from the exhibition too, like her husband?

Fresh blocks of ice had been set up around the park for carving demonstrations throughout the morning and afternoon. Candy had seen a schedule of events and knew that Felicia and the Templetons (minus Victor) were slated to give demonstrations later in the morning, while Liam Yates, Duncan, Baxter, and Colin would entertain crowds with their skills in the afternoon.

A small crowd, consisting mostly of older married couples or families with young children, had gathered expectantly in the park, viewing the already-completed sculptures and checking out the as-yet-uncarved blocks while sipping coffee or hot chocolate.

Candy checked her watch. More than forty minutes before things got started, and maybe an hour or more before they got interesting.

Making up her mind, she turned on her boot heels and headed up the gentle slope, out of Town Park and up along Ocean Avenue, moving with the crowds. At mid-block she crossed the street, checked the door that led to the *Cape Crier*'s offices, and wasn't surprised to find it unlocked.

Upstairs, she found Ben at his desk. He looked as if he'd been there for a while.

"Up early?" she asked.

"Yeah. You too?"

She nodded. "Finn's been talking to his connection, and the boys are monitoring the situation. We've heard a few details. What about you? Anything new?" She'd brought her tote bag with her, thinking she might need it sometime this morning, and now slung it down off her shoulder, resting it on the floor beside her.

"It's a male in his early forties," Ben answered, swiveling around from the computer screen to face her. He'd failed to shave or comb his hair that morning, which emphasized his rugged good looks. He checked his notes. "Above average height, fairly well dressed. No one's recognized him so far, so he's probably not from around here."

"It's not Solomon then."

"No, it's not Solomon."

Candy breathed a sigh of relief as a guilty weight, which she hadn't realized was there, suddenly lifted from her shoulders. She felt herself physically relax. "Thank goodness. I was so worried about him. It almost seemed like it'd be my fault if he . . . but he's still okay, isn't he? Or at least he's not dead."

"He's not dead," Ben confirmed. "Not that we know of," he amended.

"Then where is he?"

Ben shrugged. "I'm sure he's around here somewhere. He'll turn up. In the meantime, I have a murder story to run down."

"Need help?"

"Possibly," Ben said, "but let me get a better grasp of the situation first."

Candy nodded as she picked up her tote bag. "I'm just going to check on something in my office," she said, and started along the hall.

"Oh, hey," he called after her, sticking his head around the corner, "are we still on for our date tonight?"

She stopped and turned. "Date?"

"The Moose Fest Ball, remember? I got us two tickets a couple of weeks ago."

Candy furrowed her brow, as if trying to remember. "You did?"

"Yeah, didn't I . . . tell you?" He made a face as he considered his own words. After a moment it dawned on him. "I guess I didn't, did I?" He looked surprised. "I think I completely forgot to tell you. I can't believe it. That was actually very thoughtless of me. Candy, I'm sor—"

"So you got us tickets?" she interrupted.

He hesitated, uncertain of her reaction. "I did."

She smiled. "That was actually very sweet."

His expression turned hopeful. "You really think so?"

"Yes, I do, and I'd love to go to the ball with you, although. . . ." She paused, concern showing on her face as she turned her head in thought.

He looked at her expectantly. "What?"

She turned back to face him. "It's just . . . I don't think I have a thing to wear."

At that, he laughed. "Come on, I'm sure you can find something in your closet. Besides, you'd look good in just about anything. I bet you could get away with wearing what you've got on right now."

Skeptically, she glanced down at her ensemble, which, admittedly, did not show off her best assets. "I'm not sure jeans, boots, insulated gloves, and a fleece coat would be appropriate for a semiformal dance."

"Maybe not," he said, his tone a little more thoughtful, "but remember, this is Maine, not Boston or New York. You don't have to dress like you just came from a high-society cocktail party. And there's still time." He gave her an encouraging smile.

"Why don't you see what you can come up with this afternoon? If it doesn't work out, we'll just spend the evening in. But from my point of view, you'll look beautiful, no matter what you wear."

Her smile returned. "Well. After a statement like that, what else can I say? I guess I'll see what I can do." She thought for a moment. "Maybe Maggie can help me."

He winked at her. "I'll let you know if I hear anything else about Solomon or the body."

He tucked his head back around the corner, and Candy floated to her office.

Maybe there's hope for the two of us after all.

TWENTY

She was so engrossed in her research that she barely noticed Ben as he entered her office and plopped down in the old folding chair beside the door. "Want to hear the latest?" he asked, breaking into her thoughts, an edge of excitement evident in his voice.

She blinked several times and swiveled around toward him. Quickly she refocused. "Yes." She dropped her hands between her knees and gave him her full attention, her earlier thoughts of bafflement driven to the back of her mind for the moment.

"I just got a call from the police department. There are a few interesting things about the body they found this morning."

"Have they identified it?"

"Not yet, but they're running the fingerprints. Here's the interesting thing, though. The body had been stripped of its identification. The police found nothing to tell them who it was — no wallet, cell phone, car keys, wristwatch, comb, papers in the shirt pockets, glasses — anything that might help ID the body. The police are calling this a suspicious death." He paused. "I think they have a good idea who it is, but they're waiting for confirmation before they announce it."

"Any idea who they might be thinking of?"

He shook his head. "Could be anyone, but probably someone we don't know. That's my guess." He tilted his head, studying her, then flicked his eyes to the computer screen to see what she'd been reading. "You have any ideas?" he asked her.

She gave him a knowing smile. "I might." She swiveled back to the computer screen. "Look at this, tell me what you think about it."

She pointed to the story in the right window of the computer screen. "This is a press release from this organization called I.C.I.C.L.E. Ever hear of it?"

He shook his head. "Sounds vaguely familiar, but I don't know much about it."

"Until Thursday morning neither did I. But it's an acronym. It stands for the International Committee of Ice Carvers and Lighting Experts."

"You're joking, right?"

Candy smiled shrewdly and shook her

head. "I said exactly the same thing when I first heard of it. But apparently it's true . . . at least part of it." She pointed again at the screen as Ben pulled his folding chair closer so he could get a better look. "I found this on a popular blog for fans of ice sculpting. It's an anonymous post and includes details about this sponsorship program I.C.I.C.L.E. is putting together. Apparently some company that makes chain saws wants to hire one of the ice carvers to be its spokesperson. I've heard it could be a pretty hefty offer, though something about it doesn't feel quite right to me. This is fairly general stuff, but look at all the comments." She clicked to another screen. "Lots of posts about the sponsorship — some saying the value of the total package, with gear and all, could be worth a hundred grand or more. And look here."

She scrolled down through the comments.

"Look whose name keeps popping up, over and over."

"Victor Templeton's," Ben said, after focusing on the screen for a few moments.

"That's right. There are several key posters who are keeping this stream going, all with anonymous names, things like Power-Sculptor and SnowQueen. Most of the posts are pro-Victor, promoting his name for the spokesperson. A few here and there mention other names, primarily Liam's. There's quite a conversation going on here about something most people have never heard about. I haven't been able to identify any of the posters yet, except one. Preston Smith."

He made a face at her.

"You've heard the name, right?"

Ben shrugged. "Should I have?"

"Yes, probably, and that's what bothers me. He's been hanging around town for the past few days, mostly down in Town Park with the ice sculptors. I've e-mailed his assistant to see if I can find out more about him and his organization, but so far I haven't heard anything back. He's supposedly making some sort of announcement about the spokesperson at noon today — at least that's what it says in a press release on his website. But no one I've talked to knows anything about it. I even called Oliver over at the inn, and he says there's no announcement on the schedule. They're going to hand out a few awards at noon, mostly for a kid's ice-carving contest they're running this morning. Oliver's apparently officiating. But nothing about a sponsorship program or spokesperson for a chain saw company."

Ben shook his head. "That doesn't make sense."

"No, it doesn't," Candy agreed.

"So do you think something fishy's going on?"

Candy thought about that before she spoke. "I'm not sure yet," she said finally, "but I'm going to find out."

TWENTY-ONE

After Ben headed back to his own office, she spent another forty-five minutes digging around online, searching I.C.I.C.L.E.'s website for any additional clues and trolling through a number of other blogs and websites, especially those for chain-saw companies and tool manufacturers. But she found nothing else about the sponsorship program or spokesperson gig, nor did she find out much more about I.C.I.C.L.E. itself. There were a few obscure postings, more comments on blogs, remnants from press releases, that sort of thing. But curiously, nothing went back more than a few months.

She finally checked her watch. It was a quarter to eleven. Doc was scheduled to give his presentation in fifteen minutes at the inn, and she wanted to be there to show her support. After that, she planned on heading over to Town Park to watch the brief awards presentation and maybe grill

Preston Smith about his organization, if she could get a few words with him.

Shutting down the computer, she grabbed her tote bag, switched off the light in her office, and walked back down the hall to talk to Ben. But he was gone, though his computer was still on. It looked like he'd just stepped away briefly.

As she turned away, her gaze swept across his desk, seeing everything in a glance but nothing in particular. Several steps down the hall, however, she stopped, turned around curiously, and on an impulse returned to Ben's office.

It was an old volume that had caught her eye. Heavily bookmarked, it sat to one side of his desk, the gold lettering rubbed off of its battered, dark purple cover, its ragged-edged pages thick and brown with age. She'd never seen it before, which is probably why it jumped out at her.

She hesitated at the door only briefly before she took a few steps into his office and lifted the small, thick volume.

She tried to read the title printed on the spine, but it too was partially rubbed away, so she opened the cover and turned to the title page, taking extra care with the fragile, spotted pages.

The volume was titled *A History of the*

Early Families of Cape Willington, Maine: 1735 to 1900. With Diagrams and an Introduction by Jeremiah Sykes.

Jeremiah Sykes.

Candy shivered, and wondered if there was a connection.

She'd had a frightening encounter with a contemporary member of the Sykes family just last summer, one that had left her shaken and anxious. It had taken her months to recover mentally and emotionally from the encounter, given what she'd learned when she thought the episode was all over.

Again, she recalled an inscription she'd seen printed in the upper left corner of that set of blueprints, laid out early last summer on a table in Doc's office at home.

The inscription, written in cursive, and apparently scribbled quickly, had read: *Here are the plans. PS Make sure no one else sees this.*

PS. At first she had thought the letters referred to *postscript,* which made perfect sense. But she soon realized they meant something else.

They were initials.

She'd figured it out while reading a newspaper article about a developer named Porter Sykes, who was in the process of building a hotel and convention complex along Portland's waterfront. The project had stalled up over the past couple of years because of the economy, but she'd seen Porter Sykes's name in the papers a few times over the past nine months, assuring the citizens of Portland that he planned to make good on his promise to give the city everything it deserved.

But why would Ben have a book about the Sykes family?

Then it came to her.

The Sykes brothers had been Ben's best friends in college. They had betrayed him — or, at least, one of them had — and even tried to frame him for murder. So now he was researching their family tree, probably trying to learn more about them.

But why?

She put the book back where she'd found it and left his office with more questions than answers.

Across the street, the dry cleaner's was surprisingly busy, with an elderly couple talking to Maggie at the counter and another five or six other people standing in line, talking softly to one another or shuffling restlessly. Candy made her apologies as she hurried past them and leaned across the counter.

"I'm sorry, but this is an emergency," she said as pleasantly as possible to the elderly couple. To Maggie, she added, "I'm desperate, and I need your help. I have to find a dress for the Moose Fest Ball this evening. Everything I have is either out of date, decades old, or the wrong size. You wouldn't happen to have a little number at home you could lend me, would you?"

Maggie was about to answer when she stopped herself. "Wait a minute — you're going to the ball? When did this happen? Why didn't you tell me?"

"Just now, and I am. Ben bought tickets for us a couple of weeks ago but he forgot to tell me about it until a few minutes ago." She waved a hand impatiently. "Anyway, that's not important. What's important right now is, I need a dress! Can you help?"

"Let me think," Maggie said, regaining her composure and speaking quickly as she punched a bunch of keys on an old cash register. "To answer your question, yes, I happen to have a whole lot of cute little numbers in my closet, including that red spaghetti-strap cocktail dress I bought when we went shopping at the outlet malls. Remember? But the problem is, they're all about three or four sizes too big for you. Too bad we didn't know about this a few weeks ago. We could have picked something up."

"I know but that doesn't help me now. Isn't there something hanging in the back of your closet, or an evening dress Amanda left behind?" Candy gave her friend a pleading look.

The cash drawer rang and slid open. Maggie handed the elderly couple their change and their dry cleaning. She thanked them for their patronage before looking back over at Candy. "We'll figure something out. I close here in an hour. Stop by my place this afternoon and we'll dig through everything I have. We'll make it work."

Candy flashed her a grateful smile. "You're the best," she said, and flicked her scarf back around her neck as she dashed out of the store.

Doc was just getting started as she slipped into the small conference room at the Lightkeeper's Inn. She gave him a quick, supportive wave when he flicked his gaze toward her, took a seat by the door, and looked around. The place, with its aged oak wainscotting and dark green walls, sat about twenty or twenty-five people. A majority of the seats were filled, which obviously thrilled Doc, though he didn't show it. He looked good, dressed in a white shirt and sport jacket — the same outfit he'd worn through all his years of teaching. He stood at a podium with his notes in front of him, though he rarely glanced at them as he spoke.

"The French, led by Samuel de Champlain, were credited with the so-called European discovery of Maine and many parts of New England," Doc was telling his audience, which consisted of a good mix of generations. "They tried to establish an early settlement on Mount Desert Island but were driven off by the British. And although the British were the earliest landholders in this region, the Scotch-Irish and Germans were among the earliest European settlers here. The Scotch-Irish in particular founded a number of villages along the coast in the early to mid-seventeen hundreds, including Boothbay, which was originally called Townsend, and Belfast, named after the town in Ireland. The Germans followed and settled places like Waldoboro, which was originally called Broad Bay and initially populated by fifteen hundred German immigrant families from the Rhineland. Cape Willington, of course, started as an early British settlement, and saw activity before and during the Revolutionary War, after which it became a small fishing village for most of the nineteenth and twentieth centuries. . . ."

He continued on like that for the better part of an hour, as Candy politely listened, though her mind began to drift after a while, picking apart all the little factoids she'd gathered over the past day or two.

A few things stuck in her mind.

One of the most prominent was a recent development: *Why was Preston Smith avoiding certain people in town — like the police . . . and Ben?*

She'd seen it happen right in front of her, on the first day she met Preston, but she hadn't suspected it was a deliberate move until recently.

Two: Why the hush-hush about the sponsorship program and the naming of a new spokesperson?

The point of anything like that was to promote a specific product or company. She knew. She'd worked in marketing for more than ten years in Boston. So why bury a press release about a high-priced spokesperson you're about to spend tens, perhaps hundreds of thousands of dollars in an effort to promote your product or organization?

Third point: What was up with Liam?

The other ice sculptors seemed to be

avoiding him and were reluctant to talk about him. Why?

There were other questions on her mind as well, but she was startled when she felt her phone buzz in her pocket. She'd put it on vibrate during the lecture (um, *presentation,* she reminded herself), and it was going off.

As surreptitiously as possible, she slipped it out of her pocket and glanced down at the phone number on the screen.

It was a text message. When she flipped open her phone, she saw it was from an unknown sender: *Important announcement coming soon,* it read. *Please stand by your cell phones.*

Candy tilted her head as she read the message again. Obviously it was some sort of mistake — an ill-directed text meant for someone else, more than likely.

". . . the Sykes family originally came here as seafarers," Doc was saying. "Captain Josiah Sykes managed to purchase his own ship, a one-hundred-fifty-ton merchantman, which he called, ironically enough, *The Tempest.* It would become a metaphor for his life, and if you're familiar with Shakespeare's play, you'll see the parallels. Josiah ran timber and salted fish from New England, cloth and fine whiskey from Britain, and sugar and molasses from the West Indies, which was turned into rum in the colonies. Unfortunately, when times got tough, he also followed the Middle Passage, running slaves from Africa. It was on one of these runs that he lost his ship, breaking it on the rocky point just south of Shipwreck Cove, after dropping off his human cargo in the West Indies, and loading up on other goods in Boston. His wife, Annie, was killed during the wreck, and he thought he'd lost a daughter, Miranda, and a son, Ferdinand. But both survived, unbeknownst to him. Thinking he'd lost everything, Josiah reportedly went mad. . . ."

Candy's cell phone buzzed again.

She scowled. Who kept disturbing her in the middle of Doc's speech?

Again she fished out her phone and checked the screen.

It was another text message from the same unknown sender. She flipped open the phone and read the message.

Just ten minutes until an important announcement at the noon hour, brought to you by ICICLE!

Candy sat up in her chair.

It must be from Preston Smith.

She quickly texted back, asking for more

information and an interview, but whether it made its way to the unknown sender, she didn't know.

She held her cell phone in her hand as she waited for an answer. Doc had moved on.

"The Pruitts came to the area in the 1730s, when they built the first mill on the cape, under a contract with the Massachusetts Bay Company. Pruitts from Maine fought in both the Revolutionary and Civil Wars, and steadily acquired land in the region between those two conflicts. . . ."

The phone in her hand buzzed again.

The official announcement of our sponsorship program award winner is now only moments away, the text message read.

"The ancestors of our current Pruitts," Doc continued, "who still have sizable landholdings in and around Cape Willington, invested heavily in the region, especially in timber, and by the mid-eighteen hundreds had joined the ranks of the wealthiest families in New England. . . ."

Candy checked her watch. Five minutes to twelve.

"That should give you a brief idea about some of Cape Willington's earliest families," Doc said, wrapping up. "I'd be happy to answer any questions you might have individually, and I can recommend several books if you'd like to learn more about this fascinating material. Please see me after the presentation. Thanks very much for coming, and enjoy the day."

As a smattering of applause and chattering voices rose around her, Candy jumped up out of her chair, gave another quick wave and a thumbs-up to her father, and headed out of the inn. She thought that Preston might make his announcement along with Oliver LaForce in Town Park. But a few minutes later, as she walked down toward the ice sculptures, she saw only the innkeeper and Chef Colin, standing in front of a microphone stand and small speaker. Oliver was reading a bunch of names off a list and offering his heartfelt congratulations. Chef Colin was handing out certificates of achievement and small awards. Moms and dads applauded their talented little sculptors. The crowd was in a generally jovial mood.

But no Preston Smith.

Or Gina Templeton, Candy noticed as she scanned the crowd. Or Liam Yates. Or Felicia Gaspar.

Only Duncan Leggmeyer and Baxter Bryant were sculpting at the moment, giving demonstrations to the curious onlookers.

Her cell phone buzzed again. She flipped open her phone and read a new message.

The winner and new spokesperson is . . . , it teased.

She checked her watch and waited. It was twelve noon on the dot.

A final buzz.

. . . Liam Yates!!!

There was a final message a few seconds later.

Sorry, Victor. Better luck next time.

Candy looked at the message in disbelief. What the heck did that mean?

Her phone buzzed again, vibrating in her hand, and at first she thought it was another text message. But she realized she was getting a phone call.

It was from Finn Woodbury.

"I tried calling Doc," he told her, "but he's not answering his cell phone."

"He probably has it turned off," Candy said. "He's just finishing up his presentation."

"Oh! How was it?" Finn asked.

"Informative," Candy answered.

"Tell him I'm sorry I missed it. But it's seventy-nine degrees in Florida today. Light breeze out of the northwest. Not a cloud in the sky."

"Don't rub it in, Finn, or I'll have to come down there and give you a piece of my mind."

He chuckled. "You're welcome anytime, Candy. It'd be a nice break for you and Doc. Think about it. Anyway, I have some details for you about that body they found. They finally ID'd it. Are you ready for this?"

"I'm ready."

"Well, it was this ice sculptor guy who disappeared a few days ago. His name was Victor Templeton."

Twenty-Two

Candy had to admit she wasn't surprised. It just confirmed what she'd already suspected.

But it also opened up a whole new set of questions, adding to the ones she already had.

Was the body found by the road, now officially identified as Victor Templeton, the same one Solomon Hatch had allegedly seen in the woods? If so, how did it get from the woods to the road, where Francis Robichaud found it? Bodies didn't walk. It was a proven scientific fact — unless you read one of those zombie novels she'd seen at Pine Cone Books in town. So if it *was* the same body, someone must have dragged or carried it to its new location. And if it *wasn't* the same body, then who had Solomon found in the woods?

And where, she still wondered, was Solomon himself?

And what about Gina Templeton? Victor's death explained why the Templetons had been absent at the ice-sculpting exhibition that morning. But did Gina know more than she was telling about her husband's absence over the past few days? She had seemed distracted yesterday when Candy had talked to her. Was she hiding something?

Candy let out a breath as she folded up her phone and slipped it into her coat pocket. But it rang again almost at once.

"I should just have the darn thing implanted in my head," she grumbled as she fished it out of her pocket and checked the number on the readout.

This time she recognized it. She'd seen it yesterday. It was Annabel Foxwell.

The Psychic Sisters were paging her.

She flipped open the phone. "Hello, this is Candy Holliday."

"Miss Holliday, it's Annabel Foxwell."

After they'd exchanged brief pleasantries, Candy asked, "How can I help you, Miss Foxwell?"

"Well," Annabel said, her voice sounding a little shaky, "it's Elizabeth. She's had another one of her premonitions. This time she says she has a message for you."

"What kind of message?"

"We don't know. She'll have to tell you

that herself. I know it sounds rather odd, but she insists on seeing you in person. I wonder if you would be available to stop by the house for a visit sometime today?"

"Well, yes, I suppose I could do that."

"Wonderful. What time would you be able to come by? If it's not too much of an inconvenience."

"Not at all. I'm actually free at the moment. I could stop by in fifteen or twenty minutes."

"That would be perfect. I'll let Elizabeth know you're coming. We'll see you shortly then," Annabel said, and hung up the phone.

"Hmm. Curiouser and curiouser," Candy said to herself as she returned the cell phone to her pocket.

Before she left Town Park, she scanned the crowd one last time, looking for someone who could answer a few questions for her about Victor and Gina. Finally her eyebrows lifted. She'd spotted someone who might be able to help.

Felicia Gaspar stood off to her left, perhaps twenty-five feet away, wrapped in a long hooded cape, with the top of the hood pulled so far down over her head it almost covered her eyes. Her long, straight black hair was tucked inside, although a few strands tumbled out, partially obscuring her face. Her dark eyes, half hidden beneath the hood, swept the crowd repeatedly, as if she were in a state of constant vigilance.

Candy rubbed her hands together to warm them and, as casually as possible, started toward the dark-haired woman, moving in a wide, indirect arc around the crowd, staying on the outskirts of the activities.

She did her best not to draw attention to herself, but Felicia must have noticed the movement out of the corners of her eyes, because she spotted Candy almost instantly. She instinctively shrank back several steps, between the dark trunks of pine trees, as if attempting to hide herself.

Candy remained undeterred, pressing on and waving in as nonthreatening a manner as possible. "Felicia! Hi!" she called out in an easy tone. "I thought that was you I saw standing over here. I don't suppose I could get a few minutes of your time?"

Felicia gave no answer. Instead, she turned on her boot heels and fled back up through the park, dodging tourists as she pulled her cape and hood tighter around her in an effort to disguise herself.

Candy watched her go, mystified. "Well, what was *that* all about?" she said to herself, letting out a quick breath of frustration. "The plot thickens."

She was tempted to follow, to see if she could track Felicia down and ask her about her strange behavior, like she'd seen detectives do in the movies, but she decided against it. She was no Humphrey Bogart, or even Miss Marple.

Better to go with a known quantity — or, rather, three of them.

The Psychic Sisters awaited her, and they, at least, wanted to talk to her.

She headed out of Town Park to her Jeep.

The day had turned out cold but bright, a definite improvement over the long string of overcast days they'd had recently. For some reason she felt upbeat, which surprised her. Maybe it was just the bright sun, or the incredible landscape unfolding before her, or maybe it was something else. Maybe she felt like she was finally moving in the right direction — whatever that direction might be. She still didn't know what had happened to Solomon, or to Victor Templeton, but she was determined to find out. As she drove out of town along the southern leg of the Coastal Loop, past the small coastal cabins and the Lobster Shack, all closed up tight for the season, she gazed left, out over the ocean, which stretched away to the curve of the horizon. She never tired of seeing it. There was something special about the coast of New England, and Maine in particular. It was a place unlike anywhere else in the world. The sea here was quixotic and passionate, beautiful yet dangerous, ever changing yet forever unchanged. Somehow it made her relax, and she took a deep breath. She even rolled down the driver's-side window, just a little, so she could get some of that salt smell in her nostrils. It made her breathe a little easier and helped to clear her head. She took several quick breaths before she raised the window again. It was, after all, winter in New England. And it was cold out.

In the afternoon light, the house at Shipwreck Cove looked snug and still, its windows frosted and flower boxes stacked high with snow. But birds were at the feeders, squirrels scampered in the snowy yard after peanuts that had been thrown out for them, and a column of smoke rose from the chimney, promising warmth within.

Not only warmth, she found out as she entered the house, but more tea and treats — lemon squares this time, fresh out of the oven and dusted on top with powdered sugar. Candy had to admit, they were delicious.

"Maggie would devour them," she told the sisters, allowing herself a second one after she quickly (yet as daintily as possible) finished off the first. She suddenly realized that, with all the excitement that morning, she'd forgotten to eat lunch. *No wonder I'm famished,* she thought as she took another bite, savoring it. She turned to Isabel. "So is this from a family recipe?"

"Oh no, my dear. It came from a recipe book put out by *The Old Farmer's Almanac.* We found it at a garage sale, must have been, oh, ten or twelve years ago, wasn't it?" she asked her sisters. "It's a treasure. We've found a number of wonderful New England potluck recipes in it."

"Things like Boston baked beans, johnny-cakes, and brown bread," Annabel clarified.

"Well, these are wonderful," Candy said, finishing the lemon square. She resisted taking a third. Instead, she sipped at her tea.

They talked for a while about recipes, New England dishes, local seafood, the cost of firewood, and the charm and challenges of living in an old house. While the other women chatted, Elizabeth sat quietly by the fire in a padded wicker rocker chair, her legs tucked up underneath her. She had pulled her long gray hair into a ponytail, which spilled over her right shoulder, and was

261

wrapped tightly in a plum-colored shawl over a long white dress.

During a lull in the conversation, she finally spoke up. "Annabel has told you about my premonition."

The room grew suddenly still. Candy took the opportunity to shift her body so she could give Elizabeth her full attention. "Yes, she has. She said you had something you wanted to tell me. That's why I came over so quickly."

Elizabeth nodded. In a soft yet determined voice, she said, "I know how it must sound, me telling you all this. I don't know why it happens, or what it means. Some might consider it a curse, but I don't see it that way." She paused and gazed into the fire. "I have received two messages, and I believe I'm to direct them to you."

"Why me?"

"As I've said before, you seem to be at the center of all this."

Candy still didn't know if she believed any of this, but the sisters all seemed so sincere that she decided to give them the benefit of the doubt. "What are the messages?"

"They came to me in a dream vision," Elizabeth clarified. "I've had the same dream for several nights now. And it's always the same."

"What do you see in your dream?" Candy asked, almost in a whisper.

"Many things. Clouds. Fields. Rocks. Trees. Woods," Elizabeth said as a log in the fireplace cracked, sending out sparks, and the sea broke on the shore.

"And what's in the woods?" Annabel asked quietly, prompting her sister.

Elizabeth had a distant look in her eyes. "It's changed," she said after a few moments. "Something is different. A presence is no more. But the darkness remains." She turned to look at Candy. "And the light."

Candy leaned in a little closer. "Is that the message?"

"No," Elizabeth said. "The first message is, *Follow the light.*"

Still not totally believing what she was hearing, Candy asked, "Follow it where?"

Elizabeth shook her head but gave no other answer.

All were silent. Finally Candy spoke again. "Okay. I'm to follow the light. Was there something else?"

"Yes." Elizabeth's eyes were growing hazy. "A number." She paused, then with some effort said, "It's the number twenty-three."

Candy scrunched up her face in puzzlement. "Do you know what it refers to?"

Elizabeth closed her eyes and put the back

of a hand to her forehead. "That's all I can tell you for now." She opened her eyes and looked back at the fire. "I'm sorry. All of this has made me a little . . . tired. If you'll excuse me, I think I'll lie down for a while."

While Isabel helped her sister to the bedroom, Annabel rose and turned to Candy. "These things always exhaust her," she said by way of explanation. She held out her hand. "Thank you so much for coming today. Before you go, let me make you a small package of those lemon squares to take back to your friends."

Quicker than she knew what was happening, Candy was whisked out of the house — not impolitely, for that was not the way of the Foxwell sisters. But it was clear the audience was over. The messages had been delivered. Her purpose for being here had been fulfilled. That was all there was to it.

Back out in the Jeep, she started the engine but sat with both hands on the steering wheel for a few moments, shivering in the cold cab as she stared out at the sea.

What the heck does it all mean?

Again, more riddles without answers. In this particular case, esoteric pronouncements from a questionable woman's dreams.

How should she take these new bits of information? As clues in a larger puzzle? Or the mad ramblings of a delusional woman?

Maybe all three of them were delusional.

But maybe not.

Deep in thought, she turned the Jeep around and headed back to Blueberry Acres. Despite the lemon squares, she was hungry. She decided to stop off at the house and make something to eat, and then head over to Maggie's place and see if they could find her a dress for tonight.

Ten minutes later, her mind occupied by mysterious matters, she steered the Jeep into the snowplowed lane that led to the farmhouse at Blueberry Acres. Right after the turnoff, the lane dipped a little as it came in from the main road, resulting in a low spot where a layer of ice sat all winter long. She negotiated this section carefully, for it could be treacherous. As she drove over the icy patch, she looked down at it through the driver's-side window.

When she looked up again and out through the front windshield, she saw the white moose standing directly in her path.

Twenty-Three

Candy slammed on the brakes, causing the tires to lose their grip on the road and sending the Jeep into a skid. Had the original owner of the vehicle added the optional antilock braking system, she probably wouldn't have had much of a problem. As it was, the vehicle's tail end swung around to the right, she cranked the wheel to the left, and the back end of Jeep slid deep into a four-foot-high bank of snow piled up by the side of the road.

In a rush of light and sound, the vehicle came to a stop with a solid *whulmpf* as the back right tire wedged deeply in the tightly packed snow.

Candy had her seat belt on, so she was fine. Calmly she put the shifter into park, switched off the engine, and sat for several moments with her hands on the steering wheel and her foot still on the brake. She was more upset at herself than shaken.

She'd skidded off the road before. Just about everyone who drove in New England during the winter had at one time or another. It went with the territory. One day on the way home from work you just hit a patch of black ice and the road went out from underneath you. That's the way it happened. But this time, it had been her own fault, because she'd known she was traveling over a dangerous icy patch.

Still . . .

She turned her head as she lifted it, and looked out the right-hand side of the windshield.

The white moose stood stoically, unmoving, its head raised. It was staring off into the distance, its thickly furred ears perked, as if it had heard a sound far off.

Candy shook her head, let out a breath, unbuckled her seat belt, and climbed out of the cab.

The moose turned its head toward her.

"What are you doing here?" Candy asked, not sure whether to be angry or thrilled.

It looked at her forlornly.

"Oh boy." She suddenly remembered what Maggie and Ben had told her.

The last thing she needed right now was a lovesick moose standing between her and lunch. She tried her best not to look too attractive, which wasn't that hard today.

"Um, listen," she said gently. "I wish I didn't have to be the one to point this out, but you're blocking my path. I can't get home. And I would sure like to get inside where it's warm. So I don't suppose you could move aside?"

The moose dropped its head, searching the snow-covered ground for something to munch on. Spotting an item of interest, it took a few steps toward her, snorting as it came closer, stopping no more than a dozen feet away. It sniffed at the ground but found nothing. Giving up, it raised its head again to its full, majestic height.

Even at that distance, it seemed to tower over her. She couldn't help but take a step back as she looked up at it. "Wow, you really are a big fellow," she said, marveling at the size of the creature this close. And, to be honest, she felt a little intimidated by it. She was out here all alone, facing down a moose in the open, with no one else around to help if the animal should suddenly turn wild.

She considered climbing back into the Jeep, but hesitated.

Rather than look aggressive, the moose seemed, well, interested. Maybe even curious. It turned its head so its left eye could get a better look at her, and blinked several times.

Candy didn't know what to think.

It turned to look toward the woods, then back at her.

Candy followed its gaze, puzzled. An odd thought struck her.

It wants something, she realized. *It keeps looking toward the woods. Does that mean . . . ?*

The next moment, Elizabeth's words came to her: *Follow the light.*

Candy's head tiled. *The white moose? Was that what she meant?*

She barked out a quick laugh, which caused the moose to look at her warily. "That's crazy," she said to herself.

Moose didn't come out of the woods and beckon you to follow them. Those sorts of things just didn't happen. After all, this wasn't Lassie. The moose wasn't here to save the day. This was the real world.

Of course, this *was* Cape Willington, where strange things were known to happen — like a playboy falling off a cliff, or someone committing murder for a lobster stew recipe.

Or an old hermit stumbling across a body in the woods . . .

Abruptly the moose snorted softly, swung

its head around, and lumbered away toward the back field, moving gracefully.

It headed straight toward the spot where Solomon had emerged from the woods, two days earlier.

That struck Candy as oddly coincidental.

Or maybe it wasn't a coincidence.

She watched the moose amble away, and could practically feel the pull it had on her.

On an impulse, she hurried back to the Jeep and grabbed her tote bag. She fished out a notepad and pen, scribbled a quick note, and along with the keys, left it sitting on the driver's seat, in plain view, so Doc could see it if he looked in the window.

From the backseat, she took an extra scarf, her spare knit cap, and an extra pair of fleece gloves, all of which she shoved into her coat pockets. Just in case.

She looked up. The sky was still clear, though starting to become overcast in the west. Another cold front would move through later in the day, bringing flurries again, but she knew she had at least a few hours before the inclement weather arrived.

She'd be fine as long as it didn't snow, since anyone who came behind her would be able to follow her footprints, and she'd be able to follow her own tracks back out. Snow, of course, would cover them, making it more difficult for someone to come after her, or for her to retrace her steps.

Another thought came to her then. She looked down at her torso. She was wearing the same jacket she'd had on yesterday, when she'd gone into the woods with Ben.

She unzipped it about halfway and stuck her hand inside, feeling at an interior coat pocket. The compass Ben had given her was safely tucked away, zipped into its own compartment.

That made her feel more secure. *No matter what happens,* she thought, *I should be able to find my way out if I get turned around.*

As she zipped up again, she turned and looked out across the snowy field, toward the woods. The moose was already heading up the distant ridge toward the upper tree line, moving at a steady clip.

Candy snugged her jacket tighter around her and started after it at a brisk pace.

Twenty-Four

Once again, the woods closed in around her, though this time it felt different.

Perhaps it was the presence of the moose, which, in some way, calmed her. She felt she could trust the animal, no matter what it was up to or where it was leading her. And she felt certain it wasn't leading her into danger.

Or perhaps she felt the way she did because she knew this was exactly what she should be doing, at exactly this time. She'd asked all the questions. The answers, she'd known instinctively for a while, were here, hidden in these woods. If she wanted to know what was going on, she would have to unravel its secrets.

And who better to lead her into the secret heart of the woods than a white moose?

There was something almost mythical — and mystical — about it, she decided as she followed the creature, her boots crunching in the hard snow. She stayed a safe distance behind it, though she rarely let it out of her sight. It reminded her of a quest, perhaps one in which a misunderstood princess chased a sacred unicorn into the forbidden woods, beginning an adventure that would change her life.

That sounded strangely pleasant, a little girl's fantasies. But some fairy tales, Candy knew, had a darker side.

She wondered how this one would turn out.

Several times the moose stopped, turning its head first one way, then another, before proceeding on at its casual yet steady gait. It led her first northwest and then angled almost due west, she noted as she checked the compass. It was heading off toward the far back end of the farm's acreage and onto adjoining land, some of it belonging to neighboring farms and some set aside for conservation.

As many times as she'd been back here, it always seemed new and unexplored to her. On previous walks through these woods, she'd routinely picked out landmarks to help her determine her whereabouts, but the landmarks always seemed to change each time she passed through.

A great, low-slung pine tree with layers of

thick needled branches curving upward, like overturned umbrellas, would grab her eye one time, but try as hard as she might she'd never be able to find that tree again, as if it had moved on her or changed itself to become unrecognizable. Or a ridge would appear to face a different direction than she'd remembered, or a fallen tree trunk, rotted with age, would show up in a place completely unexpected, and she would gaze at it, wondering if it had been there and looked like that the last time she'd come through here.

The icy layers of winter made it worse. Everything seemed to have changed. Everything looked different than before. Every once in a while she would see something she'd vaguely recognize, but she could never be quite sure.

At several points she stopped to look back, wondering whether she'd be able to follow her footprints back out of the woods. For the most part, she thought she could. She knew the general direction of Blueberry Acres, at least during the early part of her journey, but once deep in the woods it was easy to become turned around.

The moose skirted an open, boggy area where tall, dry reeds poked out of the fluffy covering of snow, and angled off along a frozen stream that wound through the trees.

She followed, her body warming as she walked.

On occasion the moose would stop and linger at a particularly leafy bush or a cluster of underbrush sticking out through the snow. At these times Candy waited patiently, doing her best to stay warm, until the moose was ready to move on.

She'd lost track of time, but when she looked at her watch she realized she'd been in the woods fewer than thirty minutes. It seemed like hours, and her legs were beginning to tire.

She squinted up ahead toward the moose. "How much longer?" she asked. But if it heard her, it gave no indication.

She shoved her hands deeper into her pockets and pressed on, following the moose deeper into the woods.

They were passing through an area unfamiliar to her now. It was rockier, with high outcroppings of granite, some encrusted in ice. She felt as if the land was older here, as if it had existed longer, or maybe it was so rarely frequented by humans that it seemed ancient and timeless.

The moose stopped, but Candy continued on a few more paces, watching it and looking into the woods beyond.

"Is something up there?" she asked quietly, gazing ahead through the trees.

As if waiting for a signal, the moose continued on, though more slowly now, following a scent in the air.

A short distance later, Candy smelled it too — the smoke of a fire.

Later, she realized he'd done that on purpose, as a way to guide her — and perhaps the moose as well — to his location. For if she'd been looking for him, she had a strange suspicion she'd never find him, even if she passed him by only a few paces.

The moose climbed a rise, nudged through a thick stand of low trees and around an outcropping of rock, and came to a stop before a high, weathered wall of stone, dark gray and black, except for the places where it was spotted thickly with red, gold, and salmon-colored lichen.

Candy's gaze instinctively rose to the top of the granite wall, forty or fifty feet high, and then down along its face, her gaze following a ragged black crack. Near the base of the rock wall the crack opened into a cleft wide enough for a man to crawl through.

That's where the smoke is coming from, she thought. *The smoke of a wood fire.*

Not inside the cleft, she realized as she

got closer, but just outside. In a cleared space framed by rock and woods, someone was tending a fire.

He wore a brown woolen Russian-style winter cap with earflaps fully extended, and had tossed a green military blanket over his shoulders.

The moment he turned to face her, she knew who it was.

Solomon Hatch.

Twenty-Five

Her first reaction was one of relief. "Solomon! Here you are! I was so worried about you."

But her attitude quickly shifted to one of concern, edged with a touch of indignant anger. "What's going on? Why aren't you at your cabin?"

His face was thin, craggy, and wind-burned, showing off all the years he'd lived alone in the woods. His salt-and-pepper beard was more wild than she remembered, and the angled light coming down along the granite wall heightened the sharpness of his high, weathered cheeks, which practically cast their own shadows. He wore dark brown pants tucked into calf-high boots, and a flannel shirt so faded she couldn't be sure of its color. It might have been green once or a deep shade of gray, or perhaps even violet or blue. There was no way to tell for sure.

He scrutinized her with eyes that resembled the granite cliff behind him in both color and flintiness. "Can't go there," he announced, turning back toward the fire. He poked at it with a stick that was heavily charred at one end. A few low flames sputtered. "Too many people around there."

She let out a breath and put her hands to her sides. "Do you know they're looking for you?"

He turned halfway back toward her, lowering his eyebrows. "I figured as much."

"Solomon." Her voice softened, and she stepped around so she could get a better look at him. He had his hat on today, so she couldn't see his forehead, but she knew he had been injured. "Do you need medical care? A doctor? How's your head?"

"Oh, it's just fine. I fixed it up." He reached up and slipped off his hat so he could show her where he had put a dressing over the gash in his head.

She studied it for a few moments. "Are you injured anywhere else?"

"Nope." He lowered his hat and shrugged the blanket back over his shoulders.

"Then what's this all about?"

He gave her an odd look. "To tell you the truth, I wish I knew."

"What are you doing out here in the

woods?"

"I told you, 'cause I wanted to get some peace and quiet." He jerked a thumb behind him. "But it's all because of *that* durned creature."

Candy looked in the direction he indicated. Half hidden among the trees, the moose lingered in the woods nearby, nosing around lazily for any greenery it could find.

Thoughtfully she turned back to the old hermit. "What happened?"

He cocked an eyebrow, made a face, and motioned toward the other side of the fire. "I'll tell you, but you might as well take a load off your feet. You can sit down over there. I fixed you a place."

"You — ?" She tilted her head as her gaze shifted.

On the opposite side of the fire sat a rustic chair made from stripped tree branches of various sizes, patched together with twine and vines and probably a few old nails he had scavenged somewhere. It looked a dozen years old, and probably had been sitting out here in the weather since he'd made it from whatever he could find around the camp, she surmised. He'd dressed it up with a multicolored cushion and had laid a blanket on the seat.

It looked as if he'd been waiting for her.

"You knew I was coming?"

"I suspected you'd get here eventually," he confirmed. He pointed to a black iron kettle sitting on flat rocks at one side of the fire, steam drifting from its curved spout. "Tea?"

"Tea?" Candy's gaze shifted again. She noticed two tin mugs sitting on a larger flat rock beside the fire, and a few tea bags inside a pocket of crinkled tinfoil.

Her eyes widened. "You have tea?"

" 'Course I have tea. Coffee too. And sugar. Do you think I'm some uncivilized old coot?"

She let herself relax, unaware she'd been holding herself so stiffly, and allowed herself a small smile. She was beginning to like the old hermit.

She'd just had tea with the Psychic Sisters, but how could she refuse another cup from one of Cape Willington's most reclusive citizens? "I'd love some."

"Got some biscuits too, if you want them."

"That would be wonderful. I seem to have missed lunch."

He nodded, as if he'd expected as much, and used a coarse folded cloth to grasp the kettle's handle. He poured hot water into the mugs and added two tea bags, which he took from the tinfoil pouch. "I got the

281

biscuits inside. Might even have a little marmalade left, and maybe a few crackers. It's not fancy, but it'll fill you up."

He grunted as he rose, shrugged off the blanket, and ducked into the cleft in the rock without another word.

Alone, Candy surveyed the small, enclosed camp in which she found herself. It was sheltered on the west by the lichen-covered granite wall and on the north by a snowy embankment topped by a thick stand of squat pines. To the southeast, an outgrowth of rocks stood guard, surrounded by dense shrubbery and the encroaching forest.

It was well protected from the weather, and from any prying eyes that might pass by.

The camp itself was sparsely but adequately equipped. She saw a sledge stacked high with firewood parked next to the rock wall, to the left of the cleft. On the other side, Solomon had set up a green-roofed lean-to, backed up against the wall. Underneath it he'd put out a rickety folding table and chair, a small outdoor cookstove, and a lantern, which hung from one of the crossbars on a rusted iron hook.

The only other furniture in the camp was an old wooden three-legged stool by the fire, upon which Solomon had been sitting, and the homemade wood chair opposite it.

Candy crossed to the chair and tested it. It seemed sturdy enough. The blanket looked warm, though she suspected it hadn't been washed in a while. Nevertheless, she was grateful for a place to sit after her trek through the woods, and settled in, draping the blanket over her legs as she cozied up to the fire.

Solomon was back in a few minutes with a tin of biscuits, a jar of marmalade, and a small silver spoon. "It's the best I can do," he told her, setting out his wares. He handed her one of the mugs of tea, still steeping, and pointed to the biscuits. "Help yourself."

Under any other circumstances she might have refused, since she didn't know how long the food had been sitting around. But out here in the woods, in the fresh, cold air, after her trek with the moose, she was famished, and grateful for the old hermit's hospitality. She took a biscuit, which was wonderfully warm, and swathed marmalade on top. It tasted like a feast.

"I just made them a little earlier," Solomon said with a twinkle in his eye. "Only a half dozen or so. I wasn't sure what you'd be wanting."

Candy took another bite of the biscuit,

which was flaky and flavorful. And she couldn't help but let out a laugh. It was all so . . . unexpected.

"You're a pretty good cook," she told him.

He shrugged, but it was clear he was pleased with the compliment. "I've been taking care of myself for a long time. And I been doing a pretty good job of it too, you know."

"Don't you ever get lonely out here?"

"Bah!" he told her, emphasizing the word with an exaggerated shake of his head and a crooked wave of his hand, as if brushing away such thoughts.

She got the point and laughed briefly, but quickly became serious again. "How did you know I was coming today?"

He cackled. "That's just it! I didn't know for sure. At first I thought you were gonna get here yesterday."

"Why yesterday?"

"Because of him." Solomon pointed with his head toward the woods, in the general direction of the moose.

When the old hermit saw Candy's confused look, he laughed again, which deepened the crow's feet at the corners of his gray, wizened eyes.

"So the moose is part of all this?" she said by way of clarification as she finished the biscuit in another quick bite.

"Sure is. He's the reason I'm out here."

She swallowed and took a sip of her tea as she collected her thoughts. All this time that she'd been worrying about him, he'd been out here in the woods, hiding inside a rock wall, sipping tea and eating homemade biscuits with a moose. It was almost too funny for words.

She looked around the camp again and was amazed that he'd been able to not just survive, but to set up this small bit of civilization deep in the woods. "How long have you been out here?"

He shrugged. "A few days this time."

"You've camped here before?"

"Oh, sure, a bunch of times. It's nice out here, especially in the summer. Except for the bugs, of course. That's what makes it especially nice in the winter. It's peaceful. I fixed it up a little — just in case I needed a place to hide out."

Something in the way he said it made her shiver involuntarily. In a quieter tone, she asked, "Why do you need to hide out here now?"

He reacted physically to the question, as if it had attacked him, folding in on himself and pulling the blanket tighter around him.

When he spoke, she detected a note of

fear in his voice for the first time.

"Because," he said, eyes shifting back and forth to the woods nearby, "there's something out there. Something's after me."

She felt a chill. "What?"

He grunted and shook his head resignedly. "Damned if I know."

"Have you seen this thing that's after you?"

"No, but I heard it."

"Don't you have *any* idea what it is?"

He shook his head.

A touch of desperation crept into Candy's voice. "Solomon, you must remember *something* about it. You must have *some* idea about what's been going on in these woods."

"Sure, I have some ideas," he said, his voice rising defensively. "I got lots of ideas. But none of them makes much sense. I can't put two and two together. That's why I was hoping you could help me. Why else do you think I sent for you?"

"Sent for me? But — ?" She stopped, suddenly confused. She looked from Solomon to the moose, which still lingered in the woods just beyond the edge of the camp, and back to the old hermit, giving him a stunned look. "Do you mean to tell me that's why the moose led me here? You sent it to *fetch* me?"

"Well, what else do you think?" he asked, growing irritated. "It makes perfect sense, don't it?" He let out a snort and pulled a pipe from a hidden pocket. He clamped it between dark-stained teeth, lit it with a twig from the fire, and blew out a puff of bluish smoke as he pointed with his head toward the great white creature in the woods.

" 'Course, I don't think anyone could send *him* anywhere he didn't want to go. I just asked him politely to go fetch you and bring you here, and that's what he did, all right. Don't ask me how he did it 'cause I don't know. But you could say I always did have a way with the forest critters, so maybe he just sensed something and went to find you."

He paused a moment, thinking. "He's the one who got me into this, you know. But I'm the one who followed him. He didn't pull me along on a rope. I could have turned back anytime, but I didn't, and that was my decision, all right. I just sort of walked right into it." He stopped to take a deep puff on his pipe and looked at her pensively. "He's the one who found that body in the woods, you know. That moose led me right to it."

Candy shifted her gaze to the wild moose, foraging farther away from the camp now. It all sounded unbelievable, but somehow, for some reason, she believed him. "No, I didn't know that," she said, and found herself leaning forward a little in her chair. "So there really was a body in the woods?"

He puffed on his pipe and nodded.

"Do you know who it was?"

Solomon shook his head. "Never saw him before. He was pretty well dressed, though. Expensive clothes and boots. Must have cost him a pretty penny, I can tell you that."

"Do you know how he died?"

The old hermit nodded sagely. "Oh, sure I do. It was that hatchet in his back that done it."

TWENTY-SIX

After that, she got a fairly complete version of the story, though it took a while, since Solomon kept digressing into all sorts of subjects. Even though he lived alone, he was not completely unsociable. Candy suspected he was even enjoying talking to a young, attractive woman who was sitting comfortably in his camp, sipping tea, nibbling on biscuits, and giving him her undivided attention.

It appeared there was still some life left in the old coot.

He'd stumbled across the moose's tracks two days ago while out collecting firewood, he told her, and that had led him to the moose itself, and the body. That's when he'd been spooked by something in the woods — possibly another person, he said, or possibly something else. He had started running and thought the thing was chasing him, though he couldn't be sure.

He sounded confused when he tried to describe this part of the story. "I guess I lost my bearings in the woods and got turned around, which is a rare event for me, I can tell you that. I thought I was headed back to my home camp, but somehow I came out in your field. Could've been that bump on the head."

"How did it happen?" she asked him.

He puffed away thoughtfully before he continued. "Don't know for sure, but I think I might've run into a branch or something. Knocked my hat clean off."

"Were you attacked?"

"I don't think so," he said in a hesitating tone. "There for a while I lost track of things."

"You scared the heck out of me when you stumbled out on the field behind the house," she told him. "I was running to get the police, but when I looked around, you were gone. Where did you disappear to?"

"First I went to get my hat," he said, "and then I went back to the body. I didn't know if he was alive or dead, but I had to check. I didn't want to leave him out there alone in the woods, especially if he needed help."

"Weren't you afraid of that thing that was chasing you, whatever it was?"

"Sure I was, but I was careful. I moved

slowly and quietly, just in case it came at me again. But it must have moved on. It had been there, though. I could tell."

"What do you mean?"

Solomon shook his head. "Well, that's part of what I don't understand. You see, when I finally made it back to the body, something had changed. I figured out pretty quick what it was."

"And what was it?"

He squinted his eyes, as if recalling the scene, and shook his head. "The place had been cleaned up. And all the footprints and tracks were gone. Someone had erased them all."

Her brow furrowed. "How'd they do that?"

He shrugged. "Tree branch with some leaves left on it, or some other type of brush, sweeping it across the ground. You did that when you were a kid, didn't you? So you could hide somewhere and sneak around on your friends when you were in the woods?"

"I don't . . . well, maybe, yes. So all the tracks were gone?"

"That's right."

"But you found the body?"

"Oh yeah, I found it."

"Was he . . . still alive?"

Solomon pursed his lips and shook his head quickly. "He was dead when I got there. His face was white as the snow, and the body was turning stiff."

Candy had read about this lately. She knew a body began to stiffen fairly quickly after death, and rigor mortis began in two to four hours. After a few hours, the entire body would feel stiff, though full rigor took between twelve and twenty-four hours, as far as she could recall.

So if the body had been stiff when Solomon had found it, it had been there for a while.

"Is the body still in the woods?" she asked after a few moments.

"No, I moved it."

This surprised her. "Why did you move it?"

"It was lying in a gully. Snowmelt was starting to cover it up, and more snow was coming soon. It was about to get buried. I had to do something with it."

Candy remembered. It had snowed later that day, though not too heavily. But it was reasonable for Solomon to think the body might have been quickly covered by snow.

"How did you move it?"

Solomon nodded with his head toward the sledge, parked next to the rock wall. "It took some maneuvering," he said. Under his breath, he added, "I had to take that hatchet out of his back."

Candy was afraid he'd say something like that. "Solomon, you disturbed a murder scene." She didn't frame it as an accusation, but simply as a statement of fact.

"Yup, I know all about that," the old hermit said, "but there was no help for it. It was about to get buried, and then it'd be gone 'til spring, so I had to do something."

She understood his reasoning — he was just trying to help — but she also knew Chief Durr would be livid when he found out.

He'd also be livid when he found out she was involved in the mystery, and had stumbled across Solomon on her own. She wondered vaguely what had become of Officer Jody. Hadn't he been assigned to her so he'd be here when this sort of thing happened?

She let out a long breath. "Where did you move him to?" she asked the old hermit.

"I brought him here first," Solomon said, nodding toward the cleft in the rock. "I put him in there for a while, but it just didn't feel right."

"You moved him again," Candy said, finally beginning to understand what had happened.

"There wasn't anything I could do for him," Solomon said with a nod. "He couldn't stay here all winter. It just wasn't right. Somehow I had to get him back to the people he belonged to."

"So you put his body on the sledge and took him out to the Loop."

"It seemed like the best thing to do," the old hermit said. "I hauled him over there right before dawn this morning. The moose went with me."

She glanced again at the creature, which was almost invisible in the woods but still hung around, as if eavesdropping on their conversation.

"So it was Victor Templeton all the time then," Candy said, pondering the ramifications of this latest revelation.

"Who?"

It took Candy a few moments to respond. She was thinking. "The body you found in the woods. His name was Victor Templeton. He was one of the ice sculptors scheduled to give demonstrations in town today. Now we know why he never showed."

Solomon considered the name for a few moments before shaking his head. "Never heard of him."

"He's a tourist," Candy simplified. "He

294

was supposed to visit Cape Willington this weekend to take part in the Moose Fest. He was married to a woman named Gina." Candy paused, her mind working. When she'd asked Gina yesterday about her husband, and the fact that he had pulled out of the exhibition, she'd said it was a private matter. And she had seemed distracted and evasive when they talked. Was that because she was worried about him, or had she known more than she let on?

Candy tried to remember what else she'd heard about Victor over the past few days. She'd had so many conversations, and so many people had said so many different things to her. She couldn't remember who had said what, and when.

But then she recalled that she had all her recent interviews on her digital recorder.

She looked down at her watch. It was nearly two thirty in the afternoon.

How long would it take her to go through all her recordings? And what might she find there?

As her brow furrowed in thought, she looked back at Solomon. "You said you took the hatchet out of his back. What did you do with it?"

The old hermit pointed to a burlap bag resting by the chair under the lean-to. "I got it all right there."

"All of what?"

"All of everything. All his stuff."

"His stuff? You mean . . . ?"

Solomon held up a gloved hand and started counting off on his fingertips. "His wallet, money, cards, papers, watch, reading glasses — everything."

"You stripped the body?" Candy asked, shocked.

Solomon seemed surprised by her reaction. Somewhat defensively, he said, "What else could I do? I knew I was gonna dump it by the side of the road so someone else could find it. What if the person who discovered it was a thief who just took all his stuff? Then no one would know who he was. I couldn't take that chance."

"But . . . what did you plan to do with all of his . . . stuff?"

"Weeell" — the old hermit gave her a look that told her the answer was obvious — "I was gonna give it all to you, of course."

"To do what with?"

"Take it to the police so I don't have to," he said matter-of-factly.

Candy's face lightened. "Ahh." Now it was starting to make sense.

But Solomon must have taken her expression the wrong way and thought she was making a comment on his honesty. "I didn't steal none of it, really. It's all there." And to prove it, he waved to her. "Come on, I'll show you."

He set his pipe down, rose again, and walked to the lean-to, beckoning Candy to follow. He took up the bag and set it lightly on the table.

"I handled everything as carefully as I could," he said as he untied the bag. Slowly he began to remove items from inside it, setting them one by one on the table in front of them.

A black, well-worn leather wallet, bulging with credit cards. A wad of bills in a gold pocket clasp. A variety of coins. A comb. An Omega watch. A cell phone. Car keys. A hotel room key.

And a hatchet.

TWENTY-SEVEN

Candy stared at it, shocked.

The murder weapon.

It had fallen right into her hands.

Now what was she going to do with it?

As her gaze swept over it, she noticed several things about it. It looked nearly new, with an oak handle, free of nicks or scuffs. It had a streamlined head, half coated in red, with a sharp, polished blade at one end that practically gleamed.

That struck her as odd. This was — allegedly, she reminded herself — the weapon someone used to murder Victor Templeton. But it looked like it had just come right off the tool shelf at Gumm's Hardware Store. Shouldn't it look, well, less clean? As if it had actually been used to murder someone?

There was no blood on it. No hairs, no fibers, nothing to indicate it had been plunged into the back of its victim.

She looked up at the old hermit. "Solomon, did you wipe off this hatchet?"

He shook his head. "I didn't touch it much. Just pulled it out of the body and stuck it in the bag."

"There's no blood on it, no . . . residue," Candy said.

"Nope, there wasn't when I took it out of the body. There wasn't much blood on the body at all, come to think of it."

"Doesn't that seem strange to you?"

He shrugged. "Maybe." He motioned toward the hatchet. "You might want to take a look at the other side of that thing."

She gave him a funny look and then curiously turned her attention back to the hatchet. Gingerly, using only the tips of her gloved index finger and thumb, she reached out, took the handle by its farthest end, and flipped it over.

Immediately she saw what Solomon was referring to. Burned into the hatchet's polished wood handle, using some sort of heated engraving tool, in an old-fashioned typeface, were the words STONY RIDGE MUSEUM — HATCHET-THROWING CHAMPION, 2009.

She drew in her breath.

This was the clue, she realized with a jolt, that would lead the police to Victor Templeton's murderer.

Her hands went to her mouth.

She didn't know whether to be pleased or horrified.

She leaned forward and read the inscription again, thinking. After a moment she pointed to the inscription. "Have you ever heard of this place?" she asked Solomon. "The Stony Ridge Museum?"

He made a face, sticking out his chin and lower lip. "Nope. If it were around here, I'd know about it for sure. I've been here all my life."

"Do you have any idea who this hatchet might belong to? Have you seen it around town? Have you seen anyone carrying or using it?"

He took his time considering that. Finally he shook his head. "I don't see many people, and don't know of any hatchets except my own, and I've had that one for twenty years." He pointed at the hatchet on the table. "Never seen that one before I pulled it out of that feller's back. Don't know who it could belong to. But I'll tell you this: whoever it was, that's a pretty nice hatchet to leave out there in the woods, especially when it was sticking in the back of a dead body."

He was right about that. Candy had been thinking the same thing.

Why would someone leave an incriminating murder weapon in the back of the victim — one that could so easily be traced by anyone with an Internet connection?

She set that question aside until later, when she had some time to think about it. For now, she studied the other items Solomon had set out on the table.

The car keys, she noticed, were for a Honda. Probably a late model, from the look of them. The hotel room key also caught her eye, mostly because it looked so old. Rather than a key card, as most modern hotels used, it was an old brass key, its teeth well worn and attached to a rather battered diamond-shaped piece of plastic. The room number, which once had been stamped in the center of the plastic piece, had been worn away long ago due to heavy usage.

Her gaze focusing on it, she gently flipped it over.

The opposite side was blank. No room number.

"I wonder what hotel that's from?" she said, mostly to herself.

"There are a couple of older places up on 192," Solomon said helpfully. "Maybe it came from one of them."

Lastly, she looked at the cell phone. It was a typical Blackberry. No doubt it contained a number of clues.

Dare she switch it on?

As she pondered the question, Solomon said from beside her, "I turned it on a while ago."

"You did?"

"Took me a while to figure out. I haven't had one of those things before, though I seen my daughter using one. She's been trying to get me to buy one, but I just don't have a use for it. I don't make many calls out here in the woods, and frankly I don't care much about people calling me."

Candy understood. "And what happened when you turned it on?"

"It buzzed once or twice."

"When was that?"

Solomon thought about it. "Would've been yesterday afternoon sometime."

"Did you pick it up? Were they alerts or incoming calls?"

The old hermit shook his head. "I don't know the difference. I got tired of it after a while and turned it back off."

Candy nodded. That's the way she'd leave it.

Right now, she knew what she had to do.

"Solomon, we need to get this stuff to the police right away."

"I know that." His eyes grew hard and his

jaws tensed as he shook open the burlap bag and moved closer to the table. Carefully, he started placing the items back into the bag. "That's why I'm giving all of it to you."

"But this could lead them to Victor's killer."

"Uh-huh."

She chose her next words carefully, uncertain of his reaction. "Solomon, you have to go back with me. You have to go to the police."

She expected a strong reaction from him, but instead he was silent for a moment as he placed the wallet inside the bag. He gave her a sideways look, as if he had known her request was coming. For a moment his eyes grew dark, and she was afraid he was about to go ballistic on her. But instead the darkness receded, and he allowed a slow grin to work its way across his face. Softly, in a gravelly voice, he said, "Well, now, you know I can't do that."

"Solomon —"

He held up a hand to stop her. "It ain't no use. I ain't going to see no police."

"But you have to tell them what you saw," she pleaded. "You'll have to tell them how you found the body —"

"I already told you how I found it," he

said evenly, "and you can just pass along all those details to them."

"But they'll want to talk to you. They'll want you to show them the place in the woods where you discovered the body, and they'll want to know why you moved it out to the road."

"Like I said, I already told you all about that. As far as that gully where I found the body, I'm not even sure I could find the exact spot myself in these woods at this time of year. It's likely buried by now, or disguised somehow. These woods change a lot after a snowfall, you know. Even a little one. Makes everything look different."

"The police can help. They have all sorts of investigation methods."

"Well, there you go." Solomon's grin was gone, and he scratched the back of his neck. "You see, me and the police, we don't always get along. I leave them alone, and they leave me alone, and that's the way we like it."

He lowered his voice and leaned in close to her, and for the first time she realized he hadn't taken a bath in quite a while. "You see, I had this little problem with the police way back when. It's all settled now — at least I think it is — but there's no sense doing any *investigating* and digging it all up again, you know what I mean?"

Candy felt a breath go out of her. "Isn't there anything I can say to convince you?"

He didn't answer as he gathered up the last few items on the table.

"What are you going to do?" she asked after a few moments, watching him.

He made a sound in the back of his throat. "Well, I've been thinking about that," he said, chewing over his words carefully. "I thought about staying here — not many folks know about this place, and I'd probably be just fine. But I know of another place a little farther up in the woods, way out of town, and I've been thinking of moving up there until things quiet down."

"How long do you think you'll be gone?"

Solomon placed the last item in the bag, tied it up with a length of twine, and handed it over to her. Reluctantly she accepted it, cradling it in her two hands.

He swept off his hat, ran a hand through his disheveled hair, and looked up at the sky. "Clouds are coming in again," he said, studying them with a practiced eye. "The almanac predicted it, you know. Said we'd have this series of little snowstorms, with a few nice days in between each one."

His gaze dropped and shifted to her. "The almanac's right seventy percent of the time, you know. They got a lot of useful tips in there too. That's how I learned to cook them biscuits. I got the recipe right out of the almanac."

He chuckled, shook his head, and grew more serious as he returned to a previous question. "I don't know for sure, to tell you the truth. Maybe 'til spring. Maybe longer. Maybe not. Depends."

She nodded. "Okay. But just so you know, you can always stay with us at Blueberry Acres, if you ever need a place for a few nights. Doc and I would love to have you."

He gave her a warm smile. "I appreciate that, Candy."

She looked around the camp. "Do you have enough food?"

"Oh." He waved a hand, as if it were inconsequential. "Don't worry about that. There's always plenty of food around, if you know where to look for it. I had squirrel stew for dinner a few nights ago. Caught a wild turkey last week. I make do."

"If you ever need any staples, like sugar or flour or salt, just let me know. You can always stop by the farm. The back door's always open for you."

He nodded, but she could tell she wouldn't hear from him for a while.

She took a deep breath and looked

around. "Well, I guess I should be going. I've got to get these items to the police."

"Okay. You do that. Think you can find your way back out?"

"Sure. Just follow my footprints in the snow, right?"

"That's right. And if you get sidetracked, head south-southwest," he said helpfully, pointing in the general direction with the vertical flat of his hand. "You'll eventually come to the farm — or the sea. One or the other. Either way, you'll be fine."

She felt for the compass in her pocket and knew she had a backup in case she got lost. She nodded toward the woods. "What about our friend, the moose?"

Solomon put his hat back on and squinted at the creature. "Well, I guess that's up to him, isn't it?"

"I guess it is." She watched the moose for a few moments, still awed by its silent majesty. "Do you think that's why it came this way? Because it sensed that body out there?"

"Been wondering that myself," said Solomon thoughtfully. "It's the strangest behavior I've ever seen for an animal like that — and I've seen some strange things out in these woods. What drew it to the body, or made it come after us, I couldn't say."

"Well, I figured something was bothering him," Candy said. "He's been chasing me all over town."

Solomon chuckled. "Chased by a wild moose, huh? He must have given you quite a start." He laughed a little harder, amused by the thought.

Now it was Candy's turn to give him a sideways look. "So, you think it's funny too? My friends think he's in love with me."

Solomon laughed again. "Well," the old hermit said, slapping her on the back, "if that's true, he's not the only one."

TWENTY-EIGHT

She emerged from the woods to find it snowing again.

Somehow the weather had changed in the time it had taken her to walk from Solomon's camp to the blueberry farm. She'd been enclosed by the embrace of the woods and hadn't been aware of the gathering clouds. Looking up now, she noticed a pregnant dark cloud flitting past, one of a line of low clouds moving at a steady pace along the coast.

It was just a passing flurry, she surmised. It would probably clear up later on.

But she felt no relief in that knowledge as she cradled the burlap bag in her right arm, mindful of what it contained: evidence that would convict someone and send that person — possibly someone she knew — to jail for a long time.

There was no doubt she would turn the items over to the police today, immediately.

There was no doubt that she would spend no more time studying them. They were tied inside the bag now, and that's where they would stay, until she handed them over to the police.

Still, she couldn't help wonder what she would discover if she ran down the leads herself.

It was a tempting thought — one she resisted with all the willpower she could muster.

Doc had rescued the Jeep. It was parked in front of the house, snow caked in around its bumpers and wheel wells. He must have pulled it out with his truck while she was in the woods.

With the burlap bag under her arm, she went inside.

Doc was in his office when she entered the house, but he came running when he heard her open the door. "There you are, pumpkin. Are you all right? I was worried about you."

"I'm okay, Dad," she said as she placed the bag on the counter and made her way to the sink, peeling off her gloves so she could rinse her cold hands under the water. "It's chilly out there," she added, experiencing a few moments of sublime bliss as her fingers warmed and loosened.

"Where'd you go?"

"I found Solomon Hatch," she said simply.

Doc's eyes widened. "Where was he?"

"Hiding out in a small cave in the woods. He gave me that." She pointed to the bag and briefly explained what it contained.

"He gave you evidence? Of a murder?" Doc asked in disbelief when she'd finished.

"He said he had no interest in delivering the bag to the police himself. So naturally he thought of me."

Doc's expression changed to one of mild amusement. "You're developing quite a reputation around here, pumpkin."

"I know. Don't remind me."

He indicated the bag with a finger. "You're going to take that to the police right away, correct?"

"Correct," Candy said, "but first I have to check out one quick fact." She made a beeline for her writing desk in the living room, where she kept her laptop. They'd installed a wireless network in the house the previous summer, since they both used the Internet for research. She slipped into the straight-backed chair sitting in front of the desk, powered up the computer, and opened a browser window.

In the search field, she keyed in *stony ridge museum hatching throwing champion* and hit the return button.

Quickly she scanned the results. One link caught her eye.

It was a web page for *The Cape Crusader.* Wanda Boyle's website.

Doc watched over her shoulder as she clicked the link, opening the page.

It was one of Wanda's recent blog posts about the participants in the ice-sculpting contest. Wanda had written brief bios for several of the sculptors. One sentence in particular caught Candy's eye.

. . . won the hatchet throwing competition at the Stony Ridge Museum in Virginia three years in a row . . .

Candy's gaze shifted to the name of the sculptor highlighted at the beginning of the paragraph.

It was Duncan Leggmeyer.

TWENTY-NINE

Ninety minutes later, she sat in a small, bare conference room at the Cape Willington Police Department, sipping on a cup of bad coffee and wondering if she'd ever get out of here alive.

Doc was somewhere out front, in some waiting area, probably wondering what the hell had happened to her. She hadn't seen him since they'd whisked her away to this windowless room — decorated only with a table, a few chairs, an American flag, and a black-and-white framed portrait of the president — once they'd found out what she'd discovered.

She'd already been through the story more times than she could count, including what she'd found out about Duncan Legg-meyer, and thought she'd done a pretty good job telling it all as correctly and honestly as possible, emphasizing the parts about how hard she'd tried to stay out of it.

313

Whether they believed her or not — well, she just hoped for the best, and that it didn't involve jail time.

Chief Daryl Durr sat across from her, arms on the table, hands clasped together, and tie loosened, perhaps in an attempt to show her how he'd managed to remain calm and reasonable. He was the last of several interviewers, though they'd been more like a series of interrogators, she thought. They had started out gently enough, but each subsequent questioner had become a bit more accusatory. Despite a few tense moments, however, there'd been nothing she couldn't handle. She'd worked for the better part of a decade within the chaotic world of start-up high-tech companies in Boston. This was a piece of cake, comparatively. At least these people were sane.

Well, mostly.

A uniformed policewoman stood near the door, arms folded behind her, apparently guarding the exit in case Candy should attempt a daring daylight escape. She had actually considered it more than once over the past hour or so. But she didn't think she could make it all the way out the front door, so she reluctantly dismissed the idea.

Instead, she remained seated in her chair and took another sip of coffee, which was growing cold.

Chief Durr now gave her his full attention. He'd been distracted earlier and had been called out of the room a couple of times. Something was going on at the station, she sensed. But they apparently had no intention of telling her what it might be.

The chief leaned back in his chair, rubbing his hand across his chin. "Explain one more time this thing with the moose, Ms. Holliday. You say you followed it into the woods? And it led you to Solomon Hatch? How is that possible?"

It wasn't, Candy explained, but it had happened nonetheless. It all had happened just as she'd told them over and over again, despite how strange it sounded, she emphasized.

He gave her an "uh-huh," but she couldn't tell what was going on behind those narrowed blue eyes of his.

He asked her again about the contents of the burlap bag. Whether she'd touched any of the items. Turned on the phone. Looked into the wallet.

She answered as honestly as she could.

"Did you touch the hatchet?"

"I did, but only briefly — and with gloved fingers — to turn it over and read the inscription. Solomon touched it too, when he took it out of the bag and later when he put it back inside."

"Did he alter the evidence in any way, that you know of?"

To the best of her knowledge, she said, he hadn't.

They talked about Duncan Leggmeyer then, and what Candy had discovered about his hatchet-throwing championship. She hadn't been able to find any corroborating evidence online for that particular event, but she did find several grainy, low-resolution images of Duncan throwing axes and hatchets at other competitions. It seemed to be a hobby of his. Apparently, he was sort of the mountain-man type, as in several of the images he had longer hair and a thick beard.

But why would he have killed Victor Templeton? With a hatchet he'd won as a trophy in a contest?

That's what the police are trying to find out, she reminded herself.

She had some ideas of her own, of course, but for the moment she thought it best if she suppressed those as much as possible. At least until she was out of the police station.

The chief turned his questions back to Solomon, which made perfect sense. The old hermit was obviously a significant player in this mystery. He had found the body, and the murder weapon, and had moved the body — twice. Candy could understand how his activities over the past few days might appear more than a little suspicious. But when the questions became accusatory, hinting at the possibility of something more sinister, including a possible collusion with Duncan, Candy drew the line.

"Solomon was an innocent participant in all this, and that's all," she told the chief. "He stumbled on the body by accident and did the best he could to make sure it got back into the right hands. Maybe his decisions weren't all within the boundaries of established law, but he did in his heart what he thought was right. You can't fault him for that."

To her surprise, the chief agreed with her. "No, I can't," he said, steepling his fingers together and peering at her like a hawk. "But we also can't instantly dismiss him as a suspect. He's too heavily involved. I suppose he told you about his incident years ago, didn't he?"

"He mentioned it, but we didn't talk about specifics."

The chief lowered his arms and leaned forward, his voice dropping into a low,

folksy cadence. "He had some legal prob-
lems with us many years ago — back in the
seventies, I think it was. That was before I
got here, but I've heard about it a few times
over the years, and reviewed the files. It was
a pretty sensational event at the time. A local girl — someone close to Solomon —
was murdered. Initially he was a suspect. I
think he might've even spent some time in
jail. Not many in town rallied to his support, and I suppose it made him bitter about
it, though most of that seems to have worn
away over the years. He doesn't seem to
hold much of a grudge. Eventually he was
cleared, but as you've seen, it's affected him.
He's become a recluse, living out at the
place he inherited, and he's skittish around
the police. I suppose that's understandable
behavior, given what he's been through, and
for the most part we've left him alone out
there. Still, after what's happened here
recently, and with his history, it's only
reasonable to see if there's a connection. I
wouldn't be doing my job if I didn't follow
up on it."

Candy understood, but clarified, "There's
no way he could have done anything to hurt
that man."

"I don't disagree with you," the chief said,
"but it would be best for all parties if we

could just get together with him, talk about it, and clear this up right away."

"Yes, it would," Candy said, "but I don't think that's going to happen. He said he was leaving the area, and he didn't say where he was going."

"Do you think you could find this cave of his again?"

She actually gave that some thought. It had crossed her mind a number of times since she'd walked out of the woods. Finally she shook her head. Again, she decided complete honesty was the best approach, but she phrased it in the language of the woods, mimicking something the old hermit had said.

"Anything's possible," she told the chief, "but it started snowing right after I got back to the farm. Those woods change a lot after a snowfall, you know. Even a little one. It makes everything look different."

He wasn't completely accepting of her cryptic answer, but there wasn't much he could do about it.

After another ten minutes he ran out of questions. He rose, giving her a nod and an appreciative smile. A brief moment of understanding passed between them, and she sensed in him some admiration for what she'd done in locating the old hermit and the victim's effects. For a moment he let down his guard and allowed a weary look to cross his face.

He's probably had a rough weekend so far, she thought.

And the weekend's not even half over.

She had places to go and things to do, and it looked like the interview was done, but he had some parting words for her.

"We may need you to come back in tomorrow or Monday to clarify some points," he told her. "I guess I don't have to warn you to stay in the area. No crossing state lines or anything incriminating like that. And please, Ms. Holliday — Candy — try your very best to stay out of our investigation."

She promised she would.

"And," he continued, "if you hear of anything else — anything at all — call me immediately." He reached into his shirt pocket and took out two cards. "One's for me. One's for Officer McCroy. He's still assigned to you, though he's off on some godforsaken wild goose chase at the moment, which is just the kinda thing we don't need right now. But he'll be back a little later on. You need anything, you call one or both of us anytime. Got it?"

"Got it, Chief."

With a sigh of resignation he let her go.

She felt like she'd just been released from the principal's office.

Back in Doc's truck, she let out a deep breath of her own and could hardly contain her relief. "Wow, what an ordeal."

"You okay?" her father asked, sounding worried.

"Well, they refrained from beating me, if that's what you mean. For a while there I wasn't sure they were going to let me go."

"They were pretty hard on you, huh?"

Candy shrugged and looked out the window. "I don't know. More than anything else, I was worried about missing my date with Ben tonight. And I was worried about you sitting out there in that drafty waiting room. But in some strange way, I was okay with all of it. It's like I almost knew what to expect. I'm afraid I'm starting to get used to these sorts of things happening to me, Dad."

It was a sobering thought. They were silent the rest of the way back to the farm.

Her cell phone buzzed as she climbed out of the cab, alerting her to unread messages. While Doc walked onto the porch and unlocked the front door, Candy flipped open her phone and clicked through to the proper screen.

Ben had called almost an hour ago. He'd

left a message. And Maggie had texted her, reminding her to stop by the house to pick up her dress for the Moose Fest Ball that evening.

Needing a moment to collect her thoughts, she flipped the phone closed and looked up at the sky. It was still overcast, though the flurries had stopped. The clouds sunk low, seeming to practically graze the tops of the trees in some places. They'd have more snow this evening. She could sense it in the air, which had a raw, almost sensual feel. Perfect weather for a winter ball.

But her mind couldn't help wandering in other directions. She turned her head slightly, letting her gaze drift down from the sky, to her left, falling to the tree line on the ridge at the far side of the blueberry field behind the house.

The chief had sent more officers into the woods this afternoon, she'd heard, but she doubted they'd find anything. Solomon was probably long gone by now. They'd recovered the body and knew there was only one, that of Victor Templeton. They had the murder weapon. Any incriminating footprints or tracks around the murder scene had been covered up by . . . someone or something, according to Solomon. Candy guessed the old hermit had also covered his own tracks on the way out of town, to avoid detection and to ensure no one could follow him, wherever he'd gone. The items taken from the body had been retrieved and delivered to the proper authorities. Both she and Solomon had done their parts.

And yet, she couldn't help feeling that it wasn't over yet — at least, not for her.

She thought back over the items Solomon had laid out on the table in front of her. A wallet. Car keys. A cell phone. A brass hotel room key . . .

How many hotels around here still use keys like that? she wondered.

Almost immediately she thought of someone who might know.

Maggie had worked at Gumm's Hardware Store on Main Street all last summer and fall, until she'd switched jobs and taken the counter position at the dry cleaner's, which paid her an extra fifty cents an hour. She'd loved working for Mr. Gumm but had needed the extra few dollars a day. She'd even cried on his shoulder when she left. He threw her a party. Maggie had loved it.

She might know something about hotel room keys.

It was worth a try, Candy thought. She needed to head over there anyway to pick up the dress for the ball. So she told Doc she was running out on a quick errand, jumped into the Jeep, and drove over to Maggie's place at Fowler's Corner.

THIRTY

She found Maggie sitting in a tastefully decorated room tucked into the back corner of her two-story, green gabled house. It had once been a playroom for Amanda, Maggie's daughter, but over the years it had morphed into a family room and an office, a place where Amanda did homework and Maggie sewed on quiet evenings. When Amanda left for college, Maggie transformed it again into a cozy work space and retreat for herself. Here, she kept her small collection of business and community awards and mementos, mostly from her days at the Stone & Milbury Insurance Agency, along with her burgeoning collection of salt and pepper shakers, a small library of mystery and romance novels, a variety of scented candles of all shapes and sizes, a few hand-painted miniatures of lighthouses, and plenty of photos of Amanda, Amanda's boyfriend Cameron, and other family members and friends, including several of Maggie and Candy together, taken over the past few years.

Maggie had her nose pressed up against a computer screen. "The only way I can keep up with Amanda and Cameron is on Facebook," she said with a touch of melancholy in her voice. "At least they friended me. I think that's what they call it. Or is that tweeting? And what the heck is Skype? It sounds like a skin condition." She swept a hand back through her hair. "All this technology stuff is moving too fast. How does anyone keep up with it anymore? What happened to the good old days when we used to talk to each other on the phone?"

"Or over the backyard fence," Candy said, dropping into an upholstered chair, which had bare wood arms.

"Or on the front porch." Maggie laughed. "Listen to us, a couple of modern girls reminiscing about the old times, when things were a lot simpler. Of course, back in those days, they also lacked microwaves, garage-door openers, and Scrubbing Bubbles."

"And electronic locks," Candy said, seeing an opening to steer the conversation to a more pressing topic. "Listen, I have a question for you."

Maggie swiveled in her chair so she could give Candy her full attention. "Fire away."

"Okay." She took a quick breath and plunged right in. "Well, earlier today I found this brass hotel key, attached to one of those red plastic key tag thingies with room numbers on them. You know what I mean, right? Now, I know most hotels around here use electronic key cards, but there are probably a few places in the area that still use actual keys instead of plastic cards. Any idea which ones those might be?"

Maggie was silent for a moment, a haze of confusion clouding her face. Finally, she asked, "Is this a technical question?"

"Sort of, I suppose."

"I just wondered because, you know, you're asking me about keys. That's not a common topic of discussion. So, of course, it makes me curious: Why the sudden interest in keys?"

Candy shrugged casually. "I just like keys. Keys are interesting things."

"But you never cared about keys before."

"I've gained a new appreciation of them, due to recent developments."

"Hmm." Maggie scrutinized her friend with a narrowed gaze. She glanced down at Candy's pockets. "Do you have this mystery key with you?"

"Not at the moment."

"Why is that not surprising?" Maggie tapped her pursed lips with an index finger. "You know what I think? I think you've been nosing around — without me, I might add — and you found a clue. And now you want my help in figuring it out. Is that about right?"

The corners of Candy's mouth turned up into a conspiratorial smile. "You're not totally incorrect. I've had a busy afternoon, yes."

"You must have. I've barely seen you all day. What have you been up to?"

"Like you said — nosing around. Getting myself in trouble. And just for the record, I wasn't intentionally doing it without you — nosing around, I mean."

"I know that, honey. You can't help yourself," Maggie declared knowingly. "Just like Mr. Biggles, God rest his soul — always on the prowl. He was relentless. Nothing could stand in his way when he was on the trail of something."

She paused, grinning cagily as she sharpened her gaze on her friend. "That's how *you* get when there's a mystery in town. I admit, it's probably due to some sort of chemical imbalance in your brain or something like that, but it's why we all love you."

She smiled warmly.

"Um, thanks — I think. Anyway, back to the key question."

"Which is?"

"I'm looking for hotels that use real brass keys, like the one I saw. Any idea which ones those might be?"

"Oh, right. The key. It's probably the key to this whole thing, right?" She chuckled, amused. "That's pretty funny. The key is the key. How often does that happen? Not very often, I'd guess. Well, hmm, let me think." She closed her eyes for a few moments as she pondered the issue. With her eyes still closed, she asked, "Did you get a good look at this key?"

"Well, yes and no. I saw it, but I didn't pay that much attention to it. There were . . . distractions."

Maggie opened one eye. "Such as?"

"I'd rather not say at the moment."

Maggie opened the other eye and gave her friend a questioning look. "Withholding evidence? You've been warned about that, you know."

"I know."

"If I help you out, I could be considered an accomplice in whatever crime you're about to commit — or have already committed."

"It wouldn't be the first time."

"That's true. Okay, so, sometimes those old keys have room numbers or the name of the hotel stamped on them. Did you notice anything like that, during the distracted time this particular key was in your presence?"

Candy ignored her friend's humorous asides and stuck to the facts. "It looked like it had at one time, but it was so old that anything valuable had rubbed off."

"Okay, we'll just have to figure it out. Which hotels still use keys like that?" Maggie asked herself rhetorically as she tapped at her chin. "A few maintenance men from those places used to come into the hardware store when I worked there. One was from Hidden Valley Motel and Cabins, that place up on Route 1. And then there's the Shangri-La, that little place just outside of town. It's a little dingy, if you ask me. Probably hasn't been renovated since the sixties. One of those room-by-the-hour places, if you know what I mean. Of course, I've never been in a place like that myself. But I've heard rumors. . . ."

Maggie's eyes suddenly lit up, as if something had just clicked inside her brain. She raised a finger. "Hey, you know what, I just read something strange about that place when I was online this morning before I went to work. Now, where was it?"

She swiveled back to her computer, grabbed the mouse, and began navigating her way around the screen. After scrolling down through the browser's history and clicking the back button numerous times on the half dozen tabs she had open, she finally found the page she was looking for.

It was a bright, busy design, with flashy typefaces and bright lime green and fluorescent purple colors.

Candy had seen it before. It was Wanda Boyle's blog, *The Cape Crusader.*

Maggie looked a little embarrassed. "Oh yeah, that's right. I remember now where I saw it."

Candy waved it off. "That's okay. I've been checking Wanda's blog a lot lately myself. I hate to admit this, because if she gets any inkling it came from me, I'll never hear the end of it, but she's actually been doing some pretty good reporting, for someone just starting out."

"She's got the inside scoop on a lot of things, that's for sure." Maggie pointed at the screen. "Here's the item that caught my attention."

It was a four- or five-paragraph blog posting titled *Police Log.*

Candy leaned in for a closer look. Ben ran a similar thing in the paper, compiled by one of the volunteers. The only problem was, the paper published only twice a month in the winter, so it lost its timeliness. They'd transferred some sections online but usually updated it only once or twice a week. Wanda was posting daily, and often multiple times. The police log was one of several postings she'd made the previous evening.

"See, right here," Maggie said, pointing, and she read, " 'A guest staying at the Shangri-La Motel on North U.S. 192 reported a missing toboggan on Thursday, January 27. The guest had left the toboggan leaning against an outside wall of the motel. A brief search turned up no sign of the item. The owner later reported finding the toboggan in the woods behind the motel. Police surmised someone had taken the item and later returned it.' That's all it says. Not much, really."

Candy was silent for a long time as she pondered the implications. Finally, she said softly, "It could be nothing . . . or it could be everything."

THIRTY-ONE

As Candy was headed out the door, Maggie put a hand on her shoulder. "Don't go yet. You almost forgot the most important thing."

She ran off into her bedroom and emerged a few moments later with a slinky black dress on a hanger, covered with plastic wrapping. "I found this for you. It's your size and it should make you look beautiful. And here." Maggie handed her a long, black velvet jewelry case. "My pearls and earrings. Ed gave them to me years ago for our tenth anniversary. We were happy for a while, you know," she said wistfully. "Cost him a month's wages, if I remember correctly. I felt like a queen when I wore them. I thought they'd look spectacular on you tonight."

Candy accepted the dress and jewelry box, and gave Maggie a tight hug. "Thanks for helping me with this."

"Honey, it's my pleasure."

"Hey, you know you're always welcome to come along with me, right? I'm not quite sure where I'm headed next, or what I'll find when I get there, but no matter what it is, I can always use your help."

"Of course you could." Maggie patted her affectionately on the shoulder. "And I'd love to go tramping off with you into the snowy woods or fields or wherever you're off to. I really would. And you know I've always got your back, whenever you need me. But I have a hair appointment in forty-five minutes. Sheila managed to squeeze me in this afternoon. I was lucky to get the slot. She's booked up tight all day. The Moose Fest Ball, you know."

"You found a date?" Candy asked happily.

"I did!"

"Who is it?"

"Well, you'll just have to wait and see. I guarantee you, it'll surprise everyone! In fact, the whole thing was a surprise. He came into the cleaner's this afternoon, we got to talking, and, well, one thing led to another."

"Sure you don't want to keep the pearls and wear them tonight?" Candy asked, indicating the jewelry box she held. "It's not too late to change your mind."

"I'm going a different direction," Maggie said. "You'll see. I found the perfect ensemble. . . ."

Back outside, Candy carefully laid the black dress on the backseat, slipped the black velvet jewelry box into the glove compartment, and fired up the Jeep. Putting it into gear, she headed back out toward the Coastal Loop, also known as Route 192. At the stoplight, instead of heading back toward Blueberry Acres, she flicked on her signal and turned right, powering northward out of Cape Willington.

The road was wet from the snowfall, though the heavy traffic headed into and out of town kept it worn down to mostly clear pavement. Still, there was always the possibility of an icy patch, so she stayed under the speed limit and remained watchful as the wintertime scenery slipped past her.

The woods of Cape Willington lined the road as she drove north, although there were plenty of places along the way where someone had carved out a half acre of land or so and built a house. There were a number of historic houses along this road, old capes, cabins, and farmhouses, dating back to the earlier years of the previous century. There were barns as well, some leaning so treacherously under thick blankets of snow that they should have been condemned. But still they stood, their ancient skeletal frames refusing to give way to the onslaught of winter, or any other season, for that matter.

After a few miles she came to a filling station on the left with a small store attached, and a few hundred yards beyond that was the entrance to the motel's parking lot.

She'd seen the Shangri-La plenty of times before as she drove up and down this road but rarely paid it any attention. It was a nondescript building, with a low roof, long overhanging eaves, and a stepped construction that took the long line of rooms up a rising slope toward the woods behind it. At the back end of the property was a perpendicular row of rooms, so the building formed a long, drawn-out L shape. It was painted brick red with white-framed windows, now frosted from the weather. Out front, a terribly dated neon sign glowed morosely in the overcast day.

Candy eyed the place suspiciously through the windshield, wondering if this was a smart move. She could easily just turn around and head home. Still, she knew she had to check the place out. She had no idea what she was looking for here — but she also had a feeling she'd know it when she saw it.

Putting on her left turn signal, she eased into the motel's parking lot, driving past the office and up the slight incline toward the rooms at the back of the property. A row of high pine trees rose up on the back side of the building, framing it like something out of a postcard. There were only a few cars in the parking lot at this time of day, and she saw no one about. She wheeled the Jeep into a parking spot halfway along the building, in front of room number ten, shut off the Jeep's engine, and climbed out.

The day had grown damper and colder with the approaching weather, and Candy huddled down into her fleece jacket. She stood for a moment looking both ways, toward the office at the front of the building, and to the far end, toward the woods at the back of the property.

Despite the fact that the front of the building was so close to the road, it was fairly quiet back here, where the sounds of traffic were muted by the snow cover. She could hear the slight wind rustling through the pines behind the building and the call of a lone crow overhead, flapping past.

She started walking uphill, toward the back of the property. She passed a few cars, and a few rooms that looked occupied. She could hear the sound of a TV coming from one of the rooms, voices in another. Somewhere behind her, a door opened and closed as the occupant emerged from one of the rooms and walked down toward the office. Candy turned to watch him go, but he never noticed her.

When she reached the end of the row at room number sixteen, she came to a stop. Four more rooms angled off to her right, forming the cross arm of the L. Twenty rooms total.

She studied it all, her gaze shifting about as she focused in on the details around her, but she saw nothing out of the ordinary, nothing that could provide a clue or tell her if anything pertinent, relevant, or even vaguely interesting had happened here.

She frowned and shook her head. "Well, I guess this was just a wild goose chase," she said to herself. Resigned to the fact that she'd encountered a dead end, she turned to head back to the Jeep.

The sign on the far side of the parking lot caught her eye suddenly, as if it had practically leapt into her field of vision. It was a low wooden affair with some text and red numbers painted on it. *To Rooms 21–24* it read, and beneath that a red arrow pointed back toward *the woods.*

Candy felt her heartbeat quicken.

She noticed it now, a narrow paved road headed around the side of the building. She'd initially thought it was just a service road, perhaps for maintenance vehicles.

Apparently there were a few more rooms behind the main building.

She glanced toward the front of the motel. Not a soul in sight.

Trying her best to look as if she belonged here, she meandered around the corner of the building, following the narrow road, which led to a small back parking lot.

The lot was empty except for a single car. A Honda, Candy saw. She scanned the room numbers on the doors.

It was parked in front of room twenty-three.

She stopped and looked around.

She was all alone here, out of sight of anyone who might happen to be walking to or from the motel's office or main building. But rather than feel safe from prying eyes, she felt strangely vulnerable, though at first she didn't know why.

It took a few moments for all the pieces to click into place, and for the magnitude of what she was seeing to register in her mind.

The Honda Pilot SUV had a black roof

rack and a sporty exterior upgrade with flared fenders and black side runners — the type of vehicle a guy like Victor Templeton might drive.

Parked in front of room number twenty-three — the same number Elizabeth Foxwell had seen in her vision.

Coincidence? Candy shook her head. She didn't know.

Whatever the explanation, she had to have a quick look.

As casually as possible, she strode forward, past the door with the number twenty-three on it. The curtains were closed tight on the room's single window, making it impossible to see inside. She lingered for the briefest of moments in front of the door, cocking her ear, straining to hear a voice from inside or the sound of a TV or anything to indicate the room might be occupied. But she heard nothing.

She continued on, walking to the end of the row. There were three other rooms here, but the others seemed unoccupied, for their curtains were open, and she could see into their dark interiors. She had no idea whether room twenty-three was occupied or not.

There was an easy way to find out. She could just knock on the door and make up an excuse if someone actually opened up.

She considered that idea as she crossed to the Honda SUV. It was steel blue in color, though it needed a good washing. Crusts of black ice and salt clung to its undercarriage and wheel wells, and a layer of snow covered the roof and windshield.

Now that she noticed it, banks of snow had blown up against the tires on one side, making it look as if the car hadn't been moved in a while. Perhaps for several days.

That would fit, she thought. This could be Victor's car.

She looked in the vehicle's window, but there was not much to see. A standard blue and beige interior, with fabric seats and a plastic dash. She noticed two take-out coffee cups in the front holders between the seats, as well as sunglasses, CDs, and other items like a tire gauge. In the backseat were a few jackets, books, travel maps, and a red scarf with gold tassels.

Candy turned all the way around until she faced the woods, looking away from the building. *Which way am I facing?* she wondered. Was Blueberry Acres somewhere behind here? And where was Solomon's place from her current location?

She unzipped her jacket and felt around her inside pocket until she found the compass Ben had given her. She pulled it out, flipped open the cover, and waited until the needle settled down to focus in on it.

The red end of the needle pointed toward her right shoulder. North. She turned and looked in that direction, at an angle up across Route 192 and beyond.

She turned back around, facing out behind the motel. That meant west was vaguely to her right, and south was to her left. Or to be more accurate, she was presently facing south-southwest, approximately.

And Blueberry Acres lay in which direction?

Off to her left somewhere, she surmised, to the south or southeast.

And how far away was the farm from here? Most of the way across the Cape. A few miles, perhaps? More or less?

She thought of the missing toboggan. Why would someone borrow it, only to return it a few hours later?

She turned and looked back at the room.

I need to get a look inside, she thought.

On an impulse, she walked up to the door and knocked. She figured if anyone answered, she'd just make something up off the top of her head.

She waited. Nothing.

She knocked again.

She moved over to the window and

knocked on the cold glass, trying to peer inside to see if she could spot any movement.

It was no use. The place was buttoned up tight and apparently vacant.

She tried the doorknob. It was locked.

There was no pad or slot for an electronic key card, she noticed. Instead, the doorknob had a simple well-used keyhole.

She appeared to be in the right spot. Victor must have been here at some point over the past few days.

What might he have left behind?

She decided to try the office. Maybe she could figure out a way to get another key so she could inspect the room — maybe she would tell the person behind the counter that she was Victor's sister or cousin or something like that.

She was just coming around the corner of the building, heading into the main parking lot, when she saw a police car bearing the insignia of the Cape Willington Police Department pull into the driveway in front of the motel's office.

The vehicle came to a halt, and a few moments later, Officer Jody McCroy stepped out from the driver's seat.

Thirty-Two

As quickly and as casually as possible, so as not to draw attention to herself, Candy turned around and slipped back around the corner of the building.

Officer Jody? What the heck is he doing here?

At first she felt a deep flash of paranoia, thinking he'd come for her, but a few moments later she worked out the most likely reason for his sudden appearance.

They'd figured it out. The police had traced the hotel room key to the Shangri-La, just as she'd done. Chief Durr must have sent Officer McCroy to investigate.

More than likely he had the key with him. He'd be able to show it to the person behind the check-in counter. Would they recognize it? Would they point him back to room twenty-three?

And here she was, standing right next to what very well could be Victor Templeton's car, and in front of a room he'd likely stayed in.

She was trapped.

She'd be in a heap of trouble if Officer McCroy discovered her here, especially after the repeated warnings she'd received from Chief Durr — and her own promise to stay out of the investigation.

"Candy, what have you done?" she chided herself. She felt a moment of panic but forced herself to stay calm. "Just think. You can get out of this if you stay cool and figure it out."

After waiting for her rapidly beating heart to slow down, she edged up to the corner of the building and chanced a look around it.

Officer McCroy was just walking into the office. His back was to her as he approached an older woman behind the counter and began to talk to her, gesturing back toward the motel rooms.

His attention was focused in a different direction. If she was going to do something, now was the time, before he headed in her direction and completely cut off any avenue of escape.

Before she had time to think about what she was doing, she made her move.

She stayed close to the side of the building, turning right and right again along the

345

four rooms that made up the short end of the building's L shape, before angling left toward her teal-colored, easily identifiable Jeep. It was parked right in front of her, outside room number ten, near the center of the building. Fortunately, a beige-colored family van was parked a few spaces away on the other side, closer to the front of the motel. There was a good chance it had shielded the Jeep from Officer McCroy's view as he'd stepped out of his vehicle and made his way to the office.

Whether she could make it out of the lot without getting noticed, well, that was a different matter.

She fished the keys out of her pocket and climbed inside, glancing anxiously toward the office as she started the engine. It sputtered to life.

She put the transmission into reverse but kept her foot on the brake pedal. She knew she didn't have much time. In a matter of minutes, or seconds, Officer McCroy would come walking out of the office and head straight up the slope toward her. There'd be no way to hide from him then, and she'd have some explaining to do. She hadn't broken any laws — at least, she didn't think so — but she'd have the book thrown at her nonetheless.

It wasn't a pleasant thought. Not in the least. So it was best to get out of Dodge while the getting was good.

Still, she hesitated, waiting for the right moment. And as luck would have it, the right moment showed up sooner than she'd hoped.

A large Ford SUV came down the road, slowed, and turned into the motel's parking lot, where it crept along toward the office as the occupants of the vehicle peered about. It was a husband and wife, Candy could see, and they were trying to determine whether this was a good place to stop.

Candy used their indecision to her advantage. Pulling on her seat belt and checking over her shoulder, she backed up, shifted gears, and drove toward the front of the motel, staying to the left side of the parking lot and the SUV. This put it between her and the office, blocking the view of anyone who might look out and see her as she drove past.

She timed it as well as she could, passing by the office on the far side of the SUV. It might be enough, she hoped, to make a clean getaway.

As she reached the street, she cast a quick glance over her right shoulder. Officer Mc-Croy was still talking to the woman behind the counter, who was gesturing toward the rear of the building. He took a few steps to his side and peered out the office window, back toward room twenty-three and the spot where Candy had been sitting just a few moments earlier.

At the bottom of the parking lot she braked, carefully double-checked in both directions, turned the steering wheel to the right, and accelerated down the road toward Cape Willington, apparently unseen.

She was a good mile or two away when she finally let out her breath.

"Candy Holliday," she said with a shake of her head, "you've got to stop doing that to yourself."

THIRTY-THREE

"There," Doc said as he finally managed to secure the clasp behind her neck, after several noble yet frustrating attempts. He patted her shoulders affectionately, gave her a kiss on the side of her head, and stepped away. "Let's see how that looks."

She gently let her hair back down and felt for the string of pearls around her neck before dropping her hands to her sides and turning to face him. "So, do I look fancy enough for the ball?" she asked her father, somewhat facetiously.

Doc looked her up and down. She could see the pride in his eyes. "Sweetie, you look like a billion bucks. We've increased it, you know, due to inflation."

She beamed. "The dress *does* look good, doesn't it?"

"It's beautiful on you. It fits perfectly."

"Almost like it was tailored for me." It was expertly crafted, that was certain — a black, sleeveless Givenchy number with a form-fitting design that fell to just above her knees. She knew Maggie had good taste, but never guessed she or Amanda owned anything this nice. She must have picked it up at one of the outlets somewhere, Candy surmised, or maybe even at the Goodwill — though it must have been at a time when Candy hadn't been with her, for she'd surely have remembered if Maggie had bought a dress like this.

She'd managed to locate a fairly decent pair of black high heels at the back of her closet, and a dark gray wool business coat she'd kept from her earlier days. It felt a little loose around her but would work for tonight. She'd also pulled a silver clutch purse from the bottom drawer of an old bureau in the corner of her room, and found a black tote bag to carry her heels in. She had no intention of putting them on until she was at the ball. She'd wear her boots until then, high society be damned.

She'd done her best with her hair, which she'd kept at shoulder length for most of the past year. She'd toyed with the idea of growing it out again but liked the simplicity of simply washing it out, combing it loosely, and letting it go au naturel around the farm. For tonight, however, she'd combed it out and arranged it neatly around her face, tucking one side behind her ear. This showed off her earrings and gave her an elegant yet not too formal look. She liked it.

In fact, she liked the way she looked tonight. She'd even applied a little makeup, including red lipstick.

She hadn't dressed up this nice since she moved to Blueberry Acres, and she was pleased and a little surprised by the result. "You clean up real nice for a farmer," she said into the mirror.

Doc had his camera out and snapped a few pictures of her, and took a few more when Ben arrived, decked out in formal attire, his long hair combed back from his forehead, to take her to the ball.

He told her she looked beautiful, helped her into her coat, and shook hands with Doc before escorting her out to his warmed-up Range Rover. "I have the heat on full blast," he told her as he opened the passenger-side door. "I didn't know what you'd be wearing so I wanted you to be comfortable."

She climbed inside, and he closed the door behind her, locking out the cold. As he ran around to the other side, skirting the front of the vehicle, she arranged her dress and coat carefully around her, settling in front of the hot air vent, and turned to admire Ben in his stylish attire as he climbed into the driver's seat beside her.

"You're looking particularly dashing this evening," she told him.

He laughed as he put on his seat belt. "To be honest, I kind of feel dashing. I haven't dressed up like this in a while."

"Me neither."

"Well," he said, eyeing her one last time before he turned his attention to the road, "I'm glad we're doing this together then. I think it's long overdue for both of us."

The small yet elegant ballroom at the Lightkeeper's Inn was attached to the back of the building, though to call it an add-on would be a gross understatement. Officially referred to as the Elias J. Pruitt Ballroom, it had been built in the 1920s to Elias's precise specifications for the wedding-eve dinner of his beloved daughter, Eleanor, a debutante from Boston. The room was large enough to accommodate one hundred and sixty guests, though it seemed intimate, thanks to its design. It was decorated in sage greens, pale yellows, and muted browns, giving it a casual yet classic look, enhanced by a simply designed wainscotting of Maine pine. The multilevel ceiling, higher in the middle and lower on the sides, added a dramatic architectural element and served an important function during the day, letting in filtered light through windows high in the raised center section.

Tables draped with crisp linen cloths were carefully arranged on either side of the room, some tucked under sconces or into alcoves, leaving the center of the room open for one of its most distinguishing features, a highly polished floor of imported exotic hardwood that Elias, an international merchant, had shipped in from Africa for precisely this purpose. He'd had all the tableware brought in from England, the silverware from China, and the linens from France. He'd ordered the creation of the delicate central crystal chandelier, called the Queen by the staff, handmade in Germany, and the furniture, designed and built by the finest New England craftsmen. He'd even brought in his own mason to create the magnificent floor-to-ceiling stone fireplace, the room's centerpiece, ablaze for the evening, its flames reflected by the polished dance floor that stretched out in front of it, leading all the way to the double French doors at the opposite side of the room.

Candelabra on each of the tables were lit, giving off a soft glow, and in the corner, a string quartet played a Strauss waltz as Ben and Candy entered.

Ben stopped just inside the French doors and looked down at the card in his hand, which they'd exchanged for their thirty-dollar tickets at a table in the hallway outside, right after Candy had switched out her boots for heels and stowed her outer gear at the hat check. "We're at table seven," he said, looking around the room, which was beginning to fill with guests. He pointed to the left of the fireplace. "I think we're over that way."

Hand in hand, they started through the crowd, stopping first at the bar to pick up drinks — Champagne for Candy, a martini for Ben — and chatting along the way with those they knew. They ran into Lyra Graveton and her husband Llewellyn, Jane and Bill Chapman, Delilah Daggerstone and her ebullient husband Drew, new shop owners Ralph Henry and Malcolm Stevens Randolph decked out in their finest, town council chairman Mason Flint escorting the latest Mrs. Flint, and the Reverend James P. Daisy with his wife of nearly forty years, the delightfully regal Gabriella Daisy, who looked resplendent in a pale pink chiffon dress that showed off her straight frame and fashion-model shoulders.

In fact, Candy thought, looking around the room as she sipped Champagne, her right arm slipped in through Ben's, everyone looked amazing tonight. Somehow they'd all managed not only to find formal clothes — or clever facsimiles thereof — in the dead of winter, with half the shops in town closed down and a half-day trip at the very least to anything that could remotely pass as an actual department store, but they'd also survived the day's uncertain weather, slushy streets, slippery sidewalks, and sanded pathways to arrive here looking resplendent.

Candy suddenly felt very proud of her hearty little — and surprisingly stylish — town.

They found their table and set down their glasses, but as the string quartet launched into a popular number, a classical take on a Billy Joel song, Ben pulled Candy out onto the dance floor and put his arm firmly around her waist. "I've been wanting to do this ever since I saw you in that dress," he said as he pulled her close.

She slipped into his arms, her right hand tightly clasping his left, her left arm curling around the back of his shoulder. "Really?"

"It looks fantastic, like it was made for you. And you look fantastic in it."

She gave him an affectionate smile. "You say the sweetest things when you're wearing a tux."

He laughed. "I thought you said you didn't have anything to wear. Where did you find it?"

"The dress?" She glanced down at it, then back up at him with an amused look. In an exaggerated whisper, she said, "Would you believe it's a loaner?"

He arched an eyebrow. "From who?"

"I'll give you three guesses."

"That's too easy. And the pearls?"

"Hmm." She arched an eyebrow of her own. "You're very inquisitive tonight, aren't you?"

He smiled and shrugged. "Can't help it. It's my job."

"But a woman can't give away *all* her secrets," Candy protested lightly.

"True. That would ruin the mystery."

"And have I been so mysterious?" she said to him, only somewhat facetiously.

"You? I'm not sure I'd call you mysterious. Certainly beautiful. Definitely dependable. Tenacious at times, when you have to be. Sometimes surprising. Usually unique . . ."

"Usually?"

"Well, almost always."

"I'll take that as a compliment," she said, her smile returning. "And what about you?"

He was silent for a moment, with a look

on his face she couldn't quite read. "Hmm, yes," he said finally, "what about me?"

"Well you have to admit, you *have* been somewhat mysterious lately."

"Have I?"

"A number of people have noticed it."

"And would that number include the same person who loaned you that dress?"

She narrowed her gaze on him. "You're smarter than you look."

"I've heard that before. And more charming too."

"Yes," she said, leaning into him, "you are."

For a few moments they danced in silence, enjoying the opportunity to hold each other close after the unsettled nature of the last few days. Finally he said softly into her ear, "I don't know why it took us so long to do this."

She smiled into his shoulder. "I don't know either."

Several other couples had joined them on the dance floor, while the rest of the guests chattered in the room around them. Candles flickered, the music rose and fell, and the fire crackled, but for Candy it all seemed to recede into the background. She could feel Ben's arm around her back, strong and assured, and she could smell his cologne. His left hand felt warm in hers.

I could get used to this, she thought as she tightened her hold on him.

The music stopped, the moment passed, and they stepped apart, applauded lightly, and looked at each other.

An older woman, who had been dancing nearby with her husband, leaned over, laid a thin hand on Candy's arm, and said to her, "You two dance beautifully together."

"Oh, well, thank you very much."

She felt Ben squeeze her hand and looked up. His eyes were making strange movements sideways. It took her a few moments to turn, survey the faces around them, and realize they'd somehow become the center of attention. Ben nodded his head in awkward acknowledgement as a few people applauded, and Candy looked a little embarrassed. She squeezed his hand back. "I think we'd better sit the next one out."

He nodded. "Good idea."

As the room continued to fill and the music swelled, they lingered by the fireplace for a while before taking two seats on the back side of their table, along the wall to the left of the fireplace, where they could have a little privacy, since the other couples were still milling about, gathered in duos and groups around the room.

But several friends from work, including Betty Lynn Spar and Judy Crockett, soon wandered over to say hello, dragging along their better halves, and they all soon got to talking about the recent developments around town. They'd heard bits and pieces, and Ben listened to all the details with interest.

But it was Jesse Kidder, the paper's photographer and graphic artist, who had the juiciest piece of news. He'd stopped by the table to snap a few photos of the group for the paper's society page, though they all knew Ben would never approve the use of his photo in a non-news-related item, so a few alternatives were snapped as well.

Before Jesse wandered off to photograph the other guests, he told them, "The police are up at some motel just outside of town. Apparently they've found Victor Templeton's car and the room he was staying in. They're searching it now. The crime van's headed over from Augusta."

Instinctively Ben checked his watch. Candy noticed the gesture. She knew what he was thinking.

He's wondering if he can slip out to cover the story.

He glanced up and caught her looking at him. He gave her a knowing smile. "Don't worry. I won't disappear on you. At least not right at this moment."

She was suddenly serious. "It's an important story. If you need to cover it . . ."

He shook his head as Jesse turned back toward them. "Oh yeah, there was one more thing," he said. "The word is, they've found evidence that other people were present in that motel room with him."

Ben's brow fell, and Candy was suddenly suspicious. "Jesse, where'd you hear that?"

He shrugged. "I just read it on the Web a little while ago," he said, indicating his smart phone, and walked away.

She wanted to ask him which site, or perhaps even grab his phone and find out for herself, but he was already snapping away at the next table, and she knew she'd never get him back, not when he had his eye behind the lens of a camera.

It was probably Wanda Boyle's site, she thought darkly, turning to gaze into the fire. *Wanda.*

Why did she seem so plugged in all of a sudden? A few weeks ago she was covering doggie birthday parties and the latest selection of the local book club. Now here she was at the center of a developing news story — a murder mystery no less. How had the level of her reporting changed so quickly?

Where was she getting her information? Did she have a source inside the police department? Candy wondered — maybe the same person Finn Woodbury talked to? But that didn't make any sense. Finn would never betray his source to anyone. It was possible Wanda could have connected to the person in a different way, but Candy thought it unlikely that Wanda and Finn moved in the same circles or talked to the same people.

But then who was tipping her off? If everything Jesse said was true, Wanda was getting some pretty big scoops. How was she doing it?

Candy heard a slight disturbance by the French doors and turned to see what was going on. She heard the voice then, a penetrating tone that somehow seemed to drill right into her skin, a voice both smooth yet cackling at the same time.

". . . as most of you might know, my husband, Bart, broke his leg over the holidays while skiing at Sunday River and won't be joining us tonight, so rather than come alone, I thought I'd bring the man of the hour, the sponsorship award winner himself," said the person who was just entering the room through the French doors in a triumphant tone.

Candy let out an involuntary breath.

It was Wanda Boyle. She stopped just inside the doors, and with a flourish of her arm, announced, "Ladies and gentlemen, you all know my escort, Mr. Liam Yates!"

Candy was somewhat surprised. The woman had apparently just written and posted a breaking news story, and now here she was, decked out in a shivery blue number, looking like an overripe blueberry. Beside her, Liam wore a white dinner jacket with black pants and a black silk scarf draped around his neck. His blond, wavy hair was stylishly uncombed and still thick, despite the fact that he was probably pushing fifty. And his lined face was still tanned and handsome, with defined features. He artfully feigned mild interest in the evening's proceedings, Candy noticed.

As Wanda greeted her friends and followers, she surreptitiously scanned the room, scoping out the location of the town's important people, as if they were targets to intercept. When her gaze alighted on Candy, it paused only for an instant before moving on, without any sort of greeting or acknowledgement.

Wanda was soon deeply engrossed in her little circle of friends, crowing and launching into several loud stories. She obviously felt like the belle of the ball, due in part to her escort.

Liam stood nearby, checking the chandelier, his fingernails, the bottom of his shoe. He looked at his watch several times with exaggerated gestures and brushed absently at his clothes as he tried, and failed, to stifle a yawn.

He seemed to sense her watching him, and shifted his gaze toward her. He nodded slightly and gave her a smile before glancing at Ben and then away toward the French doors, as something suddenly drew his attention.

Candy turned to look as well. There was a shout. Murmurings.

A moment later Duncan Leggmeyer burst into the room. He paused only briefly, until he spotted Liam Yates nearby, crossed quickly to him, and slugged him firmly on his aristocratic jaw, sending Liam to the floor in a heap, unconscious.

THIRTY-FOUR

Wanda shrieked, her friends cried out, and the assembled group of guests gasped collectively. Several people rushed into the room, several people rushed out of the room, and Jesse Kidder turned toward the action, camera clicking as he documented the entire scene.

"Oh my God!" Candy said, her hand going to her face.

"What did I miss?"

She glanced back. Ben had been deep in a conversation with Judy Crockett's husband and had been facing the other direction during the confrontation.

"Duncan Leggmeyer just hit Liam Yates," she told him.

"Really?" Ben curiously studied the activity on the other side of the room. "Anyone hurt?"

"Looks like Liam was knocked out cold."

"Do you have any idea what provoked it?"

Candy didn't, but she wondered if it had something to do with the hatchet. In fact, she was surprised to see Duncan here at all. She'd told the police about Duncan's connection to the weapon, and she suspected they'd called him into the office for questioning. But what did any of that have to do with Liam?

Duncan was having harsh words with several guests, and a few moments later a security guard arrived. "He set me up!" Duncan shouted, pointing down at Liam's inert body. "The bloody bastard set me up!"

The security guard approached Duncan, held out the flat end of his hand, and spoke to him in a low, controlled manner. Duncan said something back, and the security guard's gaze turned steely. Finally Duncan backed away, bowed his head, and walked from the room without another word, the security guard close behind.

Meanwhile, a crowd of concerned people had gathered around Liam, checking him out to see if he was okay. But an even bigger group enveloped Wanda Boyle, who had had to sit down. Her closest friends fussed about her as if she were a diva who had fallen off a stage. They seemed upset at what had just occurred, obviously worried about

Wanda's well-being — as well as her reputation.

"That's what happens when you get involved with out-of-towners," Candy heard one woman, who stood nearby, whisper to her tight-jawed elderly friend.

The string quartet had stopped playing at the disruption, but they started up again, launching into Vivaldi, and the hushed room soon filled with murmuring voices.

"I'd better get over there and see what's going on," Ben said, and he rose out of his chair and headed across the room.

"Maybe we should call the paramedics," Judy Crockett said from across the table.

There was no need. A clerk appeared with smelling salts in hand, and she soon brought Liam around, though he stayed in a prone position. A guest who happened to be a nurse performed a cursory examination, feeling for his pulse and checking for injuries.

Assured the experts were on the job, most of the guests returned to their conversations, recongregating in groups and duos or heading off to the bar or to find their seats.

Maggie walked into the midst of it, bewildered.

She stood just inside the French doors, taking in the chaotic scene, her gaze wandering in disbelief from the groggy Liam to the distraught Wanda, around to all their respective attendees, and back again. Finally she looked across the room and caught Candy's eye.

Candy waved and pointed to the seat next to her. Maggie nodded and, giving the group gathered around Liam a wide berth, headed across the room.

"What in heaven's name happened here?" she asked, aghast, "and how in the heck did I miss it?"

"I've seen some strange things lately," Candy told her friend, "but this takes the cake." And quickly she explained what had happened as Maggie sank into the seat next to her.

Maggie was dressed elegantly yet rather sedately, in a stylish burgundy waist-length jacket with wide faux fur lapels, a white ruffled blouse, ankle-length gray wool skirt, and elegant silver jewelry. As Candy finished, she looked her friend up and down. "You look great, by the way. But where have you been?"

Maggie glanced around the room, as if looking for someone. "He called and said he was running late. He asked if he could meet me here. We were supposed to rendezvous at seven thirty."

Candy checked her watch. "It's just past that and —"

"Oh, there he is," Maggie said, suddenly animated. She stood and waved.

Candy turned to see Preston Smith approaching them. "Ah, here you are, Mrs. Tremont," Preston said, all smiles and twinkling eyes as he approached her. He wore a well-tailored black jacket with silk lapels, gray tie and vest, and a white shirt, well starched, giving him a crisp, classic look. His longish gray hair was disheveled, as if he'd failed to comb it that day, and he'd switch out his wire-rimmed glasses for black ones, which gave him a different look — more distinguished, perhaps. His thick gray moustache seemed thicker than usual.

But he was no less enthusiastic, and as he approached, he bowed dramatically from the waist, lifted Maggie's hand, and kissed it lightly. "My apologies, my lady, for inconveniencing you this evening. It was regrettable, I assure you, but I'm afraid it couldn't be helped. There have been a number of developments, as you may well know."

"It really wasn't much of an inconvenience at all," Maggie said, waving a hand toward the other side of the room, "except I apparently missed the only real action this town has seen in weeks — other than the murder, of course."

"Hmm, yes, nasty business that," Preston said with an air of distaste. "I've heard they have a number of suspects in mind, including" — he turned just slightly to glance over his shoulder — "some people in this very room."

"No kidding," Maggie said, and she turned toward Wanda and Liam.

Candy looked too. They had Liam sitting up and were attempting to move him to another room. Ben was talking to one of the hotel staffers, and Wanda was fanning herself dramatically, milking her role in the evening's events for all it was worth.

Candy was struck by a sudden thought, and she scanned the room. She realized several people were still missing. She double-checked herself but knew she was correct. Colin and Oliver were obviously busy behind the scenes, so their absences were explainable. Baxter Bryant had told her yesterday that he and Bernadette wouldn't be attending, as they were headed home Sunday morning and wanted to get an early start.

But that left Felicia Gaspar. And Gina Templeton.

Candy could understand why Gina wasn't

here. Her husband was dead, allegedly murdered. She was obviously distraught. Candy imagined she'd talked to the police, though there'd been no official word on that. If she wasn't currently talking to the authorities, she was probably holed up in a hotel room somewhere or making funeral arrangements for her husband.

She must be going through a terrible time, Candy thought. Her husband's body had been found in a snow bank, and abandoned in the woods earlier.

What had happened to him? Candy wondered. How had he wound up in a snowdrift at the bottom of a gully?

That was the key, she realized. If she could figure that out, it might help her solve the mystery of Victor's death. Had he been murdered in the woods with the hatchet, or had he been killed somewhere else, and then dragged into the woods and dumped?

Either scenario was possible. But Candy wondered if the stolen toboggan had anything to do with this. It all seemed a little too coincidental — the toboggan, the car, the room. Had he been murdered at the motel and then hauled into the woods on the toboggan?

That made sense, she thought. But what about the time frame? When would he have been dumped in that gully?

She considered the question for a few moments. She still didn't know Victor's time of death but figured it must have been sometime early Thursday morning.

That sparked a memory, something that had been bugging her for a while. It was a burr in her brain, a detail she had missed, a clue that seemed to lurk in some out-of-the-way corner of her consciousness. But suddenly it clicked, and she knew what it was.

She turned abruptly to Preston, who was chatting pleasantly with Maggie. "Excuse me, Preston, may I ask you a question?"

He stopped in midsentence and turned to her. "Ms. Holliday, I am your obedient servant. Please, ask away."

"Well, something's been bothering me for the past day or two, and I finally realized what it was. It involves you."

"Really? I'm intrigued. Please, continue."

"Well, correct me if I'm wrong, but yesterday morning you and I ran into each other in Town Park, and you handed me a cup of coffee. We talked for a while. Do you remember that encounter?"

"Every second of it," Preston answered truthfully.

"And you said something to me then, if I

remember correctly."

"Um, yes, and what would that be?"

"Well, you said you'd heard from Victor. You told me that he'd pulled out of the exhibition."

Preston considered her statement for a few moments and finally nodded. "Yes, I believe that's correct. Was I in error?"

"You said," Candy continued, "that you had received a communiqué — I believe that's the word you used — from Victor the previous evening, which would have been Thursday evening. But according to the timeline I've been able to establish, Victor was killed sometime early Thursday morning. The body was cold when Solomon Hatch found it, so it must have been there for a while, so let's say he died sometime around dawn on Thursday, give or take a few hours. But if that's true, it would have been impossible for him to contact you on Thursday evening, since he would have been dead about twelve or fourteen hours by then."

Maggie gave her a questioning look. "What are you saying?"

Candy shrugged. "I don't know. I'm just pointing out a few facts."

"All of which are more than likely easily explainable," Preston said.

"Really? How?"

"Well, it's quite simple. You see, Victor contacted me via e-mail, which I accessed from my iPad at a wireless café here in town — although I also have wireless in the hotel, of course. He could have sent the e-mail at an earlier time, several hours, or even several days, before I accessed it. Or he could have written it at an earlier time and delayed the sending of it via an automated setting. Or perhaps someone else sent me a phony message in Victor's name."

Candy considered that. It was possible, she thought, but she wasn't buying it. "That's not how you presented it yesterday. You inferred it was inside information — *I can assure you it's accurate,* I think you said, or something like that. So if you're right, how did you know?"

"I was obviously mistaken," he said, giving her a disinterested look and turning away. Candy shifted her gaze as well and spotted movement out of the corner of the eye. "Oh, here comes Ben."

"Ah!" Preston's eyebrows rose. "We should give you two some time together," he said smoothly. He held out a hand to Maggie. "Would you care to dance?"

Maggie gratefully placed her hand in his. "I would love to."

They were gone by the time Ben arrived at the table. "It looks like Liam's going to be all right," he said as he settled in next to her. "Nothing busted except his pride. Duncan must have hit him with a pretty good right."

Candy nodded and pointed to Maggie and Preston on the dance floor. "That's Maggie and her date," she said.

Ben squinted in their direction. "Who's that she's with?"

"It's a great question," Candy said. "Have you noticed that he's avoiding you?"

Ben made a face and shrugged. "Not particularly. But why would he avoid me?"

Candy leveled a finger at him. "That's a great question. And I think I'm going to go find out. Excuse me."

She rose from her chair and started across the room. Maggie and Preston were currently on the opposite side of the dance floor, so she angled toward them, threading her way through the other couples on the floor.

She was several couples in when she felt a hand brush across her shoulder. She stopped and turned.

A svelte woman in her mid to late fifties, dancing with her spouse, smiled at her. "I'm sorry," the woman said, "I don't mean to disturb you, but I love your dress. Where did you get it?"

"Oh, this?" Candy looked down absently. "A friend loaned it to me."

"Well, it looks lovely on you. You know, I have one exactly like it. I bought it at Neiman Marcus when we were visiting our daughter down in Boston last fall. I would have worn it tonight, but my husband forgot to pick it up at the dry cleaner's yesterday."

THIRTY-FIVE

Candy was mortified. She could feel her cheeks redden and her face grow hot. Her whole body began to tingle. She felt light-headed, and for a few moments thought she might collapse if she didn't sit down instantly.

But she steadied herself, blinked several times, forced herself to focus, and said in the most natural voice she could muster, "Well, if I had known that I would have worn something else."

"Oh, dear, don't you see?" the woman said with obvious delight. "If Sid had picked up the dry cleaning, we'd both be wearing the same dress! This way is much better. I decided to wear Chanel, which I picked up in New York the last time we were down in the city, and you look so much better in that dress than I do. Everything turned out for the best, you see!"

Candy mumbled a quiet "thank you" and

slinked away as the woman turned back to her husband, Sid, delighted at her good fortune.

Candy took a moment to get her bearings, and put Maggie clearly in her sights.

But just then the string quartet plunged into the final notes of the Vivaldi piece and ended with gusto. As the music stopped, the couples around her pulled apart as applause rippled across the dance floor and around the room. The cellist announced that the group would be taking a short break, and a staff member rang a bell, announcing that dinner was imminent and would the guests kindly take their seats so they could get started with the evening's program.

With that announcement, everyone in the room, suddenly animated, shifted en masse, and Candy was caught amid a swarm of moving bodies. She held her place, waiting for the crowd to dissipate, and when a clear line of sight finally opened up again to the far side of the dance floor, Maggie and Preston were gone.

Candy looked in both directions, searching for them. She thought she caught a glimpse of them headed out through the French doors, into the hallway beyond.

Curious, she followed. Preston's behavior

had become increasingly odd over the past day or two. It was time to find out what was behind it all.

Waiters with the first course arrived through a side door to her left, so she hurried through the French doors into the hallway beyond to avoid any more traffic jams. Only a few guests lingered here, glasses in hand, chatting away obliviously. A staff member was just coming through the hall, encouraging the guests to take their seats. Candy waved her down.

"Did you just see a middle-aged couple go through here?" She briefly described Maggie and Preston, and the staff member pointed toward the front lobby area.

"I believe I saw them headed that way."

Candy started off again, moving at a quicker pace.

Why are they headed to the lobby? she wondered. Perhaps it was nothing. Perhaps Preston simply wanted to check on a reservation, or maybe they were looking for a quiet place to talk.

But maybe it was something else. Preston's brief appearance at the ball had been too suspicious. Candy suspected he was up to something. But what was it? Where was he taking Maggie?

Her mind jumped too quickly to several

conclusions, which she forced down as she approached the lobby.

She scanned the place in a matter of milliseconds but saw no sign of her friend. Shifting direction, she was just about to ask the two women behind the front desk if they'd seen any sign of Maggie and Preston when she glanced out the inn's twin front glass doors and spotted Maggie outside under an awning, without her coat, arms wrapped tightly around herself as she stared into the darkness toward English Point Lighthouse and the coastline.

Candy ran out to her. "Mags, are you all right?" She couldn't keep the worry from her voice.

Maggie looked at her, slightly bewildered. "I'm not sure."

Candy took her by the shoulder. "What happened? Where's Preston?"

"He left."

"Where did he go?"

"I don't know, he . . . he said he wanted to show me something outside. Then he suggested we go back to his place. I told him I didn't think that would be a very good idea. And then he got very . . . strange. It's like something clicked inside him. He pulled me out here and gave me this really cold look." She turned to Candy. "To be honest, he was a little scary."

"Did he do anything to you?" Candy asked, worried for her friend.

But Maggie shook her head. "No, he . . . he told me to tell you something."

Candy felt a little chill go through her, and it had nothing to do with the fact that they were standing outside without their coats in twenty-degree weather. "What is it?"

"He said just two words, and then he —"

But Ben walked out of the door behind them just then, with an expression of concern on his face. "Candy, there you are. Is everything okay? I saw you running out of the room and I —"

He stopped as a police car turned into the driveway in front of the inn, lights flashing, and slid to a stop just a few feet from them, its rear end fishtailing a little on the ice. The door popped open and Officer Jody McCroy leapt out. He came around the car in a rush as a second police car pulled up behind him, its roof lights flashing also.

Ben instinctively put his hands on the shoulders of both Candy and Maggie, gently pulling them out of the way. As a trio, the three of them took several steps back, giving the officers plenty of room.

"Jim, what's going on?" Ben asked one of

the officers as he rushed past. The officer glanced at him but continued on as a third police car, and then a fourth, pulled into the driveway.

Chief Darryl Durr stepped out of the passenger seat of the last car and watched as his men converged on the building.

He saw Candy, Ben, and Maggie, nodded casually, and started past them toward the inn's front doors. But a question from Candy made him pause.

"Are you here to arrest Duncan Leggmeyer?" she asked.

Chief Durr turned and regarded the group for a moment before he said, "No. We're here to arrest Liam Yates."

THIRTY-SIX

The operation was performed efficiently and with minimal disruption. Most of the guests inside at the ball never knew what was happening; since the ballroom's windows faced out the back of the building, the occupants didn't see the flashing lights of the police cars out front. However, a few regular hotel guests were on hand to witness the procession as Liam Yates was escorted through the lobby about five minutes later, handcuffed, dazed by this latest development, head bowed in embarrassment, saying not a word.

Boy, he's having a bad night, Candy thought as she stood near the front desk with Maggie and Ben, watching as two uniformed officers led Liam out through the front doors to one of the waiting police cars.

A few moments later, Duncan Leggmeyer emerged from a nearby room, also with a police escort, though without the handcuffs. On his face was an expression of despair mixed with anger.

Candy's reporter instincts threatened to get the better of her, and she was tempted to start calling out questions to the officers as they passed by her. She knew Ben felt the same way, but they both held back their inquiries, at least for the moment.

Still, Ben couldn't keep still for long. "I have to find out what's going on," he told her as they watched Chief Durr nod to the inn's proprietor, Oliver LaForce, who stood with hands clasped in front of him beside the assistant innkeeper, Alby Alcott. They both appeared grim yet determined to get back to business as quickly as possible.

Candy turned to Ben. "It probably has something to do with the hatchet," she told him, and he listened with lips pursed tightly as she explained how Solomon had found the body with a hatchet in its back and had passed the murder weapon on to her so she could deliver it to the police department.

"Why didn't you tell me this before?" he asked, expressionless.

"There was so much going on. I never had a chance."

He nodded and pulled her over to one side, out of earshot of the others gathered in the lobby. "Okay, tell me everything you know," he said, and he cast his eyes downward in concentration as Candy explained what she had discovered that day, with Maggie eavesdropping on their conversation.

"I have to call Finn," Ben said when she'd finished, "and see if he's heard anything. Then I should head over to the police station." He took her hand. "I'm sorry our big night out has been ruined," he said sincerely.

She gave him an understanding look. "It was brief but wonderful. Go do what you have to do."

"I don't mean to leave you stranded. Can you find a ride home?"

"Maggie will take me." She gave him a quick hug. "Don't worry about us. We'll be fine."

"Okay. I'll call you as soon as I know something," he said, and kissed her before he ran off to grab his coat.

After he'd gone, Candy took a deep breath. "Well," she said to Maggie, "at least we got in one good dance before things got crazy."

Maggie sighed along with her. "You're lucky. I barely had that. And now it appears my date has run out on me — though I'm not sure exactly what I did. And to think I got all dressed up for this."

Candy turned toward her friend, eyes suddenly blazing. "Speaking of dresses . . ."

If Candy expected any sort of sympathy from her friend — or, heaven forbid, an apology — she was left sorely wanting, for Maggie defended herself vigorously. "Well, no, I didn't tell you about that part of it because I knew you'd have a cow," she said lightly, "but there's no harm done. She doesn't know the dress is hers — that's old Mrs. Stevenson, by the way. One of the summer people. They just came up from Connecticut for the weekend. Really nice folks. He made his money in Laundromats. Can you believe that? He's a millionaire because people plunk quarters into machines to wash their clothes. He's made his millions a quarter at a time! Anyway, they dropped off the dress the last time they were here, between Christmas and New Year's. It's been hanging back there on the unclaimed rack for weeks. And as far as they're concerned, it's still hanging there. They'll probably leave town tomorrow, and it'll hang there for another few weeks until they get back to town and finally pick it up."

"It doesn't matter," Candy said. "It's not mine. I have to get out of it at once."

"But it looks sooo good on you," Maggie protested.

That, Candy had to admit, was true. She'd received a number of compliments tonight while wearing it. "I do hate to part with it. Do you think she'd sell it to me?"

"I have a better idea," Maggie said slyly.

"What is it?" Candy asked, and abruptly paused as she reconsidered her question. "No, wait. Don't tell me. I don't want to know."

"It's nothing illegal," Maggie assured her. "I promise."

But Candy would not be swayed. "It doesn't matter. Just take the dress back, put it back on the rack — after sending it back out for cleaning, of course — and let's be done with it."

Maggie made a huge deal of sighing in a very dramatic manner. "Fine. Be that way."

"Good," Candy said, trying to convince herself that this indeed was the right course of action.

"Good," Maggie said, affirming that it was — the decision had been made, and that was that, and they were moving on.

Resigned to the fact that she had to give the dress back, Candy changed to another less sartorial subject. "Anyway, back to Preston. Outside, when Ben interrupted us, you were about to tell me something Preston had said — about a message for me?"

"What? Oh, yeah, right. *That* guy." She rolled her eyes. "How do I keep getting mixed up with guys like that?"

"It's your charm."

"True. And my good looks. I tend to attract the more dangerous types."

"So what did he say?"

"Well, like I told you, it was just two words." She lowered her voice to a hush. "He said I was supposed to tell you *white field.*"

Candy drew her head back, uncomprehending. "What the heck does that mean? What does a *white field* have to do with anything?"

"I thought it was strange too, but that's what he said."

Candy pondered the two words for a few moments as the strains of a Mozart concerto drifted down the hall. The string quartet had started up again. Her stomach growled.

She turned to Maggie. "Are you hungry?"

"Famished."

"Think we should get something to eat first?"

"I thought you'd never ask."

"After all," Candy said as they started down the hall toward the ballroom, "we *did* pay for these tickets — or at least our dates did. We might as well get what we can from them while we figure out what to do next."

THIRTY-SEVEN

"Okay," Candy said, "here's what we need to do."

She was working her way through a petite slice of blueberry cheesecake with a miniscule, token dollop of homemade whipped cream on top and a crust that was deliciously crumbly. She'd tried to deny herself dessert altogether, but she'd lost that battle, so she opted for moderation instead.

"First, we need to find out about that hatchet. We know from that online posting that Duncan was the winner of a hatchet-throwing contest about a year ago. The posting also said Duncan's winning caused some sort of friction between him and Liam — and clearly time has not healed the wound, as we saw tonight. But did Duncan really stick that thing in Victor's back? He apparently had the skill to do so, from a distance if necessary. His name is on the murder weapon. So why didn't the police arrest him or at least handcuff him?"

"Maybe he didn't do it," Maggie suggested.

"Yes, but if he didn't, who did?" She expertly pierced the cheesecake and arrowed off a thin slice, which she nibbled on as she talked. "Next, what's up with Preston? We have to get to the bottom of that. I mean, is he legitimate? Ben's barely heard of him. Same thing with the police — he's not even remotely on their radar. He seems to have slipped into town largely unnoticed, talked to only a few people — including you and me, I should point out — and avoided detection by most others. That's pretty mysterious, if you ask me. Even Officer Jody didn't pay much attention to him — he was too focused on me. Big mistake. So, what's going on with Preston? We need to check him out."

She paused. "If we ever see him again, that is. It's possible he could just disappear on us. But I have a feeling that, one way or the other, we'll hear from him again."

She thoughtfully nibbled at her cheesecake. "And third, we need to do more research on Liam. There was obviously animosity between him and the other sculptors, including Victor. And obviously the police think he had something to do with

Victor's murder. But what's the link?" She paused, pondering her own question, and finally sighed. "There are so many pieces on the table — I just can't figure out how they all fit together."

Maggie was silent for a long, stretched-out moment as she lingered over her chocolate sorbet. Her eyebrows were furrowed, and she appeared to be deep in thought.

"White field," she said finally.

Candy had begun jotting down notes on a napkin, using a pen she'd borrowed from a gentleman at the table across from her. When Maggie spoke, she looked up. "Did you just say something?"

"I think I might know what Preston meant."

"About what?

"About that message he had: *white field.*"

Candy put down the pen and leaned forward, giving her friend her full attention. "And what does it mean?"

Maggie didn't answer the question immediately. Instead, impressed with herself, she said, "I can't believe it, really. I think I actually figured something out by myself."

"And how did you do that?" Candy asked, both amused and intrigued.

Triumphantly, Maggie allowed herself a generous spoonful of sorbet, which she popped into her mouth and savored. "By paying attention," she said around the frozen dessert.

"And what did you pay attention to?"

In response, Maggie pointed at the blueberry cheesecake. "You done with that?"

At the sudden change in subject, Candy gave her friend a curious look, but she finally nodded. "It was about the most delicious thing I've ever eaten, but I'm not as active in the winter as I am in the summer, so I have to watch my figure."

Maggie sighed, set down her spoon, and pushed away the rest of her dessert. "Unfortunately I'm done as well. So, do you think they have a computer around here somewhere?"

"A computer? What for?"

"I could tell you, but it'd be easier to show you. So, where can we find one?"

Candy arched an eyebrow at her friend. "You're acting very mysterious all of a sudden," she said, "but I'll play along. I think there's a small business center off the lobby. Maybe we can find one in there."

"Good idea. Let's have a look."

Leaving their desserts behind, and after returning the pen to its owner, they made their way out of the ballroom and into the hallway leading back to the main building and the lobby.

"Are you going to fill me in on what's going on?" Candy asked as they walked.

"It suddenly dawned on me," Maggie said cryptically, "that I've seen the words *white field* before."

"And where was that?" Candy asked.

"You'll see," Maggie said with a toss of her head.

They found the business center in a small room sandwiched between the lobby's main desk and the elevators, near the concierge's station. The lights were on, but the place was vacant. A couple of nineteen-inch computer monitors sat on a side table, next to a printer and fax machine. "Here we go," Maggie said. She pulled out a chair and sat down.

"You know," she said, as she tapped at the keyboard's space bar and waited for the machine to pull itself out of hibernation, "that Preston's a cagey guy. This afternoon at the cleaner's, when we were talking, he told me that he's been keeping tabs on Cape Willington for a long time."

Candy lowered herself into a nearby chair. "Yeah, he said the same thing to me a few days ago."

With the computer awoken, Maggie launched a browser and keyed in the URL for Wanda Boyle's website. As she worked, it finally dawned on Candy what she was doing. And when she clicked on the comment section for one of Wanda's latest posts, Candy had nothing but respect for her best friend.

"You're a genius," she said.

Maggie allowed herself the merest of smiles. "Yeah, I get that a lot."

There, on the screen in front of them, was a recent comment, written in response to one of Wanda's blog posts. The comment had been written by someone named *Whitefield.*

Candy remembered now. She'd seen the same thing just a couple of days ago, on Thursday night, when she'd gone up to the *Cape Crier*'s second-floor lair, intending to sneak a look at Ben's office.

"My guess is, Preston Smith and this Whitefield person are one and the same," Maggie said, doing her best to contain the glee she felt at her discovery. "That's why he told me to you give that message. He was sending you a clue."

"And he's been posting on Wanda's blog," Candy said, impressed with her friend's astuteness.

"Indeed he has." Maggie studied the screen. "There's actually been quite a few comments from him over the past few weeks."

"He's been spying on us anonymously," Candy noted, "and stirring up trouble."

"That's right. And look at this. He posted his latest comment just about an hour ago. And I think it's personal." She leaned back and wiggled her finger, signaling that Candy should have a look.

"What does it say?"

When Maggie didn't answer, Candy leaned in closer so she could read the comment:

For the Town Crier: Check at the foot of the Ice Princess. Your destiny awaits.

"Short and sweet," Candy observed, leaning back after she'd read the message.

"Do you have any idea what it means," Maggie asked, "other than the fact that you're obviously the Town Crier. That's what he called you when you two first met, remember?"

"I do," Candy said. She leaned back in her chair and crossed her arms as she thought, but she knew almost at once what they had to do. "We need to get our coats," she said.

"And why is that?"

"Because I think the answer to at least

one of our questions is at Town Park, hidden in the ice."

Thirty-Eight

Outside, the temperature had fallen into the teens, on its way to single digits. The two women had switched out their heels for boots and pulled on their wool coats, hats, and gloves, but still braced themselves as they ventured into the cold air. Their hands tightened on their scarves and collars, pulling them a little snugger, and they blew out their breaths, which misted around them as they hurried along. They crossed the street at the light and turned into Town Park, walking carefully on the salted yet still-slippery surfaces.

Despite the chilly weather, or perhaps because of it, the place looked as festive as Candy had ever seen it. She craned her head up and around, her eyes following the strings of lights, which curved around tree trunks and swooped from tree to light post to tree.

It would have been a magical night for a

stroll here with Ben, she thought absently as they walked briskly along. But in the next moment she told herself that she couldn't think about that right now. She had other concerns. Ben was at the police station, running down the story on Liam, and she was here, searching for something hidden in the ice.

"What are we searching for?" Maggie asked, breaking into her thoughts.

Candy pointed out in front of them, where spotlights attached to posts and trees illuminated the icy works of art, perfectly preserved in the bracing air. "An ice princess."

"You think Preston left a clue for us?"

"That's what it sounds like, doesn't it? *At the foot of the Ice Princess.* That sounds like a definite invitation, and why would he invite us to look if he hadn't put something there?"

"But why would he do that? Why not just call us or text us or tell us over coffee and Danish?"

"Because I think Preston's playing a game with us," Candy said, her face turning more angular as her jaw tightened, both against the cold and what might lie ahead. "Something's been off about that guy from the beginning. It just didn't stick out that much, since there are quite a few people around here who are a little quirky. So someone like Preston fit right in."

"What do you think's going on?" Maggie asked, an edge of concern slipping into her voice.

Candy let out a deep, tight breath. "That's what we're here to find out." She nodded up ahead. "When I was out here yesterday afternoon, some of the sculptures were still unfinished. But if I remember correctly, Gina was working on something that might fit the bill."

She angled off toward the large ice sculpture of the Maine wilderness, which depicted stately Mount Katahdin and the surrounding pine- and spruce-covered slopes, reflected in a mirror lake. Separate from the main display were individual sculptures of Maine animals, as well as specialties of the ice carvers.

As they walked along, Candy scanned the area. To their left, up the slope a ways, several teens were playfully throwing handfuls of snow at each other, shouting and laughing. Couples and groups strolled along the lighted pathways and lingered around the ice sculptures, impressed with the artistry on display. A few families with smaller children, tired yet excited, roamed the park as well, hand in hand.

She shifted her gaze right and focused on the single-block ice sculptures, carved for demonstrations earlier in the day: a mountain lion, an eagle with wings spread, a pair of seals, a bear and her cubs, caribou and coyote.

Beyond that, curving around the back of the main sculpture, were the specialties of the ice carvers — their more personal works. Each sculptor had carved one or two single-block pieces, on display here. It was a diverse collection that included a curling snail adorned with a realistic textured shell and eerily probing antennae, a Sphinx with a face that resembled a national politician, an elaborate depiction of a giant shoe turned into a home for anthropomorphic woodland creatures, a surprisingly detailed tall ship, and a windblown woman who appeared to emerge from the block of ice itself.

Candy could link up most of the sculptures with their creators. Liam had obviously done the tall ship. She'd seen his detail work, and she had to admit it was impeccable. Baxter had created the giant shoe with all the critters. He'd even added little Snowball, the family dog, to the icy tableau. She could attach Duncan to the politically oriented Sphinx, and Felicia to the exquisite rendering of the snail.

The final piece was Gina's work.

It was just the woman's head and torso; the rest of her body remained submerged in the ice. But it was her windblown hair that was most intriguing. It streamed out behind her in several thick, swirling strands of ice, only to merge again with the block itself.

It had a melancholy feeling about it. The way the face seemed to pull away from the ice gave it an element of action, yet her expression was one of both resolve and resignation, as if the woman was trying to break free from the ice but was being held back by some invisible force.

She's trying to escape, but it won't let her go, Candy thought, *and she knows it.*

It was not the most elegant piece in the park, and had some crude elements to it. And it looked unfinished. Gina hadn't shown up today to complete her creation. But enough of it was there, evidence of Gina as an emerging artist. Perhaps, in some subconscious way, the ice princess expressed Gina's own inner feelings.

Is she trying to break free of something too?

Leaving the question unanswered, Candy pointed. "I think that's the one we're looking for."

"The ice princess." Maggie let out a

shivery breath as she gazed upon it.

"Let's check it out."

They circled it several times, studying it from all angles. Its ruggedness appealed to Candy, and she decided she liked it. Gina might still be developing as an artist, but she had a style all her own.

But was it hiding a clue?

Check at the foot of the Ice Princess. Your destiny awaits.

She stepped up close to the sculpture and looked at the ice down toward the bottom, near the snow-covered ground. It looked smooth and unblemished. She searched along the foundation on the second side, and the third. She ran her gloved hand over the ice, studying it in the bright light and shadows cast by the spotlights. Maggie searched as well.

They found what they were looking for on the sculpture's back side, directly beneath the woman's right ear, at the bottom near the ground.

There was something embedded in the ice.

Candy bent, and Maggie leaned forward with her hands on her knees. "What is it, and how the heck did it get in there?"

"Someone must have put it there for us to find."

"It's a bottle," Maggie said, after studying

it from several angles.

She was right, Candy realized.

It looked like a small plastic water bottle. Its transparent skin had made it difficult to identify at first.

"And I think there's some sort of note inside," Maggie added after further inspection.

Intrigued, Candy reached out a gloved hand toward it but came up against the hardened ice.

She brushed her hand over the ice several times, studying it and the bottle inside.

It finally dawned on her what she was looking at.

Maggie let out a little gasp as Candy pulled back her arm, folded her fingers into a fist, and jabbed quickly at the ice.

It cracked.

"It's just a thin covering."

The bottle wasn't embedded in the ice; it was sitting in some kind of pocket. Candy jabbed at the thin covering a couple more times, finally breaking the ice. She cleared away the shards, reached in, and withdrew the bottle.

It had once held local spring water, she saw, but now, as Maggie had said, it contained a folded sheet of paper with writing upon it.

A message in a bottle.

Maggie gazed at it, trying to decipher the writing on the note. "What do you think it says?"

"There's only one way to find out."

The cap had frozen in place, but Candy finally managed to untwist it. She tipped the bottle upside down. The note was thin and tightly folded, making it easy to slip into the bottle's small round hole. Still, she had some difficulty getting it back out, since it had unfolded during the time it had been inside. She slapped the bottom of the bottle several times, trying to get the note to pop down through the opening, but finally she had to slide her pinky far enough inside so she could compress the note down, coax it out, and snag its leading edge with her fingernails.

"Got it," she said finally.

It was a three-by-five-inch piece of paper, folded lengthwise, and a color other than white, either blue or purple. Or possibly gray. She couldn't quite tell in this light.

The message was short, written in a shaky, erratic hand, as if someone was purposely trying to disguise their handwriting style.

Hidden Valley, Cabin 9, it read.

"What's it say?" Maggie asked, looking over Candy's shoulder.

Candy read it to her.

"Hidden Valley? That's that motel up on Route 1."

"That's right," Candy said, thinking. She stooped and took another look at the pocket in the ice in which the bottle had been hidden. It looked neatly done, a hollowed-out area with smooth sides that had been professionally cut with an electric saw of some sort, not dug out from the ice with a hand pick or hatchet.

Candy studied it. Preston could have carved it out of there anytime over the past day or two. Gina hadn't been in the park that day, so she wouldn't have noticed the strange item embedded in her sculpture. And anyone who might have seen Preston creating the hollowed-out space would probably just have taken him for another sculptor. It would have been an easy task to accomplish.

But why the elaborate ruse?

Candy had the sudden, strange feeling that she was an unaware vole trying to hide under the snow, being pursued by a cunning, hungry fox.

She looked at the note in her hand again, reading the note's terse wording. Finally, shaking her head, she looked up at her friend.

"I know it's getting late, but are you up for a road trip?"

THIRTY-NINE

Despite the recent snows, the road was well cleared, salted, and sanded. They took Maggie's car, a ten-year-old Subaru wagon with all-wheel drive — the official car of Maine, as many people called it — and headed out of Cape Willington, north to Route 1. The night had cleared and the stars shone brightly, and with the heat blasting out of the wagon's interior vents, they were warm enough.

They'd made a quick stop at the dry cleaner's to change. Candy pulled on some of the clothes she'd worn to disguise herself the previous day. They didn't fit her perfectly, but they were better than a fancy dress for what they were planning on doing. Reluctantly, she left the dress on a hanger on the unclaimed rack, right where it belonged. Maggie had managed to scrounge up a pair of jeans and sweater — her own, as it turned out. They dressed quickly, pulled their boots, wool coats, and hats back on, and off they went.

They talked little on the way. Maggie turned the radio to a news channel, and they listened for any information about Liam Yates, Duncan Leggmeyer, or Victor Templeton, but instead they got an evening call-in show with periodic weather updates and a little national news.

Traffic was light at this time of the night, and they made good time. Just before nine thirty they reached Route 1. A half mile east of its intersection with Route 192, they saw the neon sign for the Hidden Valley Motel and Cabins, with the NO VACANCY light turned on.

Maggie flicked on her turn signal, checked her mirrors, and drove into the motel's parking lot. The car crept along slowly as she headed along the long row of rooms, toward the one- and two-bedroom cabins at the rear of the property, which backed up against a stream and dense, frozen woods.

"Cabin number nine's over that way," Candy said, indicating a small sign that pointed to the left. Maggie turned the car in that direction, but Candy put a hand on her shoulder. "Back up and park over there," she said softly, "just in case. I'll walk over and check it out."

Maggie backed the car between a Ford F150 pickup truck and a van, where she'd be fairly well hidden, and switched off the engine. For a few moments they sat inside, keeping warm, gazing out the windshield in the direction of the cabin.

"So what do we do now?" Maggie finally asked, her voice betraying her nervousness.

Candy let out a breath and turned toward her. "I'm going to have a look in one of those windows. You stay here."

"But what if —"

"Just stay here. I'll be right back." And before she could change her mind, Candy opened the door and stepped out of the car.

The air was crisp, but the wind had died down, so it wasn't biting. In fact, in some ways, she found it invigorating, and perhaps even mildly pleasant. Again, she thought, it would have been a wonderful night for a stroll with Ben, and wondered what he'd found out at the police station. She decided to call him as soon as she could.

Cabin number nine sat in the midst of a copse of trees, tucked at the end of a little spur of a road that hooked off the main parking lot. Candy hurried along as quietly as she could, though her boots crunched on the frozen surface. The night was surprisingly quiet, everything silenced by the cold blanket of snow. In the stillness, the sound of her boots on the icepack sounded like firearms going off, like an army was approaching the cabin.

But as she got closer, she doubted anyone would hear her, since there was no one around to notice. The cabin's windows were dark. The lights were out. There were no cars parked out front. The place looked deserted.

She stopped twenty feet away, hands tucked into her coat pockets as she debated what to do next. Should she knock? Peek into the windows? Turn around and go home?

She was still trying to decide when she heard a car approaching through the parking lot behind her. Turning, she saw headlights stabbing through the darkness. The vehicle was headed in her direction.

At first she thought it might be Maggie's car, until she realized it wasn't a wagon. Instead, it was a sleek late-model crossover vehicle with a dark exterior.

The vehicle came steadily on, passing by Maggie's car without slowing. As it approached, Candy stepped back among the trees that lined the short driveway to the cabin. The vehicle angled left and came directly toward her. Candy surreptitiously slipped behind a tree trunk as it drove past her. The rear LED brake lights came on, illuminating the night with an eerie red glow, as the vehicle stopped in front of cabin number nine.

The engine continued to run, but the taillights flicked out, and a few moments later the headlights went out too, leaving the area in semidarkness.

The driver's-side door opened, and Felicia Gaspar stepped out.

FORTY

She was alone, Candy saw. There was no one else in the vehicle with her.

Leaving the car door open, Felicia walked briskly to the cabin. She was dressed in a black hooded cloak with jeans and calf-high boots — the same outfit she'd had on earlier in the day when Candy had caught sight of her lurking among the trees in Town Park. She'd draped a gray scarf loosely around her throat and wore expensive leather gloves.

As she walked to the cabin door, she quickly looked around, but she failed to notice Candy hidden in the shadows among the trees. Felicia knocked softly, waiting only a few moments before she pushed at the cabin door, entered, and closed the door firmly behind her.

Candy saw a light flicker on inside. Cautiously she emerged from her hiding place, taking a few tentative steps toward the cabin. She was ready to dive for cover again should Felicia suddenly appear, but instead, after a few moments, she heard voices inside.

Voices? Who else was in there with her?

Curious, Candy took a few steps closer.

She could hear the voices raised in anger now. Candy listened, trying to make out the words, but they were too indistinct. Still, the second voice sounded familiar. Candy was sure she'd heard it before.

Then it dawned on her.

The more she listened, the more she was certain of it.

The argument inside had fallen into softer tones, but Candy still sensed an air of strain and desperation from the two people inside.

Again, she debated what to do. But even as she considered her options, she knew she had to take an aggressive approach. There would never be another chance. It had to be now.

With her stomach tightening in apprehension, and her throat suddenly dry in the cold, still air, she took the final few steps forward, stopped in front of the cabin door, slipped off her right-hand glove, and knocked decisively several times.

Instantly the voices inside fell into a hush, and the lights went out. Abruptly, they were all cloaked again in darkness.

Candy heard a quick toot of a horn behind her. She turned.

Maggie had been watching and was wondering if everything was okay. Candy could see her waving inside the car. Candy waved back, then turned and knocked again. "Hello, is anyone in there?" she called out. "It's Candy Holliday."

After a few moments she heard low whispers from inside. It took a while, but a latch flicked. The knob turned and the door opened a few inches. A face hovered in the shadows.

"What do you want?" a female voice asked from inside.

"I want to talk to Gina."

The face disappeared. The door closed.

Candy knocked again. "I have a friend nearby. She has the police on speed dial. You have ten seconds or I'm going to tell her to call them."

She had learned a little bit about bluffing from Doc, who played poker just about every Friday night with his buddies. She had fudged the truth, but it worked.

The door opened again.

Felicia had one hand hidden behind her cloak. She looked very unhappy. "Since you insist, you might as well come in."

Candy took a deep breath, nodded, and

stepped inside after kicking the snow off her boots.

It was a neat one-bedroom cabin, decorated in rose, sea green, and cream colors. The front room had a small sitting area with a TV and sofa, and a dining area and kitchen on the other side. Doors from the main room led into what Candy guessed were a bathroom and bedroom. The bedroom door was closed.

There was no sign of Gina.

"How did you find this place?" Felicia asked, standing nervously near the kitchen counter. But a moment later she answered her own question. "It was Preston Smith, wasn't it? I knew he was up to something sneaky. He tipped you off, right?"

Candy ignored the question as she scanned the room. "Where is she?"

Felicia forced a smile. "Where is who?"

"Gina. I heard her voice. I know she's here."

"You're mistaken."

"There are two of you in here."

"I'm here by myself. And you're not welcome here. Now get out."

Candy hesitated. She'd checked the place out. She'd done all she could. Now it was time to leave.

She was turning toward the door when

she heard a thump from the bedroom. Her gaze shifted. "Someone's in there. It's Gina, isn't it?"

Felicia threw up her arms and gave Candy an exasperated look. "Oh, for heaven's sake." She let out an exaggerated breath as she crossed to the bedroom door and swung it wide open. "You might as well come on out," she said to the person inside. "She knows you're here."

Inside, Gina Templeton was seated on the bed, hands folded in her lap. When she saw Candy, she nodded, rose, and walked out of the bedroom into the living room. Her hair was uncombed, her clothes were rumpled, and she had bags under her eyes. She looked like she had just woken up. She still wore her scarf tightly around her neck.

"Gina, what are you doing here? What's going on?" Candy asked, shooting a glance at Felicia. "Is everything okay?"

"No, everything is *not* okay," Gina pronounced firmly, her voice raspy with sleep.

"Why? What's happening?

"I'll tell you whatever you want to know," Gina said with tired eyes and a drawn face, "but you have to promise me one thing."

"And what's that?" Candy asked.

Gina rubbed her nose and sniffled. "No police."

FORTY-ONE

"Gina, I can't promise you that," Candy said honestly, "but I promise I'll hear you out."

Felicia took a few steps toward her. In a tense voice, she said, "We don't have to tell you anything." To Gina, she added, "Just remember that."

Gina Templeton folded her hands and nodded. She looked tired, frail. Her eyes had taken on a haunted look. "It's okay," she said to Felicia. "We have to talk to someone. We have to let them know what happened before. . . ."

Her voice trailed off as her gaze shifted. Candy turned to look as well. Sitting beside the door were several bags of luggage.

It took Candy a few moments to fully grasp what it meant. "You're leaving?"

"I can't stay," Gina said fretfully. "Too much has happened. I have to leave. I have to figure out what to do."

"Have you talked to the police?" Candy asked.

"Yes, but . . ." She paused, again glancing toward Felicia. "I can't go back there. I have nothing else to say to them."

"Gina, you have to talk to the police about Victor, especially if you know how he died."

At that, Gina seemed to shrink away. With all the energy she had left, she lowered herself into an upholstered armchair next to a small maple desk. "I can't believe this is happening," she said weakly, putting a hand to her forehead.

Candy was silent for a moment. She looked from Gina to Felicia and back again. "Gina," Candy said as gently as she could, "someone murdered your husband. You have to go back to the police and tell them everything you know — whatever it might be."

"I can't," Gina said, trying to hold back her emotions.

"Why not?"

"Because it's complicated," Gina said, "and it involves our friends."

"Yes, but . . ." Candy stopped and thought about it. Maybe it was time to take a different approach. "The hatchet belonged to Duncan, didn't it?" When again she received no reply, she explained, "I found Solomon

Hatch in the woods today. He had taken all Victor's belongings, plus the hatchet, off Victor's body before he moved it out to the road. The police have the hatchet now, and they know it's the murder weapon."

A defiant look crept into Gina's eyes. "I don't know anything about that."

"I checked it online. Duncan won that contest. They gave him the hatchet as an award."

"The website is wrong," Gina said, her voice cracking. "It wasn't Duncan's."

"Then whose was it?"

Felicia finally spoke up. "It was Liam's. That's what she's trying to tell you. That's what the police must have found out, and that's why they arrested him."

"Liam won that contest," Gina explained, getting some of her composure back. "He was awarded the hatchet. But it was later discovered, after complaints and reviewing videotape of the event, that he stepped over some sort of line at some point, and he was disqualified. There were allegations that he cheated, although it was quickly hushed up. Duncan came in second, so they named him the winner. But Liam kept the hatchet. He refused to return it or to pass it on to the rightful winner."

So there it is, Candy thought. Liam really

was the killer.

"That's why Duncan was so upset tonight at the ball, isn't it? That's why he hit Liam." And quickly Candy explained what had happened a short time earlier at the Moose Fest Ball.

"It all makes sense," Felicia said. "Duncan thought Liam had set him up. The records show Duncan won the contest and should have received the hatchet as an award. But only a few people know the real story. So it was natural for the police to suspect Duncan."

"But if that's true," Candy said, "the truth would have eventually come out. They would have discovered the hatchet wasn't really Duncan's in a matter of hours, if not minutes. If you're right, there must be several people who knew Liam didn't return the hatchet. He couldn't hide the fact."

"Who knows what was on Liam's mind?" Felicia said obliquely.

"Perhaps," Gina mused, "Liam thought that by using misdirection — the hatchet everyone thought was Duncan's — he could buy himself a little time until he had a chance to escape."

Candy considered that possibility but quickly dismissed it. "That doesn't make much sense. Victor was killed Thursday

420

morning. Liam was hanging around here all weekend. He was at the ball tonight with Wanda Boyle. He could be the one who's been feeding her valuable information for her blog. Why would he do all that if he murdered your husband? Why hang around for so long?"

Felicia's eyes shifted about quickly before they returned to Candy. "He's always been a glory hound," she said finally, in a harsher tone. "He can't help himself. He obviously wanted the attention."

"But why?" Candy asked. "Why would he kill Victor? For publicity? Because they're rivals? Why?"

The questions hung in the room for several beats, as all three women looked at each other. Candy heard another soft toot from outside. Maggie was getting impatient — or just worrying about her.

It was Candy who broke the silence. "All three of us need to go to the police," she said with finality. "You need to tell them everything you know."

Felicia shook her head. "I'm afraid we can't do that." She gave Candy a hard look. "As far as I see it, there are only two options here. You can let us go — or we can make this difficult." She wiggled her hand under her cloak, where it had remained since Candy had entered the cabin.

Candy got the hint. She knew they were up to something, though she hadn't quite figured out what it was yet, but she stepped back toward the door. "Okay. Maybe you're right. Maybe this was none of my business and I've gone a little too far. So, I . . . think I'll just excuse myself, and let you two get on with whatever it is you have to do."

Felicia smiled, and her eyes reflected pinpricks of light. "Thank you," she said. Under the cloak, she slipped something into a hidden pocket. She turned to Gina. "You need to finish packing. It's time to go."

Gina nodded. She rose wearily and headed toward the bedroom. "I just have one more bag to finish packing." She stopped in the doorway, turning back. "Oh, and I looked all over for that red scarf you said you lost," she told Felicia. "You know, the one with the gold tassels at the end? Well I can't find it anywhere. I'm afraid it's gone."

FORTY-TWO

Something clicked inside Candy, an almost physical feeling. The realization coursed through her being, and suddenly she saw new avenues of understanding that had not been visible before. She saw Victor's steel blue Honda Pilot SUV, sitting in front of room twenty-three at the Shangri-La Motel. And she saw a red scarf with gold tassels, tossed into the backseat.

Her body tingled. She felt like she wanted to shake out her hands to calm them. When she spoke, her voice was uneven, a little jittery, though she did her best to keep it steady as she turned her gaze to Felicia. "That's it, isn't it? That explains everything."

Felicia gave her an annoyed look. "What does?"

"It was you," Candy said breathlessly. "*You* were with Victor that morning, weren't you?"

The other two women went silent. They exchanged glances, but neither of them spoke. The room had grown deathly still.

"What makes you say that?" Felicia finally asked. Gina had gone as white as fresh snow.

"You were with him in his car, weren't you? That morning — in his Honda. He must have picked you up somewhere." Candy looked around the room quickly as the pieces started falling into place. "This is your cabin, isn't it? This is where *you* were staying? But you didn't want to be seen with him here. Maybe there are people you know staying here, and you had to be secretive. So he picked you up and you rented a room at the Shangri-La." She paused and gave Felicia a penetrating look. "But you made one mistake. You left your scarf in the back-seat of his car."

Felicia looked stunned. Gina suddenly couldn't stand on her own two feet. Eyes rolling up into her head, she wobbled to the bed, where she collapsed.

"That's it, isn't it?" Candy pressed. "You were having an affair with Victor Templeton!"

"No!" Gina cried out, and she shot to her feet again. "No!" But her emotions and weariness got the better of her, and she sank back onto the bed.

Candy turned toward Felicia.

The other woman looked strangely calm. Her black hair seemed to emphasize the severity of her jawline, her sharp nose and high cheekbones. She held her body tightly, as if ready to spring, and she had a confident look in her dark eyes.

"It was an accident," she said after a few moments.

Gina was making strange trilling noises, as if she was trying to block out all sound from her hearing, but Felicia continued. "He came after me, if you must know. But I knew he would. You see, I understood Victor. And I understood what drove him."

"And what was that?" Candy asked.

"He hated Liam. He did everything he could to beat him — but he usually came in a distant second, or even third. But he wouldn't give up. He competed against Liam for everything."

"Including women."

Felicia nodded. "Including women. Including me."

Another moment of realization. "Ah, so you were Liam's girl at one time."

"I was." In an emotional moment, Felicia averted her eyes, trying to hold back tears. "But he eventually tired of me. That's the way he is. You see, I understand what drives

Liam too."

"So once Liam cast you aside, Victor swooped in."

Felicia cast a worried look at Gina. "I didn't want any of this. You should know that. I tried to hold him off."

"How did he die?" Candy asked softly.

Felicia swallowed hard. "Like I said, it was an accident."

A trembling voice nearby, breaking into their conversation, said, "It was my fault."

Candy turned.

Gina was on her feet again. She stood in the doorway, clasping her hands tightly together in front of her. "I made him do it. I drove him mad."

"No," Felicia said.

"Yes!" She snapped out the word but forced herself to speak calmly as she continued. "I was the one who provoked him. I was the one who drove him to violence."

She paused, allowing herself a breath and a chance to collect her thoughts. She turned her weary eyes to Candy, who could see the sadness in them. "I've known for a long time about Victor's wandering eye," she said in a rush of breath, as if she was getting a great weight off her chest. "And I know I'm not the most attractive woman in the world. . . ."

"Gina —" Felicia began.

But Gina held up a hand. "No, let me finish." She turned back to Candy. "The truth is, I loved Victor. I really did. When we were first married, we were an amazing team. And when we started sculpting ice, it was even better. But when we started going out on the road, and Liam came into our lives, everything changed. Over the past few years, Victor's jealously and hatred of Liam has grown deeper with every event, every encounter. Their animosity toward each other cast a dark shadow over the entire circuit. I tried to talk to him. I pleaded with him to let it go. I even suggested we quit the circuit and go back to our normal lives. But he couldn't."

Felicia picked up the story. "So yes, Victor came after me, in part because he thought I was still Liam's woman. He insisted we get together when we arrived here. He said he'd rented us a room in the back of some sleazy hotel, where we'd have some privacy. But we didn't meet there. I suggested a neutral location — a restaurant way up Route 1."

"Did you spend the night with him?" Candy asked.

Felicia raised her eyebrows. "Things just happened. I . . . I'm not really sure I remember all the details. But yes, we went back to the room he'd rented. Gina found us in the morning. And that's when . . ."

Candy turned back to Gina. "How did you know where to find them?"

Gina's gaze had been distant, but now she refocused. "I . . . I don't know." She had to think about it. "I received a text message," she finally said.

"From who?"

"I don't know. The sender's name was blocked. But it told me where to find my husband. So I went to get him. And when I found him, he . . . he got very angry, like it was *me* who had done something wrong. He acted like I was ruining his life." She paused as a wave of emotion threatened to wash over her. "He . . . he said he didn't love me anymore." She paused again, in an effort to keep her emotions under control. "And that's when I told him I was having an affair with Liam. Just to hurt him."

Candy sensed the underlying message. "But you weren't, were you?"

Gina sniffled as she shook her head. "I knew what it would do to him if I told him. I knew how he would react. That's why I said it. It wasn't true . . . but it doesn't matter now. He . . ."

She faltered again, and Felicia continued for her. "He attacked her," Felicia said, and nodded at the scarf around Gina's throat.

"Show her."

Reluctantly Gina nodded. When she had unwrapped the scarf, Candy could see the bruises around her neck.

"He started choking her," Felicia said angrily. "He was hurting her." Her eyes grew hard. "So I had no choice. He had brought a bottle of Champagne with him, but we hadn't opened it. It was the only weapon I could find. I hit him in the head with it — hard."

"She saved my life," Gina said as her hand went involuntarily to her neck. "I'm not sure what he would have done. When Felicia hit him, all three of us fell." She held Candy's gaze, her eyes clear. "Only two of us got up."

"He must have . . . hit his head on the edge of a table as he fell. It cracked something. I . . . I don't know for sure. It was an accident," Felicia said for the third time, to solidify the point. "I'm sorry it happened. I didn't mean to hurt him. I was just trying to help Gina."

"But why didn't you just go to the police?" Candy asked.

"Because I didn't want to go to jail," Felicia said defiantly, "and because I wouldn't let him ruin the lives of two women."

When they'd told her the rest, how they'd

found a toboggan leaning up against the motel wall, how they'd bundled Victor up in a blanket, laid him out on the long flat sled, and hauled him deep into the woods, she'd listened, fascinated yet saddened, since the desperation in both women's voices was evident.

They'd taken turns pulling the toboggan, and it sounded like they'd struggled every step along the way. "We thought if someone found him in the woods they'd think his death was an accident," Gina said, sadness and regret evident in her voice. "We just didn't think he'd be found so soon."

When she finished, they were all silent again. Candy thought over everything she'd just heard, but some of it still didn't make sense to her. "I don't understand," she said after a few moments. "Victor was found with a hatchet in his back. But you didn't put it there?"

Gina shook her head. "We never had the hatchet. Victor died from a head wound."

"But how did Liam's hatchet get in Victor's back?"

"We don't know," Felicia said. "Someone must have tampered with the body. All we can tell you is that Victor went crazy and tried to hurt Gina — so we did what we had to do to defend ourselves. In some way,

Victor got what he deserved. And neither of us is going to pay for it, because we're leaving."

"But you can't," Candy said. "You have to go to the police. You have to tell them what happened."

"And go to jail for twenty years?" Felicia sneered.

"They'll understand it was in self-defense. You can't run all your lives. You have to give yourselves up."

"We're still talking jail time," Felicia said. "And why? Because of Victor? Or because of Liam? That's something neither of us is willing do."

She nodded at Gina. "We have to leave," she said, softly yet firmly.

Equally firmly, Candy said, "I can't let you go."

Felicia reached under her black cloak and withdrew a small pistol. "I was afraid you'd say that."

FORTY-THREE

Felicia motioned toward Gina with the gun. "Get your stuff. We're going."

But Gina shook her head. Her expression had changed. A few minutes earlier she'd been ready to run, but at the sight of the gun she collapsed in on herself, losing her resolve. "Felicia, put that away."

"Shut up. Just do as I say."

"But you can't hurt anyone else."

"We're in this together. You know that. We've talked about that."

"But maybe Candy is right," Gina said, sounding exhausted. "If we start running now, we'll never stop, and I don't want to live this way for the rest of my life." She looked with pleading eyes at Felicia. "I think Candy's right. We should go to the police and turn ourselves in."

"We have a car outside," Candy added in an encouraging tone. "We can all go together. I'll help you explain what happened."

"It's the right thing to do," Gina insisted. "We have to tell them."

A dark look crossed Felicia's face. "Fine," she said, shifting the gun toward Candy and back to Gina. "You go ahead and turn yourself in. Tell them everything that happened. But you're not the one who smashed in Victor's head with a bottle of Champagne. They'll let you off easy." Her voice grew tight. "But not me."

Ominously she waved the gun between the two of them. "So what am I going to do with the two of you?"

Candy tensed. "Felicia, don't do anything crazy."

"I've already done something crazy," Felicia said. "One or two more *somethings* won't make much difference at this point, will they?"

"Yes, they will," Candy said in her most convincing tone. "It's like you said. Killing Victor was an accident. The police will understand that. But killing us . . ." She let her voice trail off.

Gina continued, speaking calmly, "We'll tell them what happened. They'll understand."

But her words were lost, for Felicia was

already moving. She crossed the room in a half dozen steps, keeping the gun pointed at them the whole time. "Don't be naive, Gina. We covered up a murder. We dumped the body in the woods. They may not lock us up for the rest of our lives, but one way or another, the next few years will be hell. And I'm not going to put myself through that."

"So what are you going to do?" Candy asked, steeling herself.

Felicia thought about it briefly before she said, "I'm going away."

"But where will you go? You'll be running from the law for the rest of your life. They'll come after you. They'll find you."

"Let them try," Felicia sneered. "They'll never find me. And at least I'll be free." She motioned toward the luggage by the door, then pointed the gun at Candy. "The two bags on the left. Carry them out to the car."

Candy hesitated. In her mind she ran through a number of scenarios but quickly realized the best approach was just to do whatever Felicia asked. Still, she hesitated, which caused Felicia's dark side to flare.

"Now," she growled, "or I'll put a hole in you."

Candy doubted Felicia would take such an extreme measure but she had no interest in putting her theory to the test. She glanced at Gina, who was grim-faced, and then did as Felicia asked, moving cautiously to the door and taking one of the heavy bags in each hand. As she lifted them, she struggled and stumbled a little, causing Felicia to bark at her as she opened the door, letting in a blast of cold air. But Gina rushed forward, taking one of the bags from Candy's hand and heading out the door into the dark night.

Outside, Candy immediately thought of Maggie and surreptitiously looked over toward the far side of the parking lot, where the Subaru wagon was parked. But it was partially obscured by the trees along the front of the cabin, and she couldn't get a clear view of it.

Felicia impatiently poked her in the back with the muzzle of the gun. "Wait here," she instructed as she walked to the driver's-side door, opened it, and reached inside, pulling a small lever that popped open the rear hatchback door. "Put the bags in there."

Candy hesitated again. Felicia was several steps away from her. She toyed with the idea of dropping the bag and making a run for it, perhaps trying to get to Maggie's car, or perhaps even hefting the bag up and flinging it at Felicia in an effort to throw her off balance long enough for her and Gina to escape.

But again she quickly decided against it. She was too tired, too cold, and too cautious to put herself and Gina in further danger. So she did as Felicia instructed, and lifted the bag up into the back of the vehicle. She then helped Gina lift the other bag in.

"Close it," Felicia said.

Candy did as she was instructed.

"Now stand over there."

Felicia indicated a dimly lit spot back toward the trees. "I don't really want to do this," she said as she raised the pistol. "I'm sorry."

Candy squinted and turned her face away. Felicia wasn't really going to shoot them, was she?

Just then a blast from a car horn tore through the air. Felicia, Gina, and Candy all turned toward Maggie's car. Even through the trees, Candy could see that Maggie had jumped out of her car and was waving frantically in the opposite direction.

Candy heard another sound then, the piercing whine of a police car siren. A few seconds later, she saw the spinning red lights, and a squad car with the insignia of the Cape Willington Police Department came dashing up the parking lot, swerved into the short driveway, and skidded to a halt next to Felicia's vehicle.

The driver's-side door swung open and Officer Jody McCroy jumped out, assuming a defensive stance with his firearm in his hands. "Police!" he shouted. "Drop your weapon!"

A second police car raced into the driveway, and another officer climbed out. Candy could hear more sirens in the near distance.

Seeing the police officers, Felicia's face grew as cold as ice, and she began to back away beyond her vehicle, toward the edge of the cabin. She started to raise her arm, as if to fire, but shouts from the police stayed her hand. Finally, reluctantly, she let go of the weapon. The police rushed forward to arrest her.

Candy let out a breath and looked gratefully at Officer McCroy as he approached her at a brisk pace, holstering his weapon, ever watchful as he nodded toward her. "Ms. Holliday, are you all right?" he asked, looking from her to Gina.

Candy nodded and was surprised to find she had tears in her eyes. "Felicia told us the whole thing. She killed Victor."

"It was an accident," Gina put in.

Officer McCroy nodded. "We'll take it from here," he said, giving Candy a quick pat on the shoulder.

He started off, but Candy called after him, "Hey, how did you know we were here?"

The young officer pointed toward Maggie. "Your friend called in and told us what was going on. We got here as quickly as we could. Fortunately it looks like no one was hurt."

"Thank you!" Candy said, letting the words out in a great gush of relief. "Thank you for showing up when you did, Officer McCroy!"

He gave her a professional smile and tipped his hat. "You're welcome, ma'am, but I was just doing my job."

FORTY-FOUR

"Something's not right," Candy said.

It was near midnight, and they were back at Maggie's place, where they'd gone after spending hours at the Cape Willington Police Department. They were exhausted.

They sat on Maggie's sofa with their boots off and stocking feet up on the coffee table. Foregoing wine at such a late hour, they'd opted for hot cocoa to warm themselves, and Maggie had lit a fire. They were sharing a flannel blanket Candy had made for Maggie a few years back as a Christmas present.

Maggie had been staring into the fire, her eyelids growing heavy, but at the comment from Candy, she blinked several times, took a sip of her cocoa, and looked over at her friend with a vaguely interested expression on her face. "What do you mean?"

Candy pulled the blanket up to her chin and settled further back into the sofa as she thought. "Well, there are just too many missing pieces — the most glaring being the issue with the hatchet."

Maggie yawned. She looked bleary-eyed. "And what issue is that again?"

"Felicia and Gina wrapped Victor's body up in a blanket and dumped it in the woods using the toboggan. But when Solomon found it, it had a hatchet in its back, and Solomon didn't mention anything about a blanket. So where did the blanket go? And how did the hatchet get there? Did someone put it there after Victor died? If so, why? Then there's the issue of their tracks — why didn't the police find any when they searched the woods?"

"Easy," Maggie said tiredly. "Someone erased them using a tree branch or something like that."

"Right, but who? Solomon said he erased his own tracks but not the tracks around the body. So who did?"

"Maybe the wind," Maggie said, stifling another yawn. "You know, snowdrifts, that sort of thing."

"And what about Gina?"

"What about her?"

"Well, she said someone texted her and told her where Victor and Felicia were shacked up. Who did that?"

Maggie sighed and dropped sideways, her head falling to a pillow at the end of the sofa. "I'm too tired to worry about it tonight. Can we talk about this in the morning? You want to stay over?"

Candy seriously thought about it, but in the end decided her own bed would be best. "I don't suppose I could borrow your car one more time — that is, unless you want to drive me home?

Yawning again, Maggie handed her the keys. "I'm not going anywhere tomorrow, honey. Just drop it off whenever you get a chance."

Doc was asleep when she got home, so she locked up the house, turned out all the lights downstairs except for a night light, made sure the fire had burned down far enough, and went upstairs to her room.

The house was cold, since they kept the thermostat turned down at night to save on heating fuel. So Candy changed quickly into her flannel pajamas, turned out the light, and crawled into bed.

But a few minutes later she turned the light back on, put on her slippers and bathrobe, and padded downstairs to her desk in a corner of the living room.

She powered up her laptop, waited until it

booted up, and logged on to Wanda Boyle's site.

She couldn't get all the unanswered mysteries out of her head, and one in particular bothered her. Preston Smith. What had become of him? Why had he been acting so strange lately? And what was his role in everything that had happened this weekend?

Some of the answers, she thought, might be online.

She'd intended to search back through Whitefield's postings to see if Preston had left any other clues there. But she was surprised to find a new posting from him, dated only minutes earlier.

To Town Crier, it read. *Well done. Whitefield at 10. Ben will know the way.*

She read over the message several times. Again, it seemed obvious that it was meant for her. But what did it mean?

Whitefield at 10. Ben will know the way.

She thought of calling Ben but decided against it when she checked the clock on the fireplace mantel behind her. It was quarter to one. So, instead of calling him, she sent him an e-mail, explaining everything and telling him that she'd call him in the morning to discuss.

By the time she'd logged off, shut down the computer, and climbed back up the stairs to her bedroom, her cell phone was buzzing. She'd set it down on the top of her dresser and forgotten to turn it off or charge it.

It was a text message from Ben:

Meet me for breakfast at the diner at nine. Urgent. Dress warmly. I know what Whitefield is.

FORTY-FIVE

Candy awoke in the morning with the odd feeling that the previous day had been nothing more than a bad dream — or, more accurately, a recurring nightmare — until she'd dressed and headed downstairs. Doc had left part of the Sunday paper sitting on the kitchen table. A quick scan of the headlines revealed that, yes, indeed, it had all been for real. Felicia Gaspar was under arrest for the murder of Victor Templeton, and Gina Templeton was in custody as an accomplice.

Candy just shook her head at the truth of it all. She found it very dismaying. Sometime during the night she'd come awake with the disturbing thought that, for the third time in less than two years, she'd had a gun pointed at her and been threatened with her life. For more than ten years, she'd lived and commuted in metro Boston, renting places just outside of the city in suburbs like Arlington and Watertown, and never once had anything remotely like this happened to her. But here she was in safe, quiet, off-the-beaten-path Cape Willington, Maine, and she'd already stared death in the face three times too many.

What was happening to her beloved little town? What was happening to *her?* The realization that this staring-death-in-the-face sort of thing was starting to happen *often,* and that it might actually be turning into something of a *habit,* was enough to keep her awake during the deepest hours of the night, until she'd finally fallen asleep again right before daybreak.

Even now, as she stood next to the kitchen table, feeling off center and mentally drained after the intensity of the past few days, it was a troubling thought, causing a cold shudder to run through her bones.

Thoughtfully she dropped into a chair, taking a few minutes to scan the rest of the front-page story. It was a fairly accurate account of how Felicia had killed Victor, and of how she and Gina had dragged the body out to the woods on the toboggan and rolled it into a gully, where it had been discovered by a local hermit named Solomon Hatch, currently being sought by police for questioning.

Candy herself was not mentioned in the article, thankfully. Liam Yates was in the process of being released, it said. Chief Darryl Durr was quoted, singling out Officer Jody McCroy for special recognition in the investigation, specifically for following up an important lead, which Candy suspected was that phone call from Maggie.

There was no mention of a hatchet, or Preston Smith, or Duncan Leggmeyer and the award for the hatchet-throwing contest, or of the feud between Victor and Liam. And, of course, there was nothing about a white field, or Whitefield, or even whitefield, as Ben had referred to it in his text last night, though all his characters were lowercase, which he'd probably done for the sake of expediency.

So what, or who, was Whitefield?

Candy checked the clock on the kitchen wall. Quarter to nine.

It was time to find out.

On this particular morning, she and Doc reversed their typical roles. He was staying home, working his way through the Sunday edition of the *Boston Globe* while tuned into the morning national news commentary programs, and Candy was the one heading off to the diner for a morning breakfast rendezvous.

She found Ben, as promised, sitting in a booth by the window at Duffy's Main Street Diner, waiting for her. He'd already ordered coffee for both of them and an English muffin for her — with homemade blueberry jam on the side, of course. For himself, he'd ordered up hash browns and a breakfast steak, doused heavily with Juanita's special hot sauce.

When he looked up and saw her, he waved, half rose, and pointed to the seat opposite him. "Good morning," he said. "Hope I didn't get you out of bed too early on a Sunday."

Candy pulled off her knit cap, shaking free her hair, and tugged off her gloves as she slid into the seat. She managed to smile for him. "How could I turn down a chance to have breakfast with you? Besides, I wasn't sleeping very well anyway."

He gave her a worried look. "You've had a rough couple of days, haven't you, with Solomon, and the body, and now the whole thing with Gina and Felicia? You want me to order something else for you?"

"No, I —"

"Good morning, Candy!" said a voice to her side. Candy looked up at Juanita, the waitress.

"I brought you something, just out of the

oven," she said in a conspiratorial tone. "A fresh-baked blueberry muffin." She set a plate down in front of Candy and gave her a quick pat on the arm. "Nice job solving that murder, Candy! This is on the house. Let me know if you need anything else," she said earnestly and dashed off.

Candy stared at the muffin and let out a sigh. "I think I'm developing a reputation around town."

Ben shrugged. "People are grateful. You've done a lot of good things lately. People like to show their appreciation."

"Yes," Candy said, folding her hands on the table and leaning forward toward him so she could speak in softer tones, "but why are these things happening to me at all? Why have we had five murders in less than two years — and why have I been involved in all of them? I'm beginning to get a little" — she leaned her head even closer to his — *"paranoid."*

Ben held her eyes for the longest time, and she wondered what was going on inside his head. Finally, he said, with all seriousness, "So you think there's a connection between all these murders."

It was a statement, not a question, and it caught Candy off-guard. "What? No, I . . . you think there's a connection?" she asked, trying hard to hold back her astonishment.

He calmly sliced off a thin piece of breakfast steak, swathed it across a puddle of hot sauce, and plopped it into his mouth. "Maybe not between all of them, but between some of them, yes." He set down his knife and fork and, as he chewed, turned and reached into his briefcase, which sat on the seat beside him. He pulled out a manila folder and placed it before her. He tapped lightly at the folder's label before he went back to eating.

Her brow fell. After giving him a questioning look, she dropped her gaze so she could read the name of the file, hand-printed on the small tab.

WHITEFIELD.

She looked up at him incredulously. "You've kept a file on him?"

"It's not a *him,*" Ben said, allowing himself a mysterious smile. "It's an *it.*"

"A what?"

He nodded again toward the file. "Take a look."

So she did. She opened it and looked at its contents. She reacted with surprise, then dug down through the top pages to an aged black-and-white photograph buried inside. She pulled it out and laid it on top of the other pages. "You're kidding me," she said in surprise as she studied the old image.

Ben shook his head. "Nope, it's true. This is part of what I've been doing for the past few months — looking into all this research about the town's history, and its two wealthiest families in particular. And that's part of it."

He pointed with his chin at the old photograph sitting in front of Candy.

It was an image of a massive iron front gate and a long winding road beyond it, which led to a white pillared mansion in the distance.

Across the top of the black gate, painted in faded white capital letters, in an elaborate script, was the word *Whitefield*.

FORTY-SIX

They started out forty-five minutes later, taking Ben's Range Rover. Designed as a capable off-road vehicle, it sometimes had a harsher ride over payment, but on winter roads it excelled.

They headed up the northern leg of the Coastal Loop, Route 192, just as Candy and Maggie had traveled the night before. Shortly after leaving the outskirts of town, they passed the Shangri-La Motel on the left, where Victor Templeton had met his fate.

It looked like the area around the back motel rooms had been roped off, and Candy caught a glimpse of a warning sign, probably posted by the police department, before the place disappeared from view behind a screen of trees and shrubbery, and she turned her attention once more to the road ahead.

As he drove, Ben explained.

"This goes back a hundred, a hundred fifty years. Longer, really, to the earliest settlers in this area. Among them were the Sykes and the Pruitts."

Candy shivered. She'd met members of both clans, which had been scary enough, but who knew what might happen when the two families collided?

It had happened before, Candy remembered. Last year she'd heard a story about a clash between Cornelius Roberts Pruitt, the then-patriarch of the Pruitt clan, and Daisy Porter-Sykes, his soon-to-be ex-mistress. They'd had a falling out at the Lodge at Moosehead Lake back in the late 1940s, with dire consequences for at least two people in present-day Cape Willington.

The person behind the murders last year had been a member of the Sykes family, a descendant of Daisy Porter-Sykes. But there had been someone else. An older brother.

P.S.

Porter Sykes.

It was a mystery that still plagued her. What had been his involvement in the deaths that had occurred in Cape Willington last May?

Candy had hesitated to tell Ben the full story, but he had known enough about what had happened to be totally shocked by the betrayal of the Sykes brothers — which probably explained his interest now in the Sykes family history. And the reason she'd found that volume detailing the early history of the Sykes family on his desk yesterday morning.

"This all goes back to the original patriarch in the area, Ferdinand Sykes, the lost son of Josiah, who built Whitefield in the late 1850s, right before the war," Ben told her. "Like his father, Ferdinand was a sailor and tradesman, and by his thirties he'd amassed a fleet of ships. He'd intended Whitefield as a summer cottage, much like the Vanderbilts and Rockefellers had in New York, Maine, and Rhode Island, though the Sykeses were nowhere near those big leagues. They thought they deserved to be, though, and aspired to high society, which brought them into conflict with the far wealthier Pruitts."

Ben explained some of the highlights of the conflicts between the Sykeses and the Pruitts across the generations, providing details about bad blood between commanders in the Civil War, the race for wealth in the era of the robber barons, and the families' entwinement through the first and second world wars, including the dalliance between Cornelius Roberts Pruitt and his mistress, Daisy Porter-Sykes, at a bucolic resort in the north of Maine.

"Throughout all those years, Whitefield remained a retreat for the Sykes family. But then sometime in the early 1960s they stopped coming. They boarded up the place. A few months later it was discreetly announced that Daisy's husband, Gideon Sykes, had passed away. Whether there was a connection or not, they've never said, and I haven't been able to find one. Neither the Sykes nor the Pruitt families have released many papers, and they're both fairly proprietary with their family records. I've checked available accounts at the historical society and news clippings from the period, of course, but I've hit a dead end."

He pointed out ahead of them. "That's why I'm hoping we might find some answers at Whitefield."

Candy looked out through the windshield at the white and gray landscape, muted under a lowering sky. "Can we get into it?"

Ben shrugged. "As far as I know, the place has been abandoned for decades. Why they haven't condemned it or torn it down, I don't know. Even though the place has gone into decline, the Sykes family still owns the mansion and surrounding acreage, and as far as I can tell they've had quite a few offers for the place. But they refuse to sell."

"I wonder why," Candy said, partially to herself.

Ben had no answers for her, and kept his jaw tightly clenched as they reached Route 1 and turned eastward toward Jonesboro and Machias.

They drove for perhaps twenty or twenty-five minutes before turning south again, onto a narrow, winding road that hugged the rugged, rocky coast, until they came to a spur that cut inland to a high bluff over-looking Englishman Bay and, off to the right, Roque Island. Ben checked the GPS on his smart phone and slowed to a crawl, until he finally pointed toward a side road that looked as if it hadn't been plowed in several days. "That way."

He dropped the transmission down into low gear. "Fortunately we've got a high ground clearance in this thing," he told her as they turned onto the snow-swept road, plowing their way through blowing drifts that had crept across the road surface and frozen in place.

Two miles along, they came across a tall black iron gate set between two pillars ten feet back from the road. Weathered lettering across the top of the gate announced that they had arrived at Whitefield.

Ben slowed, pulled off to the side of the road as best he could, and pointed out past Candy through the passenger-side window. "That's her."

They both looked.

Beyond the iron gate, a snow-covered driveway wound back around a rising section of land, at the summit of which sat the mansion, facing southeastward. Candy turned back to her left. Trees blocked her view of the bay from here, but she imagined the mansion's front porch and windows offered spectacular views of the coast and the sea beyond.

"It's a prime piece of land, that's for sure," Ben said, following her gaze. "No wonder they've received offers for it."

"Probably pretty hefty ones too," Candy said, "despite the economy."

"Doesn't look like anyone's been out here in a while, though," Ben observed.

He was right. Beyond the gate, they saw no tire tracks in the snow, no footprints, nothing to indicate anyone had visited recently.

"I'll check the gate." Ben put the transmission into park but left the engine and the heater running as he opened the driver's-side door and hopped out. Despite the higher elevation, the snow wasn't too deep, probably because a good bit of it had melted down during the warming trend of the past week and a half.

Ben walked to the gate and peered through the iron bars, some of which were showing rust and disrepair. He reached out a gloved hand and grasped one of the bars, giving the gate a tentative shake. Its age and appearance belied its condition, for it held solid, giving no indication that it would give way or allow them to gain entrance to the property beyond.

A heavy chain and lock wrapped around and through several bars further prevented entry.

Ben studied it all before returning to the Range Rover. He climbed inside, and pulled the door shut behind him. "The place is locked up tight," he said, "but I think I saw a break in the fence back over that way. We're going to have to trudge through knee-deep snow. You up for it?"

Candy checked her watch. In his esoteric message, Preston had said he'd meet her here at ten. It was already quarter past. Had they missed him?

Whitefield at 10. Ben will know the way, the posting had said. Had she misread it? Had it been meant for someone else? Or was someone just leading her along?

She opened her door and climbed out, the determination clear on her face. "Let's check it out."

Ben took only a few items with him before locking up the vehicle: his 3G cell phone with GPS, which was having trouble getting a signal out here; a flashlight he'd scrounged out of the back; and a tire iron ("Just in case," he told her). She pulled a flashlight from her tote, which she'd brought with her, but left everything else in the bag on the backseat.

"All right," Ben said, turning toward the mansion on the hill, "let's see if this lady is willing to give up some of her secrets today."

FORTY-SEVEN

"There's nothing here," Ben said forty-five minutes later.

The place was abandoned — just as it had looked from the outside.

They'd trudged through the knee-deep snow to the mansion's expansive front porch, then circled around the back, soaking their jeans from midthigh down in the process, until they'd found a side door curiously unlocked. It had given them entry into a narrow passageway with a few steps that led up to the main floor. "Servants' entrance," Ben said as he pushed his way through.

The place smelled old, moldy, and unhealthy. Trash was strewn about. It was obvious squatters had been here, taking advantage of the old building as shelter and leaving their detritus behind. Ben and Candy had searched the place cautiously, thinking someone might still be here, but the place was empty — and without heat. The cold seemed to come out of the walls, as if the weather had seeped into the building's very bones.

Remembering a discovery in another old house, though one not nearly as grand as this, Candy said, "Maybe there's a hidden room, or passage or alcove — someplace where documents might be hidden."

But if there was such a place in this old mansion, they did not find it this day.

Ben looked eminently disappointed as they arrived back on the first floor after checking the upstairs bedrooms. "I was hoping we'd find something," he said, "but if this old house is still keeping secrets, she's not telling us."

Candy checked her watch again. It was just past eleven. Preston Smith — or whoever had posted that message to her — had never showed.

As if reading Candy's thoughts, Ben said, "You know, I did a quick Internet search on Preston Smith's name last night, after you sent me that message. I found a few things about him, but most seemed recent — within the past six months or so."

Candy nodded. She'd found the same thing. "Whatever's going on," she said in a resigned tone, "we're not going to find the answers here."

Ben made a quick turnaround, looking out through the windows in various directions. "There are a few more buildings outside. I'll go have a look. Want to come along?"

Candy studied the piles of snow outside and then looked down at her still-wet jeans, which had her shivering. "No thanks. I'll check upstairs again. Just swing back and get me when you're ready to go."

He told her he would, and walked back toward the rear of the building, to access the servants' entrance through the kitchen.

Candy was alone.

The house creaked around her. Outside, a frozen branch banged against a window, driven by a sudden gust of wind. She thought she heard a low moan, somewhere in the bowels of the house. And then . . . a footstep.

It seemed to have come from one of the rooms off to her right.

She heard a door close somewhere behind her.

She twisted around. "Ben?"

"Ben seems to be occupied at the moment," another voice said. "Which is just as well. You and I, we need to have a little talk."

Candy froze. She knew the voice. She'd heard it before.

Preston Smith stepped out of the shadows near her. "Hello, Ms. Holliday. We meet again."

FORTY-EIGHT

"You!" Candy said in an accusatory tone. "What are you doing here? Where did you come from?"

Preston gave her a broad grin and waved an expansive hand. "Why, I've been here all along."

"But we searched the house."

"You missed a few spots. It's a big house. It's easy to do if you're not familiar with it."

That made Candy pause. She looked at him with scrutinizing eyes. "What kind of game are you playing, Preston?"

"Hmm. Interesting choice of words." He took a few steps toward her, and she backed away.

"Come any closer and I'll scream," she warned.

But the smile did not leave Preston's face. "Well. We wouldn't want that, would we? With Ben so nearby, just outside?"

He held up a small, thin metallic object in

his hand. It was a black key.

"Unfortunately, you see, I've locked the servants' door," Preston said. "But there's no need to panic, Ms. Holliday. I'm not here to hurt you. I'm just here to talk."

Candy backed away a few more steps, casting a glance out one of the nearby windows, hoping to catch sight of Ben. But she saw no sign of him.

"The outbuildings are quite extensive," Preston said by way of explanation. "It'll take him a while to search them all. And as I recall, Ben Clayton is a very thorough individual. I'd say we have ten or twelve minutes, at least. That should be enough."

"For what?" Candy asked warily.

"As I said. For us to talk."

"And what do we have to talk about?"

"Well, a misplaced hatchet, for one thing. A hermit who encountered some sort of mysterious creature in the woods, which appeared to chase him and appropriately scared him. A mysterious donor who funded most of the ice-sculpting exhibition and lured all the participants here with visions of wealth and grandeur. An informant who's been feeding inside information to that wonderful Ms. Boyle for her popular blog. An unsubstantiated rumor about a sponsorship award program promoted by a certain dubious international ice-carving organization. And, oh yes, an anonymous blog poster and instant messenger who pointed certain key individuals in certain key directions — including you, I might add. And you followed the clues impeccably — just as I knew you would. Your growing reputation is well founded, you know. You have definitely lived up to the hype, and it's been a great joy watching you work this weekend."

He had said all of this in a casual, light-hearted sort of way, but Candy knew there was nothing innocent about what he was telling her. She glared at him. "So *you're* the one who's behind all this."

"Why, yes, I am," Preston said proudly, "although that's one mystery you haven't been able to quite figure out yet. So if I were to grade you for this weekend, I'm afraid I'd have to give you a B minus. Not quite award-winning territory yet, but you'll get there. You just need a little help every once in a while. So here's another clue for you: not everything is as it appears."

Something in the way he said it — a slight change in tone, a flicker in the eye, a word pronounced in a marginally different manner — made her look at him again, and this time she saw behind the persona, behind the public man who had been meandering not so aimlessly around town for the past few days. "It's you, isn't it?"

"Why, Ms. Holliday," he said, his voice dropping and changing noticeably now, "you've finally found me out."

He reached up and tugged at the corners of his moustache. They came away with some effort. She heard a slight tearing sound as he whisked the moustache off. The glasses next. And a prosthetic nose. The wig was the last to come off.

"You know," he said as he dramatically removed his disguise, "I had Charlotte Depew make this little getup for me. A couple of years ago, I think it was. She was skilled at that sort of thing. I used it for a masquerade party once."

He removed his fake teeth. "I went as Mark Twain to that particular event. I modified the costume a little for this weekend's impersonation. Do you think it worked?"

When his disguise was fully removed, she saw a man in his early forties, with thick brown hair, an aristocratic nose, a rugged face, and piercing blue eyes. He gave her a devious smile. "It's good to finally meet you for real, Candy. My name is Porter Sykes."

FORTY-NINE

"We don't have much time," he said, "but I wanted to let you know what was going on before I left town."

"Left town?" Candy gave him a hard look. "They're going to arrest you and throw you in prison. If you're lucky, maybe you can arrange for a family reunion."

The man formerly known as Preston Smith, but now revealed to be Porter Sykes, chuckled as he pulled a large plastic storage bag from a coat pocket, slipped the wig and other components of his disguise inside, zipped it closed, and slid it away again. "I'm afraid that won't be the case."

"And why not? What's to prevent me from yelling for Ben right now and calling the police?"

"Frankly, nothing at all. But I don't you will."

"And why not?" Candy asked.

"Because right now you're too c   y

hear what I have to say. You're wondering what my angle is — what I want. And you're trying to figure out why I would go to all this trouble."

Candy had to admit, he was right. The extent of all he'd done was impressive. She had to think it through for a few moments, until she finally looked at him with grudging respect. "It was all a lie, wasn't it? There is no I.C.I.C.L.E., is there?"

"Unfortunately, no," Porter said.

"No sponsorship program, no spokesperson, no international event that would have put our town on the map, no huge economic windfall from this wonderful ice-carving competition of yours."

He shook his head.

"But why?" Candy asked, astounded by the scope of it all. "Why go to these lengths?"

At the question, Porter Sykes shrugged. "I have my reasons. But for now, let's just say I wanted to stir things up — to get to know some of the people around town without them knowing who I was, and to see how they behaved under pressure."

A shadow crossed Candy's face. "This isn't a game. People have died."

"Yes, well, that sort of thing happens when you're playing the big game. It was unexpected, I'll admit, but I was able to take advantage of it. And it worked out quite well. You see, Victor was starting to get suspicious of me. I'd tried the Preston Smith act on some of the sculptors — Victor and Gina, especially. Felicia's too perceptive — I knew she'd see through the disguise quickly enough, so I tended to avoid her, as well as Ben. I'm sure you can understand why. As for Liam, he's a liar and a cheat. I have to admit, it was somewhat satisfying to see him in cuffs, even if it was just for a short while. And as for Duncan, well, he'll gain some notoriety out of it, which might give his career a boost."

Candy crossed her arms, reluctantly impressed by the way he'd set things up. And there was more, she suspected. She was beginning to see all the links. "You're the one who sent that text message to Gina, telling her where to find Victor and Felicia."

"She was oblivious about what was going on," Porter said. "She needed a nudge."

"And," Candy said, "you were the one who put that hatchet in Victor's back."

Porter let out a sigh. "I picked that motel strictly for its reputation. I didn't figure any of the ice carvers would stay there. So I was surprised to see Victor and Felicia driving by one night, headed for one of the back rooms. I texted Gina, and kept an eye on them. But once Gina arrived, no one left — until dawn. That's when they took the body out. I followed, of course, and when I saw where they dumped it, I sensed an opportunity. Liam's worked for me a few times down in Boston. He kept showing off that hatchet of his, and I got so tired of hearing about it that I took it from him at an event we both happened to attend."

"You stole it," Candy corrected.

"I had every intention of just getting rid of it, but I couldn't help thinking that there might be a better purpose for it. So I brought it along with me when I came to Maine. And wouldn't you know . . ."

"So you went back out to the body, taking Liam's hatchet, and plunged it into Victor's body."

Porter's face grew still. "He was already cold, and stiffening. I cleaned up my tracks — and Gina's and Felicia's. I'm not really sure what I planned to do about the body. Leave it there and let someone discover it in the spring? Perhaps it would never have been found — but it worked out for the best, didn't it?"

"And now you'll go to prison."

Porter laughed and shook his head again. "You're not seeing the reality here, Candy. I certainly won't be going to prison. And you won't tell anyone about what you've learned here today."

Candy felt a cold shiver deep inside her. "And why not, Porter?"

"Because I haven't done anything. Because I was never here — Preston was, but he's a ghost. And because if you tell anyone about me, no one will believe you."

Candy's anger flared. "You were involved in at least two murders that I know of, including Victor Templeton's," she said, "and I can prove that."

Porter Sykes sighed. "You could try, but you'd lose. I won't go into the details here. There's just not enough time. But trust me — I've taken great care to cover all my tracks. None of the clues can be traced to me, and all of the online evidence has already been erased. You'll find only residual references to Whitefield or I.C.I.C.L.E., and those will be only ghosts. Just so you know, I've technically been in Boston all weekend. I attended a fundraiser this morning and will be at another tomorrow. There's no trace of me up here. And besides, I'm sure you're aware that I own your newspaper. It's part of my family's holdings. As such, both you and Ben work for me. You wouldn't want me to shut down your own paper, would you? You wouldn't want Wanda Boyle to become the sole news reporter in town? You wouldn't want Ben to leave town for another job, and lose that extra income for yourself and Doc?"

Candy was stunned. "What are you saying?"

Porter's tone suddenly turned very serious. "Here's what I'm saying. I'm putting Cape Willington on notice. It's time for all of you to pay up for past transgressions. So I'm letting you and a few others know. Call it a simple courtesy, but do not be mistaken. For too long my family has been disgraced by the people of this town. Those days are over. And I just wanted you to know it so you could have a front-row seat as you watch it happen." He gave her a dark grin.

"But why?

He turned and looked out the window then, and checked his watch. "Our time is up. You should leave the building now. It's not safe here."

He tossed the black key to her, then turned and started to walk away, but Candy called after him: "What did your brother take from the journal that night at the lighthouse?"

She was referring to an incident that had occurred the last time she'd encountered a member of the Sykes family. And that one had been strangely similar to this.

Porter stopped and turned back to her. "It's what we're all looking for," he said enigmatically. "Even Ben. Why don't you ask him about it?"

And with that, Porter Sykes disappeared into the shadows of the house.

FIFTY

A little more than a week later, on a Monday morning, the last day of January, Candy Holliday sat at the kitchen table, paging through seed catalogs and sipping a cup of hot tea. Every once in a while, as she flipped a page or after she'd focused in on a particularly interesting description of a zucchini or a pumpkin, she'd shift her gaze out the window, toward the blueberry fields and the woods behind the house.

There had been no arrest of Porter Sykes — or someone known as Preston Smith, for that matter. There had been no word from him since she'd last seen him out at Whitefield. The Sykes mansion itself had been in the news this past week, however. Apparently some kids had broken in and started a fire to warm themselves, but things got out of hand. The fire spread to some rags and debris nearby, and soon the whole place was ablaze, quickly burning down to the ground.

The fire department arrived too late to save the old mansion, but it wasn't much of a loss, most around town agreed. The place had fallen into disrepair years ago. The following day, the Sykes family of Boston issued a statement saying they were putting the property up for sale.

Ben had shared some of his research of the Sykes and Pruitt families with her. She'd told Doc a little bit about it, and he'd done some digging in the historical society's archives. He'd come up with an interesting old newspaper clipping from the Bangor paper, with a press date in the mid-1960s.

"It's about a historian from Orono who was researching local family histories," Doc told her as he handed it to her. "This historian, a man by the name of Decker, promoted the fact that Gideon Sykes, the father of Porter and his siblings, and the husband of Daisy Porter-Sykes, had committed suicide in that old mansion. His theory was that after Gideon had taken his own life, there had been a huge cover-up, and this Decker fellow suspected it had something to do with the old man's insurance money — a sizable payout, by the way."

Candy had read the rest of the clipping and handed it back to Doc. "Bury it somewhere," she told him.

Toward the bottom of the article, she'd read that the historian named Decker had died a few weeks later, under mysterious, still-undetermined circumstances.

For now, she thought, it was best to keep that information under wraps.

For the past week she had struggled with the question of what to do about Porter and the information he'd told her. It had kept her awake nearly every night since, and had just about driven her crazy. She'd nearly spilled the beans to Doc several times, desperate for his advice. She'd avoided seeing Maggie, knowing it was next to impossible to keep anything from her friend. And she had resisted talking to Ben until she could sort out what to do and what to tell him.

The good news was that Doc barely noticed her internal agony. He was back at work on his book, and there were evenings when he brought home armloads of them from the library and historical society. He'd even made a trip to the university library up at Orono, which gave him a chance to catch up with some old friends, lifting his spirits.

Speaking of spirits, she had seen the white moose only one other time, a few nights ago from her bedroom window, as the moon drifted lazily in its arc across the sky, casting its white glow upon the frozen blueberry fields. The moose had stood in the shadows of the distant trees for the longest time, watching the house, and she had watched back, until finally her eyelids had grown heavy and she'd gone to bed.

Now she looked out at the fields and shrugged. In another few weeks winter would begin to loosen its grip on the landscape. They'd still have a storm or two in early March, usually sometime around the eighth of the month, but the cold season was coming to an end, and then the wondrous rebirth would begin.

Candy Holliday sighed deeply in anticipation and turned back to her catalogs. Spring was coming, and she had a garden to plan.

Epilogue

Ben slammed the book closed and tossed it roughly on a nearby table, which itself was laden with numerous historical works and archival manuscripts. He'd been going through the material for weeks now, searching for the one clue that would tell him what was really going on and give him some insight into the murders that had been occurring around town. His gut told him there was a pattern, a reason it was all happening, but if one existed, he still could not see it.

His search would go on, though. He was determined to find out why the Sykes family had targeted Cape Willington and what their ultimate goal was.

As his gaze scanned the desktop, he caught sight of the letter, stuffed into a cubbyhole off to one side. It was the third one he'd received in as many months. But it had been no less confounding than the first two.

There had been only a couple of lines:

There's danger for you and your girlfriend if you stay, it said. *Get out while you can.*

It was unsigned, but he had a good idea who it had come from. There had been no specific threats yet, in any of the letters — nothing he could take to the police. But even if there had been — or might be in the future — he wasn't sure he would. This wasn't a matter for the police to sort out. This was his mystery. And he would pursue it himself.

He'd thought of telling Candy several times about what he was doing, bringing her deeper into his theories and fears. But he didn't want to worry her right now. Besides, after all that had happened to her over the past two years, he didn't want to burden her with the knowledge that this could just be the beginning.

He let out a deep breath, got up to put another log on the fire, and returned to his desk.

Just another book or two, he told himself, and then he'd give up for the night.

RECIPES

SANDY'S FAVORITE WHOOPIE PIES
Whoopie pies are now the official Maine treat. These are small whoopie pies, about four bites per pie, and not as sweet as most. You'll want to make a double batch — they're that good!

For the cake, cream together
5 tablespoons cocoa powder
6 tablespoons Crisco or other shortening
1 cup sugar
1 egg
1 teaspoon vanilla

Add
2 cups flour
1 teaspoon salt
1 cup milk
1 1/4 teaspoon baking soda

Mix together.

Drop by tablespoonfuls onto a cookie sheet.

Bake at 350 degrees for 10 minutes. Place cookie sheet on wire rack and let cakes cool completely.

For the filling, cook in a medium saucepan to a paste consistency
1/2 cup milk
2 tablespoons flour

Add:
1/4 cup Crisco or other shortening
1/2 cup butter
1/2 cup sugar
1 teaspoon vanilla

Beat until smooth with an electric mixer or by hand until creamy.

Refrigerate the filling until cool.

Spread the filling on half of the cakes. Top with the remaining cakes.

Wrap individually with waxed paper and keep refrigerated.

Don't worry about how long they keep, because after a couple of days there won't be any left!

MELODY'S CHOCOLATE MOUSSE

6 ounces semisweet chocolate, chopped, or
   chocolate chips
1 ounce unsweetened chocolate, chopped
1/2 cup milk
1 teaspoon vanilla extract
1 cup heavy cream
1/4 cup confectioners' sugar

In a small saucepan, combine the semisweet and unsweetened chocolates with the milk.

Stir over low heat until melted.

Add the vanilla.

Turn off the heat and let stand until cool to the touch.

In bowl, beat the cream and the sugar with a mixer until stiff peaks form.

Add some of the chocolate mixture to the cream mixture and fold together using a wire whisk.

Add the remaining chocolate and fold in until it is all combined.

Spoon the moose into 6 serving dishes and refrigerate until ready to serve.

This delectable dessert is served daily at Melody's Café!

Marjorie Coffin's
White Moose Hot Cocoa

Combine in a small saucepan:
1/2 cup unsweetened cocoa powder
1/2 cup sugar
1/4 teaspoon ground cinnamon

Blend in 1/3 cup hot water.
Bring to a boil over medium heat, stirring constantly.
Boil and stir for 2 minutes.
Add 4 cups milk.
Stir and heat. Do not boil.
Remove from heat.
Add 3/4 teaspoon vanilla extract.
Stir with a whisk until foamy.
Pour into mugs and sprinkle with white chocolate chips.

Nanna Tibbetts's Moose Mincemeat
Use given amounts if making mincemeat preserves. Halve the amounts if using for pie filling.

3 to 4 pounds moose meat (you can substitute venison or beef)
3 to 4 pounds apples, cored, peeled, and chopped
1 pound of suet (you can substitute Crisco)

2 1/2 cups sugar
1 1/2 pounds raisins
2 1/2 cups strong coffee
2 teaspoons nutmeg
1 teaspoon cinnamon
1 teaspoon cloves

Chop moose meat after cooking.

In a large Dutch oven, combine the meat, chopped apples, and suet (or Crisco).

Stir in remaining ingredients, varying the spices.

Simmer for 1 hour, stirring occasionally.

For moose mincemeat pie, use as a filling in any piecrust.

To preserve, pack hot into pint-size canning jars. Process pints for 20 minutes at 10 pounds pressure in a pressure cooker or for 1 1/2 hours in a boiling-water-bath canner.

NANNA TIBBETTS'S MOOSE MINCEMEAT COOKIES

1 cup shortening
1/2 teaspoon vanilla
1 cup honey
3 eggs, well beaten
3 1/4 cups flour

1 teaspoon salt
1 teaspoon baking soda
1 cup chopped nuts
1 cup moose mincemeat, drained

In a large bowl, cream the shortening.
Beat in the vanilla, honey, and eggs.
In a separate bowl, sift together flour, salt, and baking soda.
Add dry ingredients to the egg mixture.
Fold in nuts and mincemeat.
Drop by teaspoonfuls on a buttered cookie sheet.
Bake at 350 degrees for 15 minutes or until delicately browned.

Makes 6 dozen cookies; halve amounts for a smaller batch.

These authentic Maine moose recipes, from the collection of Nanna Tibbetts of Denmark, Maine, were generously provided in her loving memory by her children, grandchildren, great grandchildren, and all the children she loved.

The employees of Thorndike Press hope you have enjoyed this Large Print book. All our Thorndike, Wheeler, and Kennebec Large Print titles are designed for easy reading, and all our books are made to last. Other Thorndike Press Large Print books are available at your library, through selected bookstores, or directly from us.

For information about titles, please call:
(800) 223-1244

or visit our Web site at:
http://gale.cengage.com/thorndike

To share your comments, please write:
Publisher
Thorndike Press
10 Water St., Suite 310
Waterville, ME 04901

β